THE PAWNS

THE PAWNS

RON GABRIEL

This is a work of fiction. Any references to historical events, real people, or real places are used fictitiously. Other names, characters, places and organizations portrayed in this novel are either products of the author's imagination or used fictitiously.

Edited by Julia Houston

ISBN: 978-0-9979449-5-2 (hardcover)
ISBN: 978-0-9979449-6-9 (paperback)
ISBN: 978-0-9979449-7-6 (ebook)

Published by Gramercy Fiction

The Banished (Book One of The Bucharest Witches)
The Pawns (Book Two of The Bucharest Witches)

www.rongabriel.nyc

ONE

A return visit from her dead bestie jolted Rachel awake, her pulse pounding like a stampede of wild zebras across a riverbed of wet sheets.

Why now, Sophia?

Light from a streetlamp filtered through breezy, shifting curtains in the predawn stillness as she shuffled toward the bathroom to get a towel. She pulled back the covers and spread it over the wetness as best she could. The cotton felt coarse and lumpy, but she forced herself to breathe deeply, clear her mind, and drift back to sleep.

In the morning, the towel was bunched up by her side, but at least the sheets were dry. Cool air wafted in the crack of the window. *Didn't they say it would be warmer?* She snuggled under the comforter to hide, but the dream always found her. Fragments prickled like rusted barbed wire as they invaded. More than four years had passed since Sophia went missing, but only recently had the nightmares started.

Why now, Sophia?

Depression, a familiar specter, dogged her days. So far, she'd managed to move on without Mia and Sophia. Only James understood, and that made things more complicated.

She closed her eyes and curled into a ball.

How could I have soaked the sheets? It's freezing, I still need a few seconds.

And that's when the snippets broke through.

Beams don't do much against drifting mist on a narrow mountain road. From somewhere in the tangle of trees, sobs overtake the shrill thunder of crickets. Sophia scuttles from the shadows and ducks between the headlights. There's panic on her face.

She scrambles for the cover of fog, but a woman in tatters gives chase in slow motion, hunting from above with fabric rippling and a pointed fence post poised to strike.

No one can outrun the witch in the woods, and Rachel already knows the ending.

But Sophia doesn't, and she screams as the stake impales her, and blood sprays, and then everything's swallowed—the woods, the car, and the road—a crimson murkiness.

Rachel gasped and shot up in bed, eyes wide.

There was more, but she stifled it. This had to stop, and she had to tell someone.

She checked her phone and wondered if James were awake.

TWO

JAMES LAY IN BED AND SURVEYED the music posters, football trophies, and random seashells still scattered about his old bedroom in Sussex at his mother's house. *My bros would laugh me out of Massachusetts, but I ain't redecorating just for summer.* He forced himself up, opened the blinds, and pulled sweats and a gray t-shirt over his boxer briefs. He stepped barefoot over a neon orange Bengal tiger throw rug toward the door.

Was anyone even awake? He didn't like bobbing around others in the kitchen to get a cup of coffee. His parents were spending the weekend together—again, and he was left to form his own conclusions because post-divorce his parents seemed much more chill than when they were married. He listened for voices downstairs and decided it was safe because only cicadas could be heard, awakening from a crisp night to buzz like a distant chain saw as the sun took control.

His phone dinged just as the Keurig started spouting coffee into a mug.

"It's happened again," Rachel said. "The nightmare."

"Who is this?" James paused and then chuckled. "Good morning, sunshine."

"My head is pounding, and I'm nervous."

"Take an Advil and call me in the morning." When she didn't respond, he continued. "Oh, it is morning. So, do you want to meet up?"

"Yeah, like, soon."

"I haven't even showered yet."

"Your hair always glues the same anyway."

James eyed his reflection in the window. "Fair." The Keurig finished, and he grabbed the lid for his car mug. "Your timing's good because I want to get out of here before everyone wakes up. Maple Street, our usual bench?"

"Fifteen minutes, perfect, thanks. Bye." She hung up.

James kept the gray t-shirt but bolted upstairs to change to shorts because the weather app insisted the morning would heat up. He pushed his bare feet into high-tops he'd parked near the front door and slipped outside, thankful to escape family chitchat before sufficient caffeinating.

The car his mother gave him for high-school graduation still worked fine, and he climbed behind the wheel after taking a deep swig from his mug. He looked in the rearview mirror and rubbed the sleep from his eyes after raking a hand through his short hair a few times. As his ex, Rachel still had the power to unsettle. His football days were over, but he worked out habitually; it was his thing. Meanwhile, Rachel seemed effortlessly high caliber, out of his league. *I wasn't good enough then, so why would I be now?* He backed out of the driveway and sped toward town. *Just shut up and be glad you can still hang out. You're lucky to get crumbs.*

He pulled into Maple Street Park and found a spot just below the hill to the benches. Rachel was there, poking at her phone. James took what was left of his coffee and hiked over.

Rachel put down her phone and smiled broadly; they hugged.

"Wow, a college graduate, a real adult," James said as he took a seat. "Congrats."

"Thanks."

Rachel blushed as she made room for him. Brunette waves streaked with highlights spilled out from a Red Sox cap onto a white t-shirt tucked into frayed jean cutoffs.

James swiveled to face her and took a sip. Sun rays were working their magic, and he solar paneled them in with outstretched legs, and an arm that found the wooden backrest. "You look great; glad you're sticking around for now. So, what's next?"

"Applying to jobs in Boston, Austin, even New York, whatever pops up."

"In what?"

"Marketing or some sort of branding that requires my exquisite taste and style." She puffed out her cheeks like a blowfish until a chuckle seeped out. "I don't love Social, but I can work it."

"You're a techie plus a fashion girl; everyone will want you."

"I need a bigger pond. I know there's more out there, and I need to find it while I still dare." Rachel exhaled and folded her arms. "Before my inner chicken takes over. Mia and Sophia never got the chance. I'm living for the three of us."

"It's still so freaky. It'll be better to get somewhere new, right?" James took another sip. "Are you staying in Burlington?"

"For now. Rent is cheap, and the housemates are cool." Rachel dug a pair of aviators out of her bag. "Lease runs through August. What about you?"

"I'm here until mid-August, then back to UMASS. Senior year already."

"Remember when you didn't want to apply anywhere? Now you're almost through."

"I didn't even know sports management was a thing. You opened my eyes." James leaned back and gripped the armrest. "So, tell me what's up."

"You're going to think I'm crazy; it's the nightmares again."

"I don't think you're crazy," James said. "It was worse after your car crash."

"That was PTSD."

"So, what's different now?"

Rachel rested her phone on the slats of the bench as she tilted her head back and closed her eyes. "The dream keeps coming, like six nights, the same thing." Her lids popped wide open. "It's been four years since Sophia disappeared. And now, over the past two weeks out of nowhere, the dreams started. They come with a very peculiar feeling of dread, like, I know I'm going into it, but I can't stop it and can't wake up."

He leaned in. "What do you remember?"

"I'm wandering alone on a dirt road in the middle of nowhere, surrounded by trees and drawn toward headlights. Everything's misty, but I can make out Sophia in the shadows. She's crying and cowering on the road, crouched between the light beams. And then there's a witch who lurches out of the woods and creeps along the side of the car. Sophia knows she's there and runs, but the hag flies up and chases her down the road, headed right toward me."

"You're sure it's Sophia?"

"Just wait." Rachel jiggered her aviators toward the visor of her cap. "The witch has a wooden spear that she uses to prod Sophia as she runs. Then she impales her straight through the back and drags her toward the woods. The point of the stake scrapes the road and carves a trail in the gravel. Last night I couldn't fall back to sleep and figured out it's actually a signpost."

He narrowed his eyes. "What sign?"

"That's what really creeps me out. I know the place in real life, the reservoir, down Indian Brook Road." She gently brushed his leg. "The witch rips out the post, and all that's left is Sophia crumbled in front of the reservoir sign, splayed out like she's crucified. We need to check it out."

His spine stiffened like cast iron. "Whoa, whoa, whoa, what?"

"Nightmares themselves are a sign, don't you think? Sophia's trying to reach me; it repeats for a reason. I'm going to search the woods and I want you to come with."

"Now, you sound crazy." James leaned back with legs pushed out straight and blew out a breath. "A dream doesn't mean real life, right?"

"I want to check out the woods for the sign. Maybe we'll find a clue, something, anything, to make the nightmares stop. I need a reset."

He relaxed and rubbed stubble on his jaw. "When do you want to go?"

"Soon, like now," she said, eyes wide.

He finished his coffee and checked his phone.

"Can we have breakfast first?"

Rachel nodded. "I'll allow that." She smiled and got up from the bench. "Something is making me do this, like a compulsion to find out more, some sort of calling inside."

They didn't speak as she steered them to the parking lot.

"I've never had recurring dreams in my life, especially not from a dear, dead friend. Please bear with me."

They got to their cars and decided to meet at the Firefly Diner.

As he drove to the center of town, James recalled the tough days four years ago when he helped Rachel power through the loss of her two best friends, Mia and Sophia. And she still had him. They'd dated in high school, but bonded more after the ordeal. Plus, she'd pushed him out of a rut after his parents' divorce. *How could I not be grateful?*

They'd been through so much. In the days after the car crash, just before freshman orientation, she'd snapped. For three days he watched helplessly as she cycled through bouts of mania peppered with whispers repeated with the fervor of a chant: "I got away. Fate couldn't catch me." Nothing made sense. Mia had supposedly committed suicide, but they both rejected the lame-ass police work that also concluded Sophia had run away.

After all that, I'll never pooh-pooh away a nightmare.

He parked next to Rachel as she perched on the back bumper. They entered the diner, a repurposed auto garage with the best huevos rancheros north of, well, Bennington. It was still early enough to grab a table by the window.

"So, what's up with Aaron and Paula?" Rachel asked over the top of the menu.

"Whatever's happening seems to be working. Dad's up here for the summer, same as me." James paused as the waiter came with a thermos of coffee. "It's a lot better than before the divorce; they don't fight. He seems different, more mellow."

"Are they getting back together?"

"No one knows; it's more like friends. Plus, Dad coaches in Massachusetts." He filled his cup and took a sip. "His bullying stopped. Maybe it helps me now, right? I know the ropes, not just the theory. *Something* got me into college."

"Sports propped up your grades; considering your major, it all works." She topped off her own cup. "And anyway, you're killing it now; you're in the final push."

He smiled and nodded and noticed the silence as they waited wasn't awkward.

As predicted, the morning had warmed, but the diner was cool and comfortable with the air conditioner quietly humming below the window.

The waiter returned, and they ordered. When he wandered back to the kitchen, Rachel's lips were tight, and she glanced over the mug she held with both hands.

"I want to find what's next."

He smiled. "It'll be great."

"I'm trying to move on, but fighting inertia." Her mug thumped on the wooden tabletop.

"Change takes time, right? You're the one who taught me that."

"I keep fixating on the past." Her gaze drifted out the window to the revamped parking lot that humped and got oily where the gas pumps used to be. "It can't be erased. Time helps, but it masks things over in a way that's downright deceptive and even cruel with how it makes everything seem OK, when in fact it wasn't, and it's not."

He reached across the table and touched her hand. His gaze held even as she stiffened.

"Why cruel?"

Rachel's lips tightened into a frown as she considered.

"Because you're supposed to feel OK about suffering simply because it's all gone murky. Cruel because you're robbed of closure after the grind of just surviving blunts everything away."

She cleared hair from her face and closed her eyes.

"So much doesn't make sense, and when I try to remember,

there's nothing there. It feels empty; vast like space, dark like death."

James waited for her to return, and then whispered.

"It's the same for me."

"Now I'm in limbo and anxious. And the nightmares are unbearable."

Tears pooled, and Rachel covered her face with one hand.

James squeezed the other that rested on the tabletop. "We'll look for the sign, whatever it takes, whatever might help."

She peeked out, squeezed back, and forced a smile.

THREE

JAMES AND RACHEL PARKED NEXT to each other at the reservoir in spots they found together under the trees. In the sun, it felt hot and sticky, but it was cool and clammy in the shadows, like crossing from one climate zone to another in a single step.

Rachel hoped she wasn't going too far. James had stuck by her for years, but there was a breaking point for everything, even friendship. If this indulgence uncovered nothing, she would drop it and pray the visit alone might flick off the subconscious switch behind the nightmares.

She felt better after opening to James, and at least so far, it was fun. They hiked past the security guard at the park's entrance, and she led them around a bend up Indian Brook Road.

Crickets chirruped dutifully in the shadows, battling the frenetic squawks of horny birds. Was that what made them so hyper? The brook gushed at the bottom of a ravine that sloped savagely from the road on one side, the churn of roiling water soothing in the background.

Rachel scoured the thick forest on both sides as their sneakers crunched loose stones on the hard-packed dirt road. "The sign in my dream was planted in the woods, like abandoned from old days, hand-painted, like a trail marker."

James jogged ahead toward a signpost on the side of the road, his high-tops clunky and untied, but somehow staying on. He gripped the base and playfully swung around to read the front.

"Slow."

She caught up. "Nope, not even close."

"Why would it be stuck away from the road? Sounds like a useless sign."

"Can't argue with a dream."

Cars and bikes were more sporadic than dog barks wafting through the woods, so Rachel marched down the middle of the dirt road and did a slow 360.

"It feels so familiar, like a favorite hideaway. I've come by car, but on foot it's just like the dream except now it's real. Oh my God, I sound crazy." She wiped her lips with the back of a hand.

He exaggerated a nod with eyes wide and eyebrows raised high. He followed closely behind as she dipped into the forest, pushing back tree leaves and plowing through brush, weeds, and large fallen branches.

"Why here, and not the other side?"

"The slope to the brook is wicked steep," Rachel called out without turning. "Even the witch couldn't drag her there."

"Right, of course not. And signs aren't usually stuck in the middle of the woods." He waited for a reaction, but nothing seemed to hear him but the birds. "Dreams are symbols." He stopped altogether and chuckled while she sidestepped a patch of thistles. "Watch out for ticks!"

Rachel ignored him and trudged in deeper for a minute longer until she abruptly turned and marched toward her hiking partner, who was a good distance behind.

She cupped her hands to call out. "It's pointless; you're right. I'm an idiot."

James beamed a tight smile and folded his arms as he waited for her to join him. He guffawed when she unleashed a string of expletives as she fought past the prickers.

When Rachel finally made it back, she forced herself to hold his gaze and asked, "What?"

She shrugged and bent to examine tiny scratches on her legs. He chuckled again, and without a word they'd already started back toward the road when they both heard a solid *crack* in the distance.

Rachel's heart dropped, her face went numb, and then she took a tentative step toward the sound.

It came again, this time louder. *Crack.*

Breathless, they scanned the trees while a breeze rustled the branches, and the gurgle of the brook sounded more like rapids.

"Do you hear something?" Rachel's eyes darted about.

He froze and cocked his head. "Sounded like wings flapping."

"I'm getting something more, listen."

They waited and a bird cawed and then shrieked with a flurry of black feathers in the treetops just beyond a gully.

Rachel gasped, and her heart raced.

"I saw it, but what the hell was it?" he asked and gently touched her shoulder.

"A crow or a raven?"

They strained to listen and stood motionless as a flock of starlings scattered. Sunlight filtered through towering branches that shifted on the breeze and cast a kaleidoscope of shadow.

"It's there, above the ditch." Rachel pointed, but it was hard to focus.

James shuffled closer. "It looks like a hawk, something big."

They trained their eyes, but the raptor had already disappeared into the leaves.

Rachel inhaled deeply and closed her eyes. *I know we're close; I feel it.* She pricked up her ears for a squawk or rustle. When she opened her eyes, she gasped and grabbed his arm.

He jumped. "What?"

She pointed beyond the gully. "Something's there." She focused a moment and then gently turned his head toward where they'd seen the black bird. "It could be a sign, tilted sideways; look deep." She took a few shaky steps.

"Wait up." James touched her arm and together they navigated a tangle of weeds, prickers, and gnarly roots on the forest floor. "I think I see."

There was no easy route, and the hilly terrain blocked their view behind tree trunks, but as they drew closer, the pitched post beckoned them to cross the gully.

Rachel reached it first. Chipped and faded whitewash did little to protect the weathered wood. She circled it and read the sign aloud, "*Indian Brook Reservoir.*" A pale green, hand-painted arrow pointed the way.

They locked eyes.

"It's the sign from my dream." Rachel felt short of breath.

"It's freaky." James circled around and stood next to her. "Why would it be hidden?"

"Who knows? It's old. Someone might've moved it."

James touched the faded, brush-stroke lettering. "It's like a forgotten relic."

She stepped back and surveyed the ground below the sign. "It could be a marker."

He followed her gaze. "Maybe an old hiking trail."

"Let's look for a path."

She stooped down and brushed away pinecones and twigs, then circled around. "This whole patch is smooth like an oasis."

The terrain near the sign was free of tree roots and brush, covered mostly with wispy grass and a tangle of weeds. She kicked away fallen branches and surveyed the knoll.

"It doesn't match." She tested the firmness of the soil with the heel of her sneaker and borrowed a hole. Then she crouched and dug in with her fingers. "You know I can't resist."

"Shit me." James bent next to her and probed the ground himself. "We have to dig."

"We'll come back with shovels." She jumped up; the next step was settled.

James nodded and stood next to Rachel to take in the sign.

"It's freaky enough that I'm open to it," he said. "You must've known about this somehow, right?"

"No way. I've never walked these woods, not with Sophia or anyone. I'm going hundred percent from the dream."

She reached out and took his hand. It was warm and steady.

They lingered a few moments, and then ambled back to the road, straining for any sound, any portent that might make them change plans. They leaned two large branches against a tree trunk to mark the spot where they'd need to cut through the woods when they returned.

By the time they got to their cars, they'd forgotten about the black bird.

FOUR

JAMES SLIPPED INTO THE GARAGE and grabbed a pit shovel. He stashed it in the back seat of his car. *Why am I sneaking around?* He quietly closed the door and headed up the back stairs, where he found his parents in the kitchen.

Dishes from breakfast were stacked in the sink, with no sign they'd be sorted before lunch. Game Day streamed from Aaron's phone.

Paula looked up from the newspaper. "Where'd you disappear to so early?"

James slunk toward the table. "Met up with Rachel for breakfast."

"How's she doing?" she asked as James bent to kiss her cheek.

"Good, she's graduated and is looking for a job."

"Good morning, almost afternoon," Aaron said as he got up from the table to give his son a hug. "Wow, that went fast."

"Time flies." James smiled and tapped his dad on the back with his fist as he returned to his seat.

"I remember when she started," Aaron said. "You said it spurred you into action."

James paused to consider a response that might be safe. "It was a tough time, and things at home were depressing. Are you here again for a while?"

Aaron exchanged glances with Paula, and then back. "My summer frees up when the school year ends, same as you."

"So, I guess you'll be staying?" James hoped it didn't sound as aggressive as it seemed after the question launched. He felt butterflies as he waited for an answer.

Paula said quickly, "Seems like a plan as long as it works for everyone."

"So, I guess the divorce was just for fun?" That came out worse, and James tried to soften it with raised eyebrows and a smirk as if it were obviously a joke.

Paula wet her lips. "Don't jump to conclusions. We're taking things as they come with no labels or expectations. You could call it a trial reconciliation."

"That works." He needed to say something positive. He switched his gaze to Aaron. "Don't forget, Mom's got a real job. What will you do all day?" That wasn't it. His teeth clanked shut.

Aaron's expression hardened. "Coaching's real; it just follows the school calendar."

"I know, I'm kidding, that came out wrong." Not a great start, wow, the snark came without even trying.

Aaron's voice was measured and calm. "We decided I would spend the summer here instead of my security gig in Massachusetts. Lots I can help with." He alternated his gaze between Paula and his son. "Things change."

James felt a flash of guilt. "Sorry, I didn't mean it bad."

He blamed his father for cheating on his mom and upending the family. Resentment ran deep, stoked by Aaron's hyper-competitive badgering during James's quarterback days.

"You'll have plenty to do, and you'll both enjoy the time, right?" James offered.

"I like having him around," Paula said. "It feels different now."

Aaron's cheeks flushed as he paused to consider. "It's a waste to repeat the same summer job when there's something solid here." He looked at Paula, and then shifted back to James. "We've been talking about it, and want to try."

"We've got projects lined up, things I've been putting off, like expanding the patio toward the garden," Paula said.

"That's included with my stay," Aaron added. "And I'm revisiting old friends."

James stiffened. "Like who?"

Aaron smiled. "Just buddies from before. There's a rowing club at the lake, nothing fancy. We race for fun when it's warm, just dinghies. It's like go-carts for old guys." He locked eyes with James. "Going later today if you wanna check it out."

"Sorry, already got plans. Just here for a quick bite, then gotta meet Rachel."

"I guess your breakup was just for fun?" Paula asked with a smirk.

James chuckled. "I wish." He took backward steps toward the refrigerator with his eyes on Aaron. "When's your next one? I'll make time."

"Saturdays, early evening."

"I'm off from the rink most Saturdays. Something will work." James opened the refrigerator and poked around, unpacking enough for a turkey sandwich, and then plopped things down on the counter. "Any news from Katherine?"

"She started her internship last week," Paula answered, eyes on the newspaper.

Aaron went back to Game Day.

"How's it going?" James focused on building his sandwich. "Does she like California?"

He fought to keep his voice completely neutral with no hint of shame or jealousy whatsoever. His sister was two years younger but only trailed him by a year in college because he took a gap because of the divorce. Katherine was a brain, and, of course, went to Stanford and, of course, had an internship in, of course, software engineering. Meanwhile, he worked at the hockey rink. It wasn't exactly an internship for sports management, but at least it was paid, which was more than could be said for his dad's summer job. The jocks of the family were striking out. Perfect.

"She loves it and says she's learning a lot," his mom said.

"That's great." James unscrewed the mustard.

"People are nice, and the climate's something new. It's her first summer in Palo Alto. But I think she misses home."

"Did she say so?" James asked.

"No, but she got quiet when I told her you and her dad were going to be here."

"Maybe that's why she took the internship," Aaron said with a chuckle as he stood and went to the sink. He eyed James's mess on the counter. "I'll get it with the other dishes."

"Thanks." James smiled and grabbed his plate and his father's spot at the table. "Internships put you in a different league. The race has started, and I'll never catch up."

"What race?" Paula asked and looked up.

"Seriously, Mom? The race to get ahead, to get a professional, corporate job." The look on his mother's face was one of astonishment. He found it annoying. Why such surprise? "Everything else is just crap work."

Aaron turned from the sink. "He's got a point."

"People need to be perfect, like robots, to get one of those jobs." James took a defiant bite of his sandwich. "Just look at Katherine. She's the exception, not the norm, and that's all they want."

Aaron went back to the dishes, and Paula shook her head.

"You're too young for such cynicism," she said. "Everyone takes a different path, and there's more than one route to happiness."

"But it helps if you're a robot," Aaron chimed in.

"Everything sucks for everyone young," James said. "I dread graduation, I'll probably end up right back here living with you."

Aaron laughed. "I'll join you; it'll be fun."

Paula's head kept shaking. "You both need to focus on the good you already have." She folded the paper in half. "Please remember that I'm here most of the year by myself, quite happily, and then school ends, and you come crashing in."

"Ouch," Aaron said from the sink.

"Katherine wins again," James said.

"No! I'm thrilled you're here." Her scowl boomeranged between them.

"I just might need some time to adjust when the men come thundering home."

There was a lull as Aaron finished loading the dishwasher and wiped his hands. "We won't be a burden, will, we James?" He waited for his son to shake his head. "Dishes are done, now on to the lawn." He placed his hand on James's shoulder as he passed. "See you later?"

"For sure, when you get back from the lake."

Aaron nodded, smiled, and went out the back door.

"What's it like when you're here alone?" James asked.

Paula shifted closer and lowered her voice. "I'm used to it. It's lonely sometimes, but the office keeps me busy. There's never a shortage of real estate to appraise."

"I mean, after we left the nest."

Paula's hands clasped on the table. "All mothers miss their kids when they leave for college."

"Does Dad help?"

"He does now; maybe he's a late bloomer? At first, he came up for weekends, and I started to trust him again." She smoothed her palms over the paper. "I have no expectations. I only want contentment, and I'm fine by myself. So, if that's not happening, I'll ask him to go."

James took a drink of water and plopped his napkin over the crumbs on his empty plate. "He's mellower now. I hope he stays that way. Maybe it helps I've moved on from football; we both thought it was all I could do."

"Some people can't change, but it seems like he did." Paula smiled and took his hand. "It hurt your studies back then. I know that, and so does Katherine. You shouldn't resent her."

"I don't, I'm sorry; my own fear of the future was talking more than anything."

James tightened his lips and squeezed her hand back. This was getting heavy, and it was time to pull the ripcord. "On a lighter note, can I ask a nosy question?"

The quiet of the kitchen was interrupted by the sputtering start of the lawnmower outside.

"Do you sleep together? I'm asking for Katherine." He couldn't hold back a grin.

Paula sighed and covered her mouth. "Yes, if you have to know." She whispered even though from the sound of the mower outside the coast was clear. "But it isn't everything. Before his needs came first; at least, it seemed that way to me. He's still vain, but I have a trick."

James raised his eyebrows.

"I don't pine for him. A cheater might cheat again, but now I don't care. If we sleep together, it's on my terms. He's a sexy ex with benefits, and for now, that's enough. I'm afraid if we formalized things the same bad patterns would repeat. I think that means I'm not fully recovered from the divorce."

Paula shrugged almost out of reflex. "I'm doing my best."

"That sounds good. I want you to be happy." He got up slowly and brought his plate to the dishwasher. "Thanks for sharing. I'm going to jump in the shower before meeting Rachel."

Paula smiled and folded her arms. "I'm glad you're still friends."

"So am I."

"I give you both credit for overcoming—"

James hugged Paula and she stopped, then he pointed out the window to the backyard.

"You should keep that guy extremely busy."

FIVE

RACHEL OFTEN DROVE WHITE-KNUCKLED even when she was the only one on the road. She blamed the accident, and the strangest part was she could only remember fragments of the crash so why would it still scare her so much? For that matter, many memories from that summer were spotty, and it irked her. Doctors said the memories would return, but they never did.

Rachel found herself speeding up and eased off the pedal. She had a shovel in the trunk. Her housemates used it in winter to clear snow from the driveway, so why wouldn't it work in the forest? There was a ridge on its top to stomp on.

She wasn't crazy. That much she hoped because she'd graduated with honors and had no memory glitches whatsoever except for details surrounding the week before college started, the end of the dark summer that killed her two best friends and left her hospitalized after crashing through a stockade fence for no apparent reason.

Rachel signaled left and turned onto Indian Brook. Gravel crackled under the tires as soon as she hit the packed-dirt road. Tall, billowy clouds mostly blocked the sun, but when it broke through, flares like spotlights blasted through the tree cover.

About a mile down the slope she spied James's car pulled over with the hazards flashing. She came up behind him and waved and left the engine running as she popped the trunk and hopped out. They'd agreed in advance to stash the shovels so the security guard at the entry gate wouldn't get suspicious. Rachel grabbed hers and hustled to the tree they'd marked. She hid it in a ditch right next to James's.

As she scurried back, James peeled out and headed for the parking lot, and she trailed close behind.

Rachel smiled at the security guard who checked the window decal and waved her through while James waited with his arms folded, leaning against his car.

"Thanks for doing this," Rachel said as she got out and secured the door. She popped her phone and keys into a red shoulder sling that crisscrossed her tank top. "I worried you might change your mind or get pulled into something with Paula and Aaron."

"No problem; of course not. I'm glad I had an excuse to get out of there." He wore a blue North Face backpack over a white v-neck tee with black shorts. "It's still a bit awkward with them. I'm not used to him being back, not yet. I was kind of a bitch."

He smiled and started jogging ahead.

Rachel caught right up and poked him. They made it past the security gate and jogged beyond the bend before slowing to walk.

"Do you think this will work," James asked, "satisfying your curiosity?"

"I'm hoping just acting on the dream will clear it." She shot him a wary look. "I know it's annoying, but I can't take another nightmare."

As a slower pace kicked in, their breathing made it easier to talk. "I hope the dream will lose its power source because there's nothing to the sign. Or maybe I can trick my mind to wake up as soon as the dream starts."

James shot her a smile. "OK, let's do this and set you free."

Rachel felt a rush of warmth. He was solid, just like always, plus looking good.

She shot him a smile back. "I'd love to prove I'm rational."

When they reached the marked tree, they cut left without a word, grabbed the shovels they'd stashed, and marched into the woods. Fallen branches and dried leaves crunched underfoot.

Their strides melded with cricket chirrups, assorted avian songs and shrieks, and the rush of the brook. Before long, they spied the silhouette of the sign in the distance.

"Does anyone but us even know it's there?" Rachel asked.

"I doubt it." He caught up and wiped the sweat from his forehead. "We could jimmy it out and no one would care."

Rachel nodded and pressed on, sidestepping a pricker bush. They crossed the gully and when they reached the crooked sign, she gripped the post. Though it appeared to be falling over, it was stuck firmly in place. She tried to wiggle it as she studied the lettering.

"Hand-painted over whitewash, definitely wicked old." She narrowed her eyes. "I'm burning the image into my subconscious to make sure it sticks."

James circled behind her and watched as she spoke to herself.

"OK, nightmare? I followed your breadcrumbs. Now, leave me alone."

She paused to take in the moment and listen to the soothing falls.

James gently touched her shoulder. "Do you still want to dig?"

Rachel bit her lip and surveyed the knoll. "Yeah, I do, just for the hell of it."

James nodded, took a few steps past the sign, and plunged his shovel into the ground. It didn't go deep, so he stamped down, shimmied the hardwood handle, and hoisted out some shovelfuls. He did a few more, and Rachel joined in. They found a rhythm and created a decent pile of dirt. The hard-packed top layer of weeds and roots gave way to moist earth below that was looser and easier to dislodge.

"Not a bad start." James took a breather to wipe his forehead. "Let me know when we're done."

Rachel stuck the shovel in the ground and propped herself against the handle. She took a deep breath and exhaled slowly. "I guess that's enough. Thanks for humoring me."

James pulled a water bottle from his backpack and took a swig before handing it to Rachel. "You take a break. I'll do a few more, as many as you want to kill the nightmare."

He grinned maniacally and attacked the hole they'd started with exaggerated vigor.

Rachel smiled as she watched him and took a drink. The best part of it all clearly was James and his muscles forced into manual labor in a clingy outfit. Why not let him continue for a while? She chuckled in spite of herself.

"What?" James looked up from the hole.

"I'm a bitch for making you do this."

"Just a little deeper; you tell me when." James scraped the side of his shovel along the bottom of the hole to smooth it out and tossed loose dirt onto the pile.

Rachel eyed the mound with dread. She realized they'd have to put it all back. "I think we're done. I'll start filling it in while you take a rest."

James suddenly roared and planted his legs while hoisting the shovel above his head with both hands. He scrunched up his nose, bared his teeth, and stared at Rachel as he proclaimed:

"Spirits from Rachel's nightmares, be gone! I cast thee out! With this thrust, you are exorcised from this place, and Rachel's brain is free forever!"

He ceremoniously plunged the shovel into the hole with all his might. He grunted and almost fell as it struck with a thud and abruptly halted with the spade halfway in.

"Ouch! Fucking rock." James shook out his left arm. After a pause, he tried again with significantly less bravado.

Rachel bent over the hole to watch as he hoisted out more dirt and scraped the shovel against the obstruction. He bent down and poked around with his fingers.

"It seems like wood."

He cleared more away and exposed some length, wriggling his fingers around it.

"It's a stick, like a plank."

Rachel knelt down on the other side of the hole to help. They both kept digging and exposed a thin weathered board. James shimmied it to loosen the end that was still buried, stooped down, and slowly pulled. The plank came to a whittled point.

"An old fence post," James said as he rubbed off caked-on mud, "like a stake."

He held it up.

"Listen—" Rachel said and covered her mouth before reaching out to grab it. "It's like the dream, the witch had it. This isn't fun anymore."

He poked in the trough with the tip of the shovel. After a few strokes, he felt it bump and scrape against something. He flung loose dirt with abandon.

Rachel watched and held her breath; her grip tightening on the fence post.

James kneeled and dug with both hands, his fingers probing to make it wider.

Something shifted in the dirt. He cleared away more and tugged at it.

"It feels like fabric. You gotta look."

Rachel dropped the post and kneeled on the opposite side of the ditch. She stared as James burrowed deeper and wriggled enough free to grasp.

Rachel reached in and touched it. They brushed away debris and exposed a swath of black satin. She tugged at the fabric, pressed down, and felt something hard and lumpy.

And then something thin, curved, and calcified poked through.

Rachel flinched when she touched it.

"Shit me deep," James said. He clamped on to jigger it with a circular motion out of the muck below the tear in the fabric. It resisted but loosened so he used more force and then all at once it broke free and he fell back.

She screamed and recoiled when he held up what looked like a rib bone thick with clumps of muddy sinew.

SIX

Five months earlier, Bucharest

TRAVIS CONSIDERED GERI UNREFINED because she didn't much care for the mortals living alongside them. They were interesting enough, but since some wound up as feed, she didn't empathize with the whole lot. He took this crudeness as part of the package and figured he'd strive to soften her over time. The goal was worthy: helping a fellow witch elevate from ingrained, baser instincts. So, he signed the contract despite misgivings.

He pushed the papers aside and waited as Geri served dinner in her renovated flat north of central Bucharest near the lakes. A fire crackled in a large stone hearth; golden light wavered on sloping masonry walls and chocolate-stained timber beams. Warmth wafted across the expanse of the main room toward the dining area, and mingled with a meaty aroma with notes of paprika, oregano, and sage.

"Are the papers in order?" She eyed the contract as she maneuvered the steaming Dutch oven onto a trivet on the table. "Coven law sometimes intrudes on otherwise private matters."

Travis swiveled sideways as his eyes shifted from the papers to meet hers.

"It protects us both because relationships are fraught with danger. I'm bad at them, most witches are. My parents were an exception, but I haven't even come close. Love can be illusory, and sometimes fleeting, even for mortals. The contract might help us both, a safety net."

She exaggerated a frown. "Is love what you're going for?"

"If I believed it might be real."

Geri reached out to rake the stubble on her mate's jawline. "Wiring for love doesn't always come naturally, especially given a witch's focus on matters of craft."

Travis filled their glasses with Bordeaux, and Geri took a sip before continuing.

"We could end up childless, a fate much worse than a contractual arrangement. We are bearers of potent bloodlines that otherwise will fall to waste."

Travis leaned back in the sturdy wooden chair and folded his arms. Meeting another witch from a family as powerful as his own would be difficult within the relatively small coven pool, especially considering physical attraction. And he knew openness, sharing, and warmth were definite stumbling blocks. How would one learn that? It was prudent to lock someone in.

"Squandering the work of my parents is not an option," he said. "The older I get, the less my power means without also connecting to something else. The contract helps us both."

The firelight danced on Geri's high cheeks and forehead. "Of course it does, and it's not uncommon for witches like us. We will retain rights to the child, whether or not we choose to stay together, and magic from both sides can be taught. Our heir will be empowered by both bloodlines, exactly as the coven wishes. Everyone wins."

He felt himself relax. It wasn't like he was used to this: planning a future with another person, witch or mortal. Was trust happening? He reached across the table to take her hand.

Potent bloodlines that otherwise will fall to waste.

He knew he might lose everything, just like his parents. Life was difficult for witches with no guarantees and capped by an eternity of darkness if you failed.

The hardwood floor creaked as he pushed back from the table

and went to Geri's side. He embraced her from behind the wooden slats of her chair and savored her citrusy scent.

"It's not a mortal's fairy tale, and not even close to what my parents shared, but it works."

He lingered a moment, and she bent backward to watch him as she squeezed his forearm.

"Don't torture yourself," she whispered. "Enjoy a nice dinner."

Travis nodded and sat back down as she served the braised lamb she'd obviously taken pains to prepare. He tasted it and let his thoughts drift from the contract to his plate. It was OK to relax. Life changes were stressful, especially when they came fast. And given his newcomer status in Bucharest, what more could he expect?

He was a bit of a coven celebrity, having rejoined it four years ago after experiments in a secluded Vermont town proved the potency of his family magic. The coven encouraged his reintegration, and in a year's time, he'd met Geri, a mysterious beauty from afar, also rootless and ripe.

Travis wanted an heir, especially given his brush with mortality during his American excursion, and it motivated him to act. Geri seemed to like the remoteness he attributed to his orphan status growing up. And here he was in her flat in Primăverii, an elegant neighborhood with a lake and shady strolls.

All at once, his psychology training kicked in.

Get out of your head and back to Geri. Focus on the present and give others the friendly focus that forms a connection. He genuinely wanted to do better, and forced himself forward.

"Shouldn't magic be something we aim to do together?" Travis asked as he scooched back from his plate. "We could collaborate now that we're united."

"I suppose we could. But we're both ambitious and pulled in different directions." She took a sip of wine. "Our family magic is predetermined; you know that better than anyone. Mine's mainstream, yours is mutant, but it's what you got from your ancestors."

"I could teach you," Travis said. "The threads would grant new options."

"Maybe someday. Right now, it's too crude and rough for my taste."

"The goal is to integrate, to make our need to refuel minimally invasive. My magic doesn't kill mortals. We are far outnumbered and can lose everything if we're discovered."

"I'll leave you to your noble work if you'll leave me to my dinner."

She smiled, but Travis took the hint and retreated to the lamb and his thoughts.

Coven walls no longer confined witches, and the mortals who lived alongside them were oblivious to their presence. However, witches faced a never-ending need to replenish power to sustain an immortal lifespan, and spells drained reserves. So did weapons like his bolts.

Travis had completed his PhD and worked at the general hospital's center for child trauma and resilience. Psychology provided fertile ground for intercepting human angst. He didn't create pain and fear himself; it came into his office. His goal was to retool his magic to feed from whatever trauma was already there.

Geri's work as an adjunct professor of management theory granted her access to a diverse pool of locals. Her magic was traditional, woven widely throughout the coven, meaning she needed to sometimes murder to refuel, or got an energy boost from the suffering she created.

"Do you consider your mate barbaric?" Geri asked with a playful grin. She flinched and then froze. "Damn, I forgot the arugula." As she jumped up from her chair, a Pucci print dress clung to her tiny baby bump and shifted as she raced to the kitchen.

Travis cupped his hands around his mouth so the words would carry.

"Don't run, and you might question if you are being complacent, defensive, and resistant to change," he called out with a snigger in his voice. "I know just the fix. Free classes in my family magic, limited time offer."

He waited until he saw her coming back.

"Well, for you, the offer's always open."

Geri sauntered in with the salad bowl. "I know I should want to, but I'll wait until it works. Right now I've got bigger worries." She eyed her stomach with a sly grin.

Travis stood and pattered his fingertips across her belly. "I understand. I'm the outlier who got stuck with black pearls." They locked eyes, and he smiled. "They're an acquired taste. I don't blame you for not trying, especially not right now. Maybe someday when the baby is older."

Geri took his hand. "I wish you could relent."

"So do I, but not until I understand more. I'm on the cusp of a big advance for the whole coven if it secures our replenishment without inflicting pain."

"I hope you're right." She raised her chin to meet Travis's eyes, and he smiled.

"I hope so too, but there are still kinks."

"What kinks?"

He combed for the right words, and shifted his gaze to the ceiling beams.

"A danger lurks behind the spell." A spark popped from a log, and he went back to his chair to serve the salad as Geri settled into her seat. "My parents faced it too when they lost control of three conjurings here in Bucharest."

"I heard about it," Geri whispered. "It's coven legend now, a cautionary tale."

"There were kinks of my own in America." Travis took in Geri's gaze. "Conjured souls suspended in hell while completing my spell's cycle. I was blindsided."

Geri's eyes narrowed. "Can you isolate the suspicious threads?"

"Not yet, so I've switched tactics entirely." Travis put down his fork. "I'll use existing pain instead of creating it myself. I posit that will tame it."

"Tell me more."

"There's an orb, a crystal ball of sorts, that doesn't tell the future but reveals the past."

Geri exhaled slowly and laid her fork down as she waited for him to continue.

"It extracts deeply guarded secrets, much like hypnosis, and festering pain is unearthed without creating more. I refuel from it while the subject releases inner demons. We both benefit."

Geri refocused on her salad. "Our magic is black and can only be so tepid; this sounds rather benign. Is it even witchcraft? Sounds more like standard psychotherapy. Instead of fueling the doctor's ego, the released trauma replenishes his power."

"It's a sustainable way to coexist. The coven needs to remember we are far outnumbered. Insights from the patient will hasten treatment and the magic advances therapeutic goals."

Geri smiled and refreshed his glass of wine. "You're a witch and now an expectant father. Don't forget you need to refuel or die."

Travis frowned and almost imperceptibly nodded. "I understand."

"Would you kill for me or your baby?"

Travis prodded the lamb bone with his fork. "For me to murder goes against everything my parents and their own ancestors worked for." He took a healthy sip of wine. "They knew they were on the cusp of a revolution and left it to me to advance."

"You might need to bend, as well." She leaned back and rubbed her belly. "There may be times when you'll need to empower us both."

Travis exhaled slowly, raised his eyebrows, and smiled with clamped lips.

When they finished dinner, he reread the contract, and then let his mind drift to baby names. He'd share two favorites with Geri once he'd nailed them.

Milena? Constantin?

SEVEN

TRAVIS WATCHED THE BOY FIDGET, close enough to touch but far enough away to be in another world. His new patient wouldn't lock eyes and shot furtive glances though a straggle of raven hair as he withered on the sofa seat cushion.

"How are you?" Travis's voice was deep and soothing and blended with the whir of the heater motor.

The student stiffened, and clutched at the sleeve of his sweater that was too short to reach his narrow wrist. "Fine, Dr. Coman."

"You can call me Travis." The psychologist beamed the friendliest smile he could muster and held it. "Do you like Andrei or Andy?"

"I don't care," Andrei whispered as he shook his head to nudge hair out of his eyes.

Travis eyeballed the folder on the edge of his desk.

"Mrs. Berceanu brought you because your father couldn't come."

The student shuffled and peeked out again. "He works at the restaurant."

"I know." Travis smiled again and leaned back in his chair. "I wonder why Mrs. Berceanu wants us to talk."

Andrei tugged at both sweater sleeves and seemed bothered they didn't reach far enough.

"She teaches social studies and wants me to speak up in class. She thinks I'm shy or distracted and not listening."

He dared to look up. "She says I look sad, but I'm not. I'm just tired. I don't always sleep well."

"I wonder why?"

Andrei crinkled his thin, aquiline nose and exhaled through his plump lips. "No reason."

Travis took in his patient's tone and body language, which signaled discomfort.

"Do you feel sad?"

"No."

"Then what?" Travis leaned back and gave the boy time to think.

Andrei shifted in his chair and looked past Travis to something outside the window. High cheekbones created a hollowness that made him appear undernourished and younger than fifteen. His eyes narrowed. "Sometimes I daydream. I get tired, and I can't pay attention. I think that's why Mrs. Berceanu got mad. I didn't answer the question. Well, I couldn't because I didn't hear it."

Travis paused and let the heating fan disperse calm before he continued. "She isn't mad. She's very nice and volunteered to wait outside. She cares about you. She thinks this winter break would be the perfect time for us to meet."

"She shouldn't have called my father." The boy's eyes darted from Travis to the window.

Travis folded his hands, smiled, and leaned toward his patient. "She needed his permission to bring you. She's worried about the daydreams."

Andrei peeked at Travis then looked away again.

"Daydreams are cool," Travis continued. "I like them too. It's healthy to let your mind roam. But sometimes you can miss important stuff, like the talking in a movie or a classroom, if you don't pay attention." He waited until the boy looked up. "Do you like movies?"

Andrei frowned for a moment. "Yes."

"What kind?"

"Action, I think, with explosions and fights."

"Who takes you?"

Andrei puzzled again. "What do you mean?"

"To the movies: who brings you there?"

"No one. I watch them on TV."

Travis smiled and wheeled his chair a bit closer. He watched Andrei settle against the arm rest. There was a bruise blending with his patient's eyebrow, and a scrape on his nose. Mrs. Berceanu had mentioned them over the phone.

"What's your favorite subject?" Travis asked, upbeat and probing.

"Math."

"Who's your favorite teacher?"

Andrei considered it. "I guess Mrs. Berceanu." He shifted on the couch. "But she shouldn't have called my father."

"Why?"

Andrei crinkled his nose. "It's bad when a teacher calls."

"Bad, how?"

For the first time, Andrei seemed to study Travis from head to toe.

"Do you play sports?" he asked.

"Yes, sometimes. It's important for everyone to make time for exercise." Travis smiled and leaned forward. "Do you like sports?"

His patient bit his lower lip. "I like my bike."

"Oh, wow, tell me about that." Travis leaned back with his fingers locked over his knee.

Andrei's gaze drifted to the window. "I ride all around Bucharest."

"With who?"

"Friends from school."

Travis waited for more, but nothing came. "Where did you get the bike?"

"My dad," Andrei said and shifted his eyes back to Travis. "It was a present."

"For what?"

There was a long pause. "After my mom died."

Travis maintained a steady, even tone.

"Can you tell me about that?"

Andrei shook his head and then went still. He stared out the window and blinked away tears.

Travis passed him a box of tissues and tightened his lips. He wouldn't push any further, there would be plenty of time to talk, little by little. He waited, and Andrei was soon still as stone.

"Maybe someday your dad will come to join us. I already spoke to him."

Andrei recoiled, eyes wide. "You told him?"

"Yes, it's normal to invite the parent to meetings, especially in the beginning."

Andrei exhaled loudly and slowly. "He won't like it."

"Why?"

"I have to be good at school." Andrei wiped his nose, bunched up the tissue, and tossed it in the can beside the couch.

Travis spoke quietly and leaned in. "You're not in trouble."

"I think I am with Mrs. Berceanu."

"Not at all. Don't forget, she cares about you. You're a great student. She doesn't want you to miss important things in class. The daydreaming makes things harder."

Andrei sat quietly to consider, then his words came in a burst. "I'm sorry! Sometimes I don't pay attention, but that's it, that's the only problem. I promise I'll do better."

Travis watched his patient carefully and hoped for eye contact, but the boy's gaze remained fixed out the window. There wasn't a view.

Travis spoke again when it became clear the boy was finished. "You did really well. This was a great first session. I'll look forward to seeing you next week. Your father told me I could find him at the restaurant to talk about how meetings might work." Travis smiled widely. "Someday he might come too. Are you ready to go back outside?"

Andrei nodded, and Travis led his patient to the waiting room to rejoin his teacher. Andrei flashed a shy grin and a quick glance at the doctor before he shuffled to the door with Mrs. Berceanu. Travis saw them out and returned to his office to write up notes.

When he finished, he poked at his cellphone, verified an address, and checked the time. He'd have to rush because Andrei's father had made it very clear he could only meet before the dinnertime crunch.

EIGHT

THE CAB DRIVER TOOK TRAVIS along the busy thoroughfare of Calea Victoriei, which carved through the city's architectural heart, the "Little Paris" of Bucharest. The peak of the Romanian Athenaeum triggered a memory. The columns and metallic lyres on each identical portal window spanning its circular dome, oddly, made him think of his dog, Luca. Travis figured the coven compound of his youth couldn't have been far away. The Carpathian sheepdog had torn about the open courtyard in front of the concert hall, now a manicured glow of holiday lights.

He arrived in the Old Town center, and Travis strolled along the cobblestones of Strada Stavropoleos, guided by ornate, wrought-iron street lamps in the wintry dusk of late afternoon. Andrei's father worked nearby at Caru' cu bere—The Beer Wagon—a traditional Romanian restaurant popular with locals and favored by tourists. When he entered, a woman at a thick, walnut-stained podium greeted him below the oiled wooden arches and ornate supports that rose to emerald-green ceiling domes covered with hand-painted coats of arms.

"I'm looking for Stefan," Travis said. "He's expecting me."

"Of course. You'll find him at the bar." She pointed to the back of the cavernous space.

Travis smiled, craned his neck, and then made his way across intricate blue and gold tiles. A ruggedly handsome worker with broad shoulders and a snug uniform perched alone on a barstool.

His knee twitched as it bent over the padded seat beneath the rounded corner of an enormous wooden island that anchored eight ornamental draught beer fonts.

Travis bellied up to the bar.

"Pardon me. I'm looking for Stefan."

The man turned his head and raised his eyebrows. "That's me."

Travis extended his hand. "Nice to meet you. I'm Dr. Coman; we spoke earlier. I've just started seeing Andrei."

Stefan smiled, stood, and extended his hand. "Of course. It's nice to meet you, too, Dr. Coman."

Travis shook hands. "Thanks for taking a moment to meet. You can call me Travis."

Stefan took a step away from his stool. "Sometimes I feel silly in the uniform," he said as he smoothed the front of his checkered shirt into his black trousers, and tugged at his bowtie. "They even make us wear suspenders. Tourists like the details; it's more of an event."

Travis took a step back and signaled his appraisal with a nod. "You look nice. Is this a good time?"

"Right now is fine unless a tour bus hits."

Travis surveyed the room. "It's a very popular place. I hope that means good tips."

"Sometimes it does, but it's never enough. Life is expensive."

Travis leaned in closer. "Can we talk about Andrei?"

Stefan turned his head toward the back. "It's better if we go upstairs."

Travis nodded and followed the waiter as he walked to a winding wooden staircase that led to a balcony level overlooking the bar. Stefan grabbed the first table, comfortably wedged between an intricately painted support beam, and a thick, hand-carved wooden banister that guarded the ledge.

"We'll have some privacy here." Stefan pulled out a chair and motioned for Travis to sit at the round, walnut-stained table. "I work this section. It's closed for a while longer."

Travis settled into his chair and folded his arms.

"So, what's the issue with Andrei?" Stefan asked.

Travis exhaled slowly. "His teacher, Mrs. Berceanu, is worried about him."

Stefan stiffened in his seat. "She shouldn't be; he's got good grades."

"Yes, he's an excellent student. But she thinks he could do even better. Trouble is he's distracted and missing things because he can't pay attention."

"Can't or won't?" Stefan scoffed and rolled his eyes. "He does the same thing at home."

Travis took in the body language of the boy's father. "I wonder why?"

Stefan nudged his chair back a bit. "ADD. Ever hear of it?"

"I think it could be more than that." Travis paused and leaned in. "Marks on his face, bruises, low self-esteem."

The waiter exhaled slowly. "Boys are accident-prone; just last week he fell off his bike, almost needed stitches."

Travis bit his tongue and nodded as he focused on Stefan's face. His strong jaw was clamped tight, and his eyes darted about. "Can you tell me about his mother, what happened?"

"You mean my wife?" The consonants popped out loud and sharp.

"Yes."

Stefan took a deep breath and gazed into the soft light of the golden chandelier floating in the expanse across from them. "She died last year."

"I'm sorry." Travis continued to watch him. "Can you talk about it?"

Stefan placed his arms in his lap and spoke quietly. "There was an accident; a drunk driver swiped her while she was crossing an intersection. Well, we think the driver was drunk because the police never caught the perpetrator. The car didn't stop; maybe didn't even know."

Travis rocked forward in his chair. "That's horrible, I'm very sorry."

The boy's father nodded slowly. "Thank you, it's still raw."

There was silence except for the murmur of voices on the lower level and the occasional clatter of dishes and stemware.

"Maybe you could come in with Andrei." Travis raised his eyebrows and did his best to appear mildly upbeat. "You can both talk about it."

"For what? Adversity stalks everyone. You suck it up and move on otherwise it bites you, too." He seemed distracted by the patrons below. "You haven't figured that out by now?"

Travis was adept at keeping a measured voice. "Things can fester and go bad if you don't talk."

"That's easier said than done. If you feel you need to talk to Andrei, fine, but don't expect me to join in." The clanking of glassware got louder, or else seemed to. "I still think it's ADD. Let's get him medicated like they do in America." Stefan's breathing quickened, and his focus drifted back to the chandelier.

"I'm sure it's hard on Andrei too."

"It's worse for a husband." Stefan rolled up the sleeves of his checkered shirt, revealing a tattoo on one thick forearm.

"Why would it be harder for you than Andrei?"

Travis kept his voice neutral and studied the man's face. He looked vaguely familiar, like a square-jawed generic movie actor who had to wait tables on the side. He might be famous one day or broke the next.

Stefan gave the psychologist an annoyed look. "I'm sure it isn't easy for him, but he only knew her for a few years. He's adopted, a gypsy, he's lucky he got away."

Travis took a deep breath. "That's wonderful, I didn't know. How did you find him?"

The boy's father rubbed his temples and then focused across the table. "We couldn't conceive, and, believe me, we tried. So, we went to an agency. Do you have to know everything?"

Travis smiled. "No, I'm sorry. I'm just eager to learn all I can. It's part of my job."

"And what exactly is that?"

"To help your son." Travis watched Stefan stiffen. "He's hurting."

"We're all hurting. He'll toughen up. He's young and 'resilient.' Isn't that the word?"

"Yes, but it doesn't happen by itself. I'm going to see him regularly. You are welcome to join us."

Stefan folded his arms and gripped tight. "I don't like whining to strangers."

"It will help Andrei." Travis felt the tightness of his own smile and held the waiter's gaze.

"And what exactly do you think is the problem?"

Travis narrowed his eyes and shook his head. "I don't know yet. But the disassociation, diffidence, and withdrawal are consistent with symptoms of abuse." He watched for a reaction, but the boy's father sat motionlessly. "And the bruises are troubling."

"I already told you, he falls off his bike; he hurts himself."

A spasm below the table rocked it, and the plates clattered. "You should've seen him when we got him. He was like a scarecrow. Anything messed up about him happened before he came to us."

Stefan's fingers thumped the tabletop and his eyes darted about the balcony level before he unleashed more.

"Yes, he's quiet. Except when he isn't and bursts out and refuses to listen. He wasn't raised right. Gypsies have their own ways. He's got to learn things now, and catch up, or it's going to be too late. I'm doing the best I can by myself."

Travis watched quietly.

"I'm sorry, I feel pressure to raise him. I know he needs to do well in school. If you don't think it's ADD, then maybe you can help him." Stefan looked through the carved rails of the banister. "We're filling up, and my shift's going to start soon. Let me bring you dinner, one of our specialties."

Travis checked the time on his phone. He liked the idea of observing Stefan at work.

"Sure, it's practically dinnertime. But only if it's OK for you, and I pay the regular price."

"Great, you're the first one in my section, and at my favorite table. You eat meat, yes?"

Travis nodded, and Stefan smiled broadly for the first time, his lips thick, and his desire to please a welcome, if abrupt, change of mood.

Travis watched him descend the winding, wooden staircase, dart across the tiled floor, joke with a bartender, and then disappear into the kitchen.

There's a snake charmer somewhere inside there.

His mind raced. How hard should he push to get Stefan to join his son's sessions? The man was obviously dodgy and defensive. It might be best to get Andrei to open up alone first, and magic would do the rest. He could test drive the orb. Andrei would open to him and expose the source of his trauma. Any abuse from Stefan would come out. And the process would spin fuel. It was a win/win and potentially a huge time saver; talk therapy might not even break the boy's defenses.

By the time Stefan ascended the winding staircase, Travis was ready for him. He watched his waiter approach with a boyish charm, pleased as he presented a platter of grilled skewers.

"Here we are," Stefan said with a flourish. "One chicken, pork, veal, and turkey." He pointed out each perfectly charred chunk wedged between onions and peppers. "And, of course, our home-made bread."

"Thank you. It looks great." Travis widened his obsidian eyes and smiled warmly.

Stefan's expression turned from satisfaction to shock. "My God, and to drink? I completely forgot. I got busy with other tables, and I knew you were waiting and the usual order of things changed because the food came before—"

"It's perfectly fine, no worries. Flat water would be great."

"And wine? Do you want the list?"

"A glass of red? Any cabernet you can recommend."

"Of course. I have a favorite." Stefan backed up. "I'll be right back."

A smile returned to his face, and he disappeared down the stairs.

The skewers were hot, and Travis carefully served himself as he pondered over Stefan's apology and panic from a simple oversight. Now it seemed clear the man might benefit from meetings of his own without his son. Anger and alarm lurked just below the surface.

Before long Stefan returned to plunk a chilled liter of water on the table and then presented the wine like a surprise from behind his back.

"This is a reserve, and it's one of our best. I want you to have it." Stefan flashed the charming grin again. He opened the bottle, poured a sample, and waited for Travis.

"Wow, an excellent choice; can I afford it?" Travis smiled as he swirled it.

"It's just a demi. I want to offer something."

Travis took another sip and leaned back. "I appreciate it; thanks so much."

"My pleasure. I hope you enjoy." Stefan filled his glass and left the bottle beside the water. "Do you need anything else?"

Travis surveyed the spread in front of him.

"No, this is perfect."

Stefan's focus shifted, and he nodded to acknowledge the hostess who led four patrons to a nearby table. "We're getting busy now. I'll check back later."

Travis smiled and raised his glass as he sped off.

Over the course of the meal, Travis watched Andrei's father as he navigated the dining room to take orders and serve guests that started to fill up the balcony. His hunch that Stefan was a charmer bore out. The waiter solicited hoots from a table of Brits with his fine English and good-natured willingness to please.

"How are you doing here?" Stefan asked as he swooped in a while later seemingly from nowhere and surveyed the table.

"I think that's about all I can manage." He'd polished off most of his meal. "I can see why this place is popular."

"Do you want me to wrap it up?" Stefan refilled the water glass.

"No, there's not enough to trouble you."

"More wine?"

"No, all set. It is wonderful. Just the check when you can."

Stefan nodded and cleared the table. "Of course, I'll be right back."

Travis watched Stefan whizz down the stairs and disappear through swinging doors into the kitchen.

Should I try to get him to come in alone?

The restaurant buzzed with activity while Travis finished the last of the wine, and Stefan returned with the bill. He passed Stefan his credit card to run through the reader and handed him a business card.

"Here's my information. I see Andrei on Tuesdays at 2 p.m."

Stefan scrutinized it while they waited for the transaction to complete.

"Don't forget he has an active imagination. He exaggerates, just so you know."

The waiter tucked Travis's contact info into his shirt pocket.

The doctor studied Stefan's face and noted a shift in mood; dark brows creased as he tugged at the receipt that spat from the card reader.

"Do you want to join next time?" Travis was upbeat despite the troubled look on the waiter's face. "Or you could come alone. There are many things we could talk about. The goal is to share with someone and feel known; it can change everything. I'm sure I can help."

There was a pause as Stefan ripped the receipt free. "I haven't agreed to anything. I need time to think." Stefan forced a smile as he slid the paper and pen to Travis. "I'll talk to Andrei in the morning about the trouble he's caused. I don't get off until after midnight."

Travis shot a wary look at Stefan as he signed the receipt.

"He hasn't caused any trouble."

"Hasn't he? His daydreams? This meeting?" Stefan's lips locked tight.

"Daydreams aren't unusual." Travis didn't want the encounter to end on a sour note. He smiled. "We'll get to the bottom of it."

"You might not like what you find."

"How's that?"

Travis's alarm sounded. Now he wanted to leave before things degenerated further.

Stefan bit his lip and looked away. "The gypsy in him, something wasn't right."

Travis stood as he pushed his chair back from the table. "Then that's exactly why some attention is appropriate. My job is to help him understand his feelings better, which leads to growth. And the proper term is Romani, not gypsy, which is pejorative."

The psychologist smiled and held out his hand. "It was a great pleasure meeting you. Thanks for your hospitality. I really enjoyed everything."

Stefan gripped Travis's hand tightly and held it until a patron nearby waved for service.

"I'm very glad you came in. I'll talk to Andrei, and I'll do better. I won't call him Gypsy Boy. I'm sure I'll see you again. I might even come in, but I need some time."

Stefan turned away.

Travis lingered for a moment and then wound down the staircase. He waited near the entry podium and watched as Stefan looped into the kitchen.

He would stop calling Andrei 'Gypsy Boy'?

That's great work, Doctor, congratulations.

Travis cringed and slunk out of the restaurant.

NINE

SORINAH HELPED MARKU TIDY his favorite spot in the world: the far corner of his room with the rocking chair. Housekeeping wasn't part of her job, but she pitied the mortal. He had no friends, and after observing him for months, she figured it was because he liked being alone. Time wasn't a luxury residents at Floreasca Manor could afford to waste on a loner.

She'd taken the nursing home job to establish a base to help Travis so that when the spell he was devising was ready, she could join him with his experiments.

Marku sat in the wooden rocker and watched her as she made the bed.

"You don't have to do that," he said after clearing his throat. "I don't mind it messy."

"Things are quiet today; I've got extra time." Sorinah smoothed out the bedspread, surveyed the room, then unfolded a metal chair, and sat next to him. "Want to play hearts?"

Marku smiled shyly and shook his head. He wore a stained, white t-shirt that clung to the slight paunch above his belt. Close-cropped silver hair was full and youthful. She wondered why he was in a home for the elderly at all. Sure, he was seventy-five, but also healthy and sharp. Some people had nowhere else to go, she decided.

"Have you made any friends?" Sorinah shuffled the deck of cards.

Marku shook his head again and looked toward the window.

"You told me you were going to work on that."

Marku's eyes met hers as he considered. "It's harder than it sounds."

"Access to others is one of the perks of being here." Sorinah widened her eyes and smiled. "Otherwise, you could live by yourself or with family."

"There's no one else; my wife left me."

"What about your sister?" She tapped the cards on the metal seat to line them up.

Marku struggled to sit higher on the polished wood of his rocker. "She was older and died two years ago. I have some cousins, but they moved to the Eurozone."

"I'm not sure I realized she'd passed. I'm sorry."

"I don't think I told you." Marku's lips formed a tight smile, and he gazed toward Sorinah but avoided her eyes. "She took me in after the revolution and never asked for anything. But I earned my keep. I ran her store. And when she got older, I took care of everything. I gave her retirement from the headaches of the store."

Sorinah paused and held a smile. "I'm sure she was very grateful."

"It was hard to get around, and in the end, she had a walker. But I got her to the monastery at least once a week." The man's eyes drifted from Sorinah to the window. "Stones and stairs aren't easy. She would have liked this much better; there's an elevator, and the monastery's close."

The heater near the window kicked on, and no one spoke for a moment.

"I wouldn't be alone if she had lasted longer," Marku whispered.

Sorinah leaned forward. "You shouldn't be."

"It's a choice." He rocked slowly in the chair. "I trust no one."

"That isn't healthy. Everyone needs other people." She shimmied the cards back into the box. "I know someone you can talk to."

Marku raised his eyebrows and sat straighter. "A priest? That's what I need."

Sorinah tightened her lips and gently shook her head. "He's like a priest in that he's trained to listen very carefully. He's a professional, a doctor, a psychologist."

He started rocking again. "You already listen enough."

She smiled gently. "But it's not really helping, is it? You need real friends, and I'm just a worker. I haven't seen you meet anyone or even try to mingle in the dining room. You sit by yourself, and when someone comes near, you scowl. It scares them away."

"That's just the way I am."

Sorinah put her hand on the arm of the rocker. "It doesn't have to be that way. My friend, the doctor, can teach you to share without being afraid."

The man smiled and stopped the chair again. "Now you sound like my sister." He eyed the cards on her chair. "Do you want to play hearts? You can tell me more about this psychologist."

Sorinah nodded and passed him the box.

"His name is Travis, and he's also my teacher. He works with an orb that opens people up. It's fun, like a game, a crystal ball. You like games. I'll bring him to meet you whenever you're ready." She watched his eyes dart about as he considered.

Marku slid out the cards, shuffled, and smiled a little as he dealt them on the bedspread.

"I do enjoy games."

TEN

RACHEL'S HOUSEMATES WERE AWAY for the weekend, so she and James crashed at her apartment to analyze their grisly discovery in the woods and self-medicate with alcohol. James even grabbed a change of clothes so he wouldn't have to drive home. His parents didn't question his motives, and he guessed they hoped he and Rachel were getting back together.

"The Sussex police think I'm crazy, again." Rachel propped herself against pillows on the living room couch, hoisting a heavy pour of white wine. A chilled bottle on a side table was within reach. "I have quite a record." She paused. "Let me see. There's Mia and Sophia, then the car crash, and then the hospital. Oh, and they pointed out my persistent one degree of separation from the worst crimes this town has seen in generations, and now this."

"It's better if they think you're crazy." James sat on an easy chair with thick leather cushions. He drank a Heady Topper and kicked off his high tops. "You can't find corpses based on a dream, right? It's suspicious and sounds alarms."

"Maybe I'm psychic." Rachel watched him stretch out. "Be careful."

"That might be the one thing keeping you out of jail." Rachel's jaw dropped, and James smirked. "Joking." He took a sip of beer. "It's more likely that someone mentioned the reservoir and it stuck in your subconscious. Now that it's summer again, the memory got triggered, though what we found is spooky AF."

When they'd uncovered the remains, they'd called 911. James stopped digging and they waited in mostly stunned silence until the police arrived. Shadows got dark, every creak, rustle, and gurgle suddenly sinister. Rachel stared at the bone and black satin in the ditch and was certain it was Sophia. The dreams had led her there, the enormity of the uncanny discovery just beginning to sink in.

And the police and forensics team had questions.

"Why would you guess it's Sophia Hurley?" a detective asked Rachel.

"She was my close friend, and I had nightmares about her."

"So, why here?"

"The sign was in every dream, like an omen. It begged me to find it."

"Again, why would you suggest these remains are Ms. Hurley's?"

"The black dress she wore to our last dinner. There's no way I could forget it. We had just come from our friend's funeral. I know in my bones it's her."

The forensics team later uncovered a skeleton draped in formal wear exactly as Rachel described.

James showed the police the fence post he'd pulled from the ditch, and it was entered into evidence. And within hours, breaking news reports confirmed a corpse had been found in the woods near the reservoir. For a community the size of Sussex this was big, and soon an unnamed source leaked they believed it to be the long-missing Sophia Hurley, pending the results of DNA evidence. Another leak proposed a cause of death: she'd been impaled by a fencepost and buried along with it in a shallow grave. The whole town was abuzz. Web and TV reports showed yellow police tape roping off a swath of the Indian Brook woods with plenty of onlookers and cameras.

"Someone in the station has loose lips," Rachel said and took a sip of Pinot Grigio.

James nodded and bit his lower lip. "Just wait until we get

pulled in deeper. When I stopped home to grab stuff, I didn't leak a word to my parents. It's just a matter of time."

"And then the drama will start again. Don't forget, I'm still the 'last clique member' concealing a suicide pact." She downed her glass and refilled it. "They say we planned it, but now the skeleton in the woods changes the narrative. I hate that I've done this without even trying. How the hell could my dream know? It scares me to death."

"Try to keep calm." James put down his beer can, folded his hands, and leaned toward her. "How are you doing?" She just looked at him. "You actually seem better than this morning, some progress, right? It makes me hope now the dreams will stop."

"I don't know what to make of anything. I'm trembling a little. It's the shock of finding Sophia after all this time." She held his gaze. "What if everything in the dream really happened? I always knew she didn't just disappear or run away, and so did you. Finding her body gives a smidgen of release. Maybe now they can catch the killer. Her parents deserve closure. They never held a funeral because they hoped she'd turn up one day."

"But not like this. It opens a shit ton of questions." James reached for his beer.

"What if a witch really chased her, like in my dream? Why wouldn't it be true, as real as her skeleton? And it makes me wonder about Mia too. I know she didn't kill herself."

They sat without speaking for a moment. A car idled on the street outside and then passed when the light changed, projecting shadows through the picture window onto the ceiling. Everything felt spooky again.

Rachel swiveled to sit straight on the cushion with her legs folded beneath her.

"I really wonder what happened after we left the tavern. Why did Sophia turn onto Indian Brook when she should have continued straight? The killer might be local. Someone who could randomly lurk, then act, and then return home unnoticed. I don't know what's worse, the witch from my dream or someone she knew."

"Let's hope the police step up. I want the killer to pay." He took a long, slow drink. "It's been four years. What if the trail's gone cold?"

Rachel clicked on the TV. "Let's see if there's an update. I'm glad you can stay." She cycled through the menu listing.

James drained the can. "I'm glad I'm not driving," he said, catching her eye. "I'm going to pop another Heady. Need anything?"

Rachel examined her supply. "I'm fine for now, thanks. Grab whatever you want."

James went to the kitchen, and Rachel flicked to the local news. She eyed the ticker on the bottom of the screen, but nothing had changed.

Besides, there was James. The attraction was back and not only because he hadn't laughed off her nightmares. Together they'd discovered the impossible, a knoll in the woods between dream and reality. Life was strange and scary and fleeting and she wanted to act.

"Anything new?" James asked as he entered with a fresh beer and studied the screen.

"No, I'm muting it." Rachel grabbed the remote, and then poked at her phone. A playlist started from a speaker in the far corner of the living room. "We deserve to chill. It's been quite a day." She tapped the cushion next to her. "Want to join me?"

James concealed a grin behind the rim of the can, and went to the couch. He sat and pulled one leg up as he swiveled toward her. "I wasn't sure I was allowed."

Rachel smiled and rested her hand on his thigh below the edge of his shorts. "Neither was I." She leaned toward him, and their noses touched. He moved close and wrapped his arm around her shoulder. "That feels nice, familiar like before, but different now."

James leaned in to kiss her. "I know what you mean."

Rachel felt the firmness of his full lips press against hers and remembered his taste. Her hand moved from his thigh to his chest and any distance between them melted.

"I'd like to think we're allowed to be happy, at least sometimes."

He pulled back slightly to fix on her brown eyes. "After all we've been through."

"It feels like nothing's changed, except everything."

Rachel smiled and stroked his close-cropped hair. "I don't want to ruin whatever I touch. You know I believe in fate, the scary kind that doesn't let you escape. I feel that tingling again like the summer when Mia died. Please let this be different." She paused, and their eyes locked. "Maybe finding Sophia set a new pattern in motion, a healing one, you know?"

Rachel felt James push forward, and she leaned back as he shifted on top, his weight warm, solid, and welcome. As they kissed, she felt his hand reach below her shirt and a slow, steady pulsing that synched with each breath. She wanted to forget everything except the feeling of safety that came with a connection restored.

"The real test is tonight, the nightmares," she whispered. "Please, God, let me sleep."

And then James soothed away any desire to say another word.

ELEVEN

THE LAST WEEKEND IN MAY brought Sussex a welcome taste of summer.

James agreed to help his father Aaron with the garden they'd planted on Mother's Day. Bags of mulch and a pair of shovels waited on the lawn next to the recently tilled soil. Aaron cut one of the bags open with scissors and pulled on work gloves.

"Do you think Katherine's staying away just to avoid me?"

James loaded a shovel with mulch and piled some next to a row of eight-inch tomato seedlings. "No, Dad, she's got a great internship. It has nothing to do with you."

"I hope you're right." He kneeled next to his son, and they carefully smoothed handfuls of mulch around the plant stems. "I still have the guilt thing going."

James turned to face his father. "I like having you back, if that matters."

Aaron's lips clenched into a tight grin. "Of course, it does."

James felt close with his dad again, a welcome shift after years of resentment. "It seems like Mom does, too. That's the most important."

"I can't expect forgiveness. I just want to do better." Aaron packed down the fresh layer and grabbed another handful. "I was wrong, and really lucky to get another chance. The therapy helps me look at my impact on others. I'm different now, I hope you can see that."

"I don't know if I'm ready for this much bonding." James jumped up to shovel another load and shot Aaron a smirk. "Seriously though, I get what you're saying about second chances. Rachel and I are back together."

"I wondered if that were happening," Aaron said. "You're both back in the Sophia story."

"We've been through too much to ignore." James shimmied on his knees further down the row. "We're both freaked out by the dreams, the hidden corpse, the whole thing."

For a moment there was only a breeze that rustled the tree branches.

"So there's a killer on the loose?" Aaron asked.

"Well, there was four years ago. The trail's dead now. I doubt they'll catch anyone."

"It must be hard on Rachel. Strange she dreamed it. Everyone agrees it sounds spooky or suspicious. Wish I could say it didn't."

"People still blame her. There's a need to pin this on someone, and she's an open target. It isn't fair. She's completely innocent; she's the victim here."

Aaron shuffled closer and put his hand on James's shoulder. "I know that."

James felt his face flush and closed his eyes.

"I'm sorry," Aaron said. "It's all fresh and raw. We can change the subject."

An unbalanced bag of mulch flopped over.

"Mom said you'll both join for the boat race," Aaron offered, "and a lakeside cookout."

"We'll go in June when the water's warmer. Thanks for the invite."

Aaron smiled and winked and waited before patting down more mulch.

It occurred to James he liked his dad again.

TWELVE

THE LAST WEEKEND IN MAY brought Bucharest a lingering chill.

Geri had grown increasingly withdrawn, humorless, and tired as her due date drew closer. Travis noticed a change in her mood and attributed it to seasonal depression, given the cloudy, dreary spring. She blamed hormones, and he'd never been party to a pregnancy firsthand so had no reason to assume otherwise.

On a Friday when afternoon sessions were unexpectedly canceled, he raced home from his office with flowers, chocolates, and lavender bath salts, small luxuries he hoped might be diverting. He climbed the front steps, and a brown paper *PostEurop* parcel waited outside the door. He scooped it up along with the presents.

Travis sealed the front door against the damp, blustery wind and crept into the living room, wary of the stillness. The room was dark, and Geri lay on her back on the couch, seemingly breathless, with her legs propped up on pillows. He shuffled as quietly as he could to the kitchen so he wouldn't disturb her nap.

"Don't worry. I'm awake," Geri said after he'd already passed. She hoisted herself with both elbows and strained a smile. "I didn't expect you so early."

He swiveled toward her. "I wanted to surprise you."

"Cramps and fatigue, it's not a great day." She folded into the sofa cushion.

Travis doubled back. He bent down to kiss her and put the parcel and the gifts on the coffee table. "I hope these will cheer you when you're ready for a distraction." He stooped down. "You're barely dressed and perspiring, what's happened?" He touched her forehead and smoothed away tiny droplets just below her silken bra. "It's cold in here. Do you have a fever?"

"The cramps make me sweat," she managed and closed her eyes. "Thank you for the presents."

"Can I get you anything?" When Geri didn't answer, Travis reached for the bouquet. "I'll put these in water." Travis noted her detachment, the same as before work, the same as the past week, and it unnerved him. Clearly there was something he should be doing better. His magic was useless against psychological walls, and the resulting emotional sinkhole made life heavy and joyless. Wasn't this supposed to be uplifting? He felt stalled out and impotent, hardly an expectant father and the scion the coven expected to forge a future path. "Do you want me to crack the window?"

A pair of bored eyes looked back at him. "I'm just tired and achy and grumpy."

"Do you want to see a doctor?"

She took a deep breath and exhaled slowly. "I just wasn't ready for you."

Travis went to the kitchen to fill a vase and plopped in the flowers without removing the paper. Maybe foul moods were completely normal. It wasn't like he'd had much luck nurturing intimacy during the pregnancy. He blamed the contract because it didn't generate love, despite generating an heir. He blamed himself for not knowing how to get Geri to love him. He'd hoped he would learn the secret, a foolish notion. So what now?

"Let me know if there's anything I can do," Travis said as he reentered the living room.

"I'm always tired, to my core, and I'm not talking about needing another nap." She flopped sideways on the pillow to face him. "I should have refueled before this point. My instincts urged me to prepare. Operating as a duo doesn't sit well."

Travis sat in a chair opposite the couch. "We're going there again?"

"If I hadn't listened to you, I'd be in a much better state." She anchored an elbow and propped herself up. "I needed to refuel, and now I'm weak, and it's too late to do anything." She wiped sweat from her brow. "I'm sorry, I'm not at my best. Maybe you should take a walk around town and come back in an hour. I'll be better. I promise."

"We both worried about a spell's effect on the baby," Travis said as he folded his arms. "Especially with your brand of magic."

"Have you made any progress with your own?" Geri swiveled to sit straight and placed both hands below the baby bump. "She needs a strong father."

"I'm ready with the orb."

Geri's face tightened into scorn. "The crystal ball? Sounds formidable. It's a good thing one of us won't shy from helping her."

"Really? Now? I don't want to argue." Travis scowled and gripped the armrests.

"The pregnancy's sharpened my focus on an inescapable truth we need to face."

Travis shook his head very slowly and clenched his teeth. Maybe this flare-up would burn out on its own. Or maybe her advice to leave for an hour was spot on.

Geri locked eyes with him. "I am not a dependent. I'm perfectly capable of fending for myself and our daughter as I proved for years before ever meeting you. It's a simple reality."

She breathed deeply and exhaled slowly. When he didn't speak, she continued.

"I respect that you are forging a new path. I know it takes time and is difficult work. But all creatures rise or wither, and I'm not prepared to languish while you tinker with a crystal ball. Lulia deserves powerful parents."

Travis sat up straight and glared. "You've settled on a name? Yourself?"

"I see a vision of her face." Geri closed her eyes and massaged her belly. "She's Lulia."

"We are equal partners per the contract. I have a say in her name."

"You don't like it? Then suggest something else."

Travis scoffed as he felt his ire rise. "That is not the point."

"I feel her essence, and the name fits."

His heart pounded, but he forced himself to remain composed. "It's rude to dismiss my place in this, or for that matter, the direction of my work."

"I'm not dismissing you." Geri's eyes sprang wide. "I'm asserting myself given that she's inside my body, and I can see her and feel her, but you can't."

"You don't want to share something so basic?"

"The contract doesn't require sharing. It's about survival and propagation for the good of the coven." She pressed against the cushion and leaned her head back. A deep breath pushed past her pursed lips, slow and hissing like a steam pipe. "I didn't expect such sensitivity. You're powerful, but don't act like it. So concerned about the rights of mortals over your own daughter. If you want to share, we'll share. Names, please."

Travis fought the urge to snap. "Survival isn't enough. Don't you want something more?"

"Anything beyond survival is ephemeral."

"Perhaps, but I want more for her, at least what I had with my parents."

Geri gasped, and her face tightened. "Sorry, I cramped."

Travis waited for her expression to relax.

"Aren't you forgetting something?" Sweat beads formed on her forehead. "The black magic part, critical ancestral threads, and bloodlines we are bound to?"

Travis watched her. "I'm not certain any of that preordains emptiness."

"Of course not. I'm overreacting. It's the hormones. I'm sorry." Geri's eyes widened; she groaned and curled into a ball. "Something's wrong."

Travis sprang to his feet and kneeled near her head as she gripped her abdomen. She moaned quietly and then seemed to relax, until she coiled and leaped up, tottering toward the bathroom, rubbing her belly with both hands. She bit her lower lip as Travis followed right behind, panicked and frustrated.

"I don't want you to see me like this." She rushed in and locked the door behind her. "I'm not weak."

"Please, let me do something." Travis waited a moment and then tapped. "Are you OK?"

Geri screamed.

Travis banged on the door. "What's happening?"

When she didn't answer, Travis slammed against the door with the full force of his shoulder. It didn't give, so he took a running start, and the latch bolt jumped the housing. He burst into the bathroom, somehow recovering his balance without stumbling to the white marble floor.

Geri sat on the toilet with her head cradled in both hands. She didn't look up.

He ran to her and put his hand on her shoulder. "What can I do?"

It took a moment for Geri to answer. "I think we lost the baby."

"Why do you say that?"

"Something doesn't feel right, and the blood smells septic."

"Let's get you to the hospital."

Geri exhaled a long breath and her arms trembled.

"I want you checked."

She raised her head and met his eyes. "Let me clean up first. I need a moment."

Travis squeezed her shoulder and closed the door. "Sure, I'll be right outside."

After a few minutes, he heard the bathtub fill as he paced the living room. He looked at the unopened presents on the side table. What the hell had happened? In the morning they were expecting a daughter, and by afternoon she might be gone? Nice try and better luck next time? He didn't feel equipped to parse his emotions. How could he hold a PhD in clinical psychology if he couldn't discern fear from anger or sadness?

"Maybe it's not too late," he called out toward the bathroom.

And then poison barbed him: *What if she somehow did it on purpose?*

He shook his head and cleared it away. Why would he think that? Whatever disagreements they'd had, it made no sense for her to carry a baby for months only to self-induce a miscarriage—none at all. Why waste time with the contract? He paced the living room in a confused shuffle, but then froze when he heard a snort. He darted to the bathroom door, but there was only the rush of bathwater.

"Everything OK?"

When she didn't answer, Travis closed his eyes and strained to listen and this time heard a low groan. He followed the sound and crept toward the kitchen. The door to the basement was open. His heart raced, and he clicked on the light.

A man lay on the floor at the bottom of the stairs.

Travis descended step-by-step, watching the stranger who was unconscious or entranced. Travis stood over him and looked for blood or twisted limbs. He found the man's shirt on the floor near his feet. Travis grabbed it and noted the *PostEurop* insignia above the pocket. He exhaled, exasperated, left the man to his dreams, and trudged back up.

Travis fumed as he waited in a brown leather armchair. How could she not mention the man at the base of the stairs? Whatever the explanation, barging into the bathroom wouldn't help. He forced himself to wait, numbed by cognitive-behavioral restraint like a robot.

A small eternity passed before Geri emerged in a cloud of steamy lavender. Her hair was slicked back, straight and wet.

"How are you feeling?"

Geri took slow steps into the living room.

"Much better, the cramps are gone, and the bleeding's stopped. We can go to the doctor now."

Travis paused and held up the uniform.

"Care to explain this?"

Geri froze and then crossed the living room. "I didn't have the energy to get into it." She sat on the sofa and folded her arms. "You came home early, so upbeat and helpful. It caught me by surprise, and I was in such pain. For a few minutes, I forgot all about him."

Travis was unimpressed. "What happened?"

"The postman threatened me, there was a struggle."

Travis grimaced and shook his head. "Keep trying."

"I opened the door to sign, and he forced his way in."

Geri took a deep breath and closed her eyes.

"It was awful. He grabbed me and slammed the door and somehow swung me around and squeezed. I couldn't breathe, and I was terrified for Lulia. He pressed forward and held me against the wall. His sweat and scent were all I needed to freeze him. Then came an infusion as he lost control."

Travis exhaled and raised his eyebrows. "How did he wind up in the basement?"

"I forced him toward the kitchen, step-by-step, backward. He was helpless, and he knew it and took to the stairs. His panic sprayed like a fire hose, so I put him under to stop it."

Travis's eyebrows narrowed.

"I'm beginning to understand. The cramps?"

Geri paused to consider.

"The surge was strong and I was stunned. I haven't refueled for months, and once it started, I was so depleted, it really hit."

She studied his face and surmised she had to keep going.

"You were home early and caught me by surprise. I would have sent him away, and you'd be none the wiser." She whispered the last part. "But then came a stabbing sensation."

Travis stiffened and stood and took a step toward her.

"You endangered our baby."

Geri pursed her lips and shook her head. "He attacked me."

"We talked about the risks." Travis glared at Geri. "You didn't care and indulged anyway."

"I didn't believe it might happen." Geri pulled the towel tight.

Travis dropped the shirt he'd balled up and stormed out.

THIRTEEN

FOR HOW LONG HE WANDERED, Travis didn't know, but he found himself on a park bench near the lake. He'd passed the *PostEurop* delivery truck on the way; at least it was properly parked, and the engine wasn't running. He was seething and took deep breaths to keep from turning back and lashing out. Geri's recklessness was to blame for whatever happened to the baby, he was certain.

And it stung that she had already chosen a name.

He had nothing against it, but it was clear his opinion didn't matter. He didn't matter. In one afternoon, the contract had collapsed into a foolish waste of time. Doubts came true. Everything was void.

The solution hit him at once: Sorinah. She'd saved him before, and he needed her again. He could get away from Geri; the move didn't have to be permanent, just immediate.

It's all gone wrong, Travis transferred silently to his mentor as he stared out at the whitecaps on the lake. *Can you take me in for a while? The arrangement failed.*

A surge of warmth and a tingle between his eyes settled in.

Of course. You always have a place. When can I expect you?

I can be there tomorrow evening. I'll explain everything.

He smiled to himself and held a deep breath. Some shred of a plan, a simple option to leave, helped steady him enough to stand and force his legs toward Geri's flat.

When Travis returned, the *PostEurop* man was gone, and

the bedroom door was closed. Travis inspected the basement and found evidence of nothing, as Geri had intended.

He drank a glass of water in the kitchen then knocked on the bedroom door. A moment later Geri opened it, backed up to the bed, and sat.

"I'm sorry," she whispered.

He studied her face, and she couldn't fake sadness. He came close and leaned against the bureau with his arms folded. Professional presence and calm were required.

"Let's take you to the hospital," he said. "How do you feel?"

Geri slowly shook her head. "I'd rather not. There's no pain, and the bleeding's stopped." She reached out and touched his arm. "Worse, I can't see her face." Tears pooled in her eyes, and she continued through sobs. "Already I am healing from the replenishment, and my physical condition won't reflect a mortal's late-term miscarriage. There is no equivalent, no explanation."

Travis steadied himself, shook his head, and took her hand.

When he didn't speak, Geri continued. "I'm so sorry, I know I should have listened. The refueling jolted me. It stung, but I've been so drained and desperate to regain some shred of my former self. I should have ignored the man, but his audacity took me by surprise. In an instant, he became everything I craved. I doubted the risk. I even thought it might do the baby good." She looked into his eyes. "I don't blame you for hating me. I really don't. But the intruder instigated it; I was terrified, and forced to react."

Travis's lips were tight, and he backed up to plant himself against the bureau. "The man was handsome. I'm unconvinced of your helplessness."

"Against an intruder almost twice my size?"

Travis felt his face flush.

"When you answered the door, did you bait him?" His black, angry eyebrows arched.

Geri's eyes widened. "How would I?"

"Sexually. Your shirt was oddly absent."

"What a thing to say," Geri whispered.

"Because now we have no child, no heir, everything wasted. I need to know."

There was silence as she searched for words. "I'm in here alone all day. It was like a sleek cobra attacked and lost to a pregnant mongoose. The allure was irresistible, my judgment got cloudy."

"Was it a game to you?"

"It happened very quickly, and I couldn't stop once a flow of power started. I recognize now how wrong it was."

Travis went stone-faced.

Geri noticed and jumped back in. "I've learned a horrible lesson," she said. "We could try again in a few weeks' time."

Travis exhaled slowly through pursed lips that hollowed out his cheeks.

"Not after this. It's a deal-breaker." Travis smoothed back his straight, black hair. "You're high-risk, volatile, incapable of restraint, disinterested in compromise, and not a good bet for a mother." Travis frowned and shook his head. "Obviously the contract is null and void."

Geri's face fell to the floor. "I understand."

No one spoke for a moment, and Travis sidled toward the door.

"I'm moving and Sorinah will take me in. I will be gone tomorrow before dark."

Geri lay back on the bed and exhaled. "I'll explain the situation to the elders. I won't bother you with anything. When the contract is annulled, you can sign anytime you're ready."

"Let's just do it quickly and be done with it."

"I'll contact Elisabeta and try to have it before you go."

Geri sat up and watched as Travis stood framed in the archway. He realized he was trembling as the door closed behind him. What next? On reflex, he trudged to his office to pack what he held most precious: his parents' manuscripts. But without an heir to pass them to, doubt took hold and the emotional sinkhole reopened to swallow him.

He filled a wheeled suitcase with the volumes and carefully wrapped the crystalline orb he was ready to test. For now, he would focus on the advancement of his ancestral magic. There was nothing else. Correction, he could also focus on packing. So the living room floor was soon cluttered with piles of clothes, footwear, and a few bottles of wine.

Geri retreated to the kitchen and they didn't exchange a word. It was clear she was feeling no pain. Severe physical injury could kill any witch, but an infusion of mortal essence rapidly healed anything less. He focused on clamping shut a suitcase while she crept in to watch. She lingered a moment before shuffling to the front door, and it sealed quietly behind her.

By late afternoon the next day, Travis's belongings were in the driveway, and he was loading his sedan when Geri pulled in. He'd spent the night on the couch and heard her leave the house around 10 a.m. She approached where he stood behind the trunk.

She stood back and waited for an opening. "Things unravel so fast."

He turned his head to answer. "So I am learning."

She held his gaze. "You can always come back for anything you've forgotten."

Travis clenched his jaw and nodded.

Geri held out a manila envelope with a pen clipped to it. "I've got the contract if you'd like to sign. I explained to them the situation, as best I could. I'm very sorry it didn't work out and my actions contributed to the miscarriage."

"Your actions obviously caused it," Travis said with annoyance.

"You can refuse to sign, and I will be obligated to try once more."

Travis paused to consider. He wanted an heir, but not like this.

"I'd rather move on. We have significant philosophical differences that would have interfered later."

Travis took the envelope and eyeballed the paper inside. He skipped to the last paragraph where it stated they both agreed to dissolve the partnership. There would be no shared heir. They were both released from further commitment. Geri's signature was in blue ink, next to Elisabeta's, the coven's supreme.

Travis signed and handed everything back.

"Done," Travis said, and he took in her face, etched with a sadness that looked genuine.

"Thank you. I will be leaving for some time to stay with my mother in Cluj-Napoca. She wants me to contemplate what I've done, so I learn to control my urges. She shares your view of me as a mother and a witch." She paused to wipe a tear from her cheek. "Keep your key in case you need to retrieve something."

Travis looked away and nodded.

Geri sealed the envelope and stuck the pen into her purse. Travis closed the trunk and rejiggered a laundry bag full of clothes that spilled out the back seat.

"I thought you were fanatical, but I'm not so different." Geri walked to the front of the car, and Travis watched her as she spoke. "Overcoming instinct isn't easy for a witch."

She turned and went up the front steps.

Travis held his breath until she disappeared inside.

FOURTEEN

SORINAH LIVED NOT SO FAR AWAY. Travis climbed the steps of her villa and recalled the fear of raising the iron knocker to her front door as a youth in Bratislava. She was once his only hope, and here he was again.

The door slowly opened, and Travis knew he'd arrived at the right place, an elegant red velvet settee along with the golden wallpaper of the entry salon offering a clue. Sorinah beamed and extended her arms to embrace him. A thick wave of burnt caramel hair spilled behind her shoulders.

"I hope this isn't an imposition," Travis said as he held her close and recognized her scent of cardamom.

"You are family to me." She moved backward through the doorway but still led him by his forearms. "Can I help you with anything?"

"No, there's not so much. Just show me where to go."

"Yours will be the first bedroom on the right at the top of the stairs, the same as in Bratislava." She placed his hand on the oiled oak banister and pointed beyond the curve of the stairwell.

"Perfect. This means a lot." He smiled, turned toward the entrance, and crossed the regal living room back to his sedan. He popped the trunk, heaved out the heaviest suitcase with the manuscripts, wheeled it to the base of the steps, and hauled it up.

Sorinah was waiting in the hallway outside the room she'd prepared for his arrival. Dying sunlight streamed in a vaulted window flanked by chocolaty, tweed curtains. Fresh linens on the four poster bed smelled of trimmed cedar, mixing with notes of suede from an abundant sheepskin throw.

"I'll let you finish and get settled. I can hardly wait to catch up over dinner." Sorinah peeked in the doorway as he parked the suitcase flat on the floor under the oversized window. "Find me in the dining room when you're ready. I'm sure you're hungry, and there's plenty of wine." She beamed warmly then disappeared down the stairs.

Travis made several trips to his sedan and roughly unpacked, leaving a few piles around the room that could wait. He showered and changed for dinner into jeans and a navy polo with bare feet tucked into dark tan Birkenstocks.

On his way down the stairs, he recognized the ornate crystal lamps, paintings with thick, gilded frames, and Victorian red velvet furniture from Sorinah's former residence in Bratislava. He lingered until the clatter of dishes and a tantalizing aroma of toasted spices beckoned from somewhere down a narrow hallway. He found Sorinah in the dining room lighting a candelabra in the center of a round marble table with two meticulous silver place settings.

"Did you settle in?" she asked with a smile to greet him.

Travis nodded. "The whole place is incredible. Thank you, again. What can I do to help?"

"Pick out a wine, and let's get to it." Sorinah pointed him toward a mahogany cabinet. "I need to hear everything."

Travis examined the neatly stacked bottles and pulled one out to study the label.

"I should have listened to you from the beginning." He returned one bottle to its assigned slot in the rack to check out another. "A contract can't bind opposites. And in the end, Geri's lack of self-discipline and cravings cost us our baby." He selected a Cabernet and brought it to the table with a corkscrew. "She seduced a *PostEurop* worker and then fueled from him. A forceful absorption caused her to miscarry. Obviously, the contract was annulled."

The candles were lit, and Sorinah waited for Travis to pour. "I never approved of the arrangement, but I suppose it was worth a try so you could learn there are no shortcuts. You need a mate who is compatible mentally, physically, and magically. This wasn't right at all."

Travis handed her a glass. "Let's toast to the next chapter." They clinked glasses and took a sip. "I need to focus on the magic again; for now an heir will have to wait."

His gaze drifted to the candelabra, and Sorinah watched him. "Geri chose a name without me. That hurt much more than I would have expected. And now Lulia isn't to be."

"I'm very sorry for your loss." She motioned for Travis to sit. "I was proud of the progress you'd made trying to form a union with another witch, contractual or not, because I always advocated self-reliance. So, of course, I am partly to blame."

Travis narrowed his eyes and held hers. "For what?"

"I shielded you all those years from emotional connections. That kind of isolation works for me, but it left you rudderless, vulnerable, and with poor judgment in personal matters."

Travis swirled the wine gently and took a sip. "Next time I'll do better. Compatibility is as important as bloodline power because a child deserves a stable home. I see that now."

Sorinah's face hinted a smile as she studied his face. "You're looking good, as handsome as ever. For now, take the time you need to recover and find your way."

Travis pushed out a deep breath that wobbled a flame. "Time isn't what it used to be. And how quickly fortune shifts."

Sorinah's auburn eyes were wide and placid. "Given our ability to replenish, time is in your favor. Stay focused on evolving your ancestral magic; it's still important."

Travis leaned back in his chair and folded his arms. "And you?"

"Without a son or daughter to equip for a lifetime of magic, I replenish just enough to keep myself from fading."

She took a sip of wine. "Battle-ready, I'm not. I would be hard-pressed to immobilize another witch, and forget about mustering a bolt to fire. But I'm inspired by your orb technique. I feel needed again. I've been practicing, and I'm ready to demonstrate. I was waiting to surprise you when my subject feels ready. I'm flattered to be your first test."

"We'll discover if my family magic can be adopted by other witches." He raised his brows and fixed on a tiny rivulet of hot wax starting down a candlestick.

She extended her hand across the table. "I'm not from your bloodline, but family nonetheless. You shared your secret bolts when I was strong enough to launch one."

Travis smiled and took it. "Somehow this feels exactly right, being with you, reunited in experimental work like old times."

"I'm sorry for your loss, but thrilled to have you close again."

Travis refilled their glasses. "I'm grateful and excited for your test. Any idea when?"

Sorinah's eyes danced about the room as she calculated.

"I have a subject in mind, a resident at Floreasca Manor. His inner demons might be exactly what your spell prescribes. He's in my ward and seems willing to meet you. He knows you're a psychotherapist and told me he doesn't dare share what haunts him with anyone, ever, and never will."

Travis nodded with lips tight. "The orb will open him, or at least lubricate the process."

"We can try in the next few weeks." Sorinah raised her glass and took a sip.

Travis held her gaze and joined her. Diving back into his parents' work was exactly what he needed to move past yesterday's pain, and he felt a stirring of hope.

FIFTEEN

"I WONDER WHY RESIDENTS WITH the strongest religious convictions suffer the worst fear of death?" Sorinah asked as they entered the nursing home. "It's so counter-intuitive."

Travis followed her to the front desk of Floreasca Manor where he was listed as a visitor. Their footsteps echoed as they crossed a cavernous expanse of polished terrazzo floor tile to the elevator bank.

"Tell me about Marku," Travis said as they entered the cab. "Why is he the one?"

Sorinah waited until they started moving. "Something inside consumes him, so he self-isolates and won't share a thing. Meanwhile, he's staunchly religious but tortured."

When the doors shuddered open on the third floor, they crossed a lengthy, mint-green corridor and passed identical beige metal doors sealed tightly. A monotone of the muffled chatter of televisions wafted through.

"He's wracked with guilt, or shame even," Sorinah offered as she led the way. "It's obvious he's suffering. He likes to play cards and tell stories, and I'm a good listener. But he never lets on what happened, and he won't mix with anyone. I'm hopeful your globe will uncover what's eating him. And if it fuels us at the same time, it will be an important harbinger of the magic that might sustain the entire coven."

"We could coexist with mortals harmlessly. Undetected; our methods disguised."

"And be robust rather than insipid. Choosing weakness is hardly life at all."

Sorinah stopped at the end of the hall, Door 339. She knocked firmly and waited until a voice croaked from within, and they entered politely.

Thin, dusty curtains were drawn against indirect daylight that struggled through splotchy lead pane windows. A wire fan buzzed and swiveled on the floor but did little to relieve the uncomfortable stuffiness as winter leaped to summer, seemingly overnight.

Marku sat in the wooden rocking chair across the room and beckoned them forward with uneven circular waves of his tattooed left arm. He wore an untucked short-sleeve dress shirt with jeans and slippers.

Sorinah crept toward him with Travis close behind. "Hi, Marku. It's so nice to see you. This is Dr. Coman, the friend I mentioned would be joining me."

She smiled and stepped aside so the two men could shake hands.

"Are you the magician?" Marku strained upward and studied the witch closely.

"No, I'm a psychologist, not the same thing." Travis gave Sorinah a wary look.

Marku frowned. He ran a hand through his short, straight, silver hair and locked eyes with Sorinah. "I was hoping for some tricks or maybe a priest."

Sorinah pursed her lips and gently shook her head. "I told you he's trained to listen, and not to judge, almost like a priest. But he's teaching me a technique we hope can help you."

Marku exhaled audibly but seemed satisfied enough to lean against the back of the rocker. He looked at Travis and motioned to a folding chair near the window. "You can sit."

The metal chair legs creaked under Travis's weight as he positioned himself on the narrow seat. Sorinah sat close to Marku and focused on him. "How are you today?"

"I feel nervous in front of a stranger. It's always just us."

"You can ignore me," Travis said. "Just pretend I'm not here. In fact, maybe it's better if I move." He lifted the folding chair and crossed to the other side of the bed. "I'm here only to observe, and then see how I might help with future sessions of our own. I won't interfere."

Marku eyed Travis. "Observe what?"

"Sharing releases torment that's toxic while it's bottled up."

"I told you he's trained to listen," Sorinah said to Marku. "It's part of his job. When you share what's painful, you begin to move beyond it. Over time, he can help you make sense of it."

"Who cares what I have to say? I'm growing old and don't want much. I go to the monastery. I go to the kitchen. And I talk to you. I don't do much else, neither do I want to."

Marku took his time to take in his visitors. When no one spoke, he continued, "I don't trust anyone. Why would they give a damn? There's no reason to care; they don't know me."

Pain shot from the man. Both witches smelled it, and Sorinah leaned closer. "Why wouldn't someone care?"

"Is there a chance for redemption?"

"You go to the monastery every day," Sorinah said. "I'm sure you're already forgiven."

Marku held a deep breath and then exhaled with an agitated head shake.

"There's a life you don't know and things I won't tell. Everyone has secrets. I thought time would bleach the stain, but it doesn't. I need absolution before I die. Praying for it isn't enough."

Marku shot his eyes to Travis. "You look nothing like a priest."

Travis smiled and shook his head. "I'm not. But sharing is healing in itself. No one is beyond forgiveness. Take your time and say whatever you wish. You're doing great."

Sorinah reached into her bag and pulled out what looked like a crystal ball with a grooved channel that twisted, and a few strands of silver hair inside. She handed it to Marku.

"This is the game I mentioned. It makes it easier to talk."

She murmured something so quietly it was impossible to hear.

Marku seemed to relax with the silent prayer as he slowly rotated the orb between his thick-knuckled fingers.

"The hairs inside, they look like mine. And now they're floating. Where does the color come from? The vapor?"

He inhaled sharply and held the breath.

"There's a tingling, some kind of current." He began to rock slowly in the chair as he gazed, and an ultraviolet light gently illuminated his lap, torso, and weathered face.

"It's oddly soothing."

Travis leaned toward him with his hands clasped.

"Let's talk about forgiveness; that's where you always get stuck." Sorinah's voice was calm and reassuring as she studied Marku. "I'm confused why a sweet man like you should fear death. You pray in the monastery every day. Heaven shall welcome you."

Marku shook his head and scoffed. "It's not so simple. No one can pave their way with monastery visits. Trust me, I've been trying. It's not a matter of quantity."

He grew silent as Sorinah studied his quivering lips.

"It's OK; just relax," she said. "Gaze into the vibrating glow. The words will come."

Sorinah's hand grazed Marku's knee. If the old man felt her touch, he didn't show it. His eyes narrowed, and his brows creased above the bridge of his nose.

"There is nothing I can do. I am separate from all others in a class alone. People can sense it, and they keep their distance, even here, in the dining room."

His breathing quickened, and the witches felt an infusion as energy spun from the orb.

"Why separate, why the distinction?" Sorinah asked. "I sometimes think you imagine the distance, and it keeps people away because you've created a canyon."

Marku didn't blink and was lost in the globe. Despite his trembling grip, it rose by itself to the level of his eyes. The black light intensified and bathed his corner of the murky room. "There are things you can't understand because you don't know."

Travis spoke quietly. "Secrets corrode from within unless you let them out."

Marku's eyes widened, and he gasped, his face reflecting marvel and wonder.

"There's a parade in the street, a grand procession. Why are they all cheering while evil comes their way? Are they daft? I need to hide."

Travis noted Marku's breathing, twitches, and lack of control.

"I'm trying to lose myself in the crowd, but the beast is getting close. Maybe he can't see through so many bodies. Do I dare peek? It's impossible to resist the sparkle of jewels above a black mask with lion teeth. So tall he is, majestic."

Marku paused, his eyes wild and his breathing fast like a sprinter.

"It was a split second! That's it! He caught me! Fuck, fuck, fuck! I know it's bad. I won't look again. I'll pretend I'm invisible." Marku clamped his eyes shut and his arms pulsed in sync with flashes of black light. Then his lids went wide.

"He's staring now. I hear a snigger. He wants me to know I can't hide. Why won't anyone help? Don't they see? He marches by like a king with leather armor. I'm singled out amid all these people. The Devil is inside me now!"

An otherworldly voice, deep and resonant, escaped the man's lips.

Marku. I know about Darius.

Marku sucked in a breath, and he trembled as his own voice sputtered back.

"Get out of my way, I need to escape. He knows! I can't fool him."

Marku began to pant like a dog with his tongue extended, and sweat beaded along the lines on his forehead. His lips parted as he gripped the orb, and it seemed he might crush it. Fear spewed from the old man like a geyser.

Are you getting it? Sorinah transferred to Travis, and they locked eyes as he nodded.

Marku grimaced and stopped talking. Drool dripped from his lower lip.

"Where are you?" Sorinah whispered. "We need to stop."

"No, everything's changing," he said as his expression shifted from terror to awe. "Timișoara, I see the streets like it was yesterday." His words came slow and quiet now. "I know them well from tracking Darius, a ring leader, a radical. We have orders to stop the protestors."

The chair rocked in sync with Marku's breaths.

"But the crowd is wild, and the big march on the square turns dangerous. The *Securitate* has a duty, and I shoot him openly, proudly, along with two of his compatriots. Terror on their faces says they didn't think we would do it, but we have permission from the top. Their screams don't stop us and we mow down dozens."

Sorinah put her hand on his knee and nudged it. "There's a lot to unpack here. Dr. Coman will help you work through this. It's a great first step, and a start toward recovery."

Marku continued, lost in a trance. His voice quavered.

"Shots, moans, blood, and death, all in front of the television cameras. The government orders a cover-up, and I volunteer because there will be rewards. I burn Darius's body in a quarry with the others. We cremate them to make them disappear so the massacre won't look so bad."

Marku's face was red, and he held his breath before whispering. "I should have stayed to face my punishment. Now the Devil waits instead."

That's not right, Travis transferred to Sorinah. *End it.*

Sorinah's lids went wide and her lips moved in a silent murmur.

Marku stiffened and the globe flew to the bed. His hands plopped in his lap. He gulped some breaths and took a while to open his eyes.

"What's happened? Why are you staring at me?" He looked about the room and then noticed the front of his shirt trailed sweat down the buttons.

"No one is staring." Sorinah recovered the orb and stuck it away in her bag. "We were listening, you're back in your room and away from danger. You did great."

He shook his head furiously from side to side.

"Something is very wrong. I feel it, a presence inside. Someone still knows where I am."

Marku leaped from the rocker, tore to the other side of the bed, and kneeled in front of Travis.

"What did I say? What did you hear? Tell me what you saw." His eyes were wild. "Tell me it's not too late. You're the doctor; can you help me?"

"Calm yourself, Marku," Travis said as he took the man's hands and squeezed them gently. "Take deep breaths to help the panic pass."

Travis stood and lifted Marku from the floor.

"He came to me in your globe. He found me." The old man's legs wobbled like stilts as he wheezed. "His black, piercing eyes over the mask, I still see them and feel his hatred. He wants me to know I'm marked and there's nothing I can do. He finds it humorous. How do I know that?"

Travis steadied him by grasping the underside of both arms up to the elbows. "Who?"

"The Devil!" Marku shouted. "Aren't you listening? What's wrong with everyone, the townspeople?"

"You need to lie down." Travis guided him to the side of his bed and to a sitting position, then lifted his legs on top of the quilt. "Breathe deep, hold it, and exhale slowly."

Marku did as instructed, twice, but his head rocked from side to side.

"This won't help. He's found me. His eyes burn behind my own." He whimpered as his gaze shot around the room. "Get him out! Sorinah?"

She ran to his side and stroked his arm.

"I have to get away," he whispered. "This room is tainted. He's here. Maybe I can hide in the monastery. Yes, that's the answer. He can't go inside. We have to leave, now."

Marku jumped up and hobbled toward the closet to kick off his slippers and pull worn sneakers onto his bare feet.

Travis opened the door and waited for Sorinah and Marku to follow. He trailed them into the hallway as they made for the elevator. He heard the man murmur to himself, but didn't understand the words until they stood side-by-side and waited for the doors to close.

"I didn't see you; it wasn't me."

Travis eyed Sorinah warily, and she frowned.

The doors opened and Sorinah charged out, reached behind, and took Marku by the hand. She marched toward the entrance lobby, past the main desk, and out the front doors. Marku shook free and raced toward the monastery with wide eyes that darted about as if scouring for danger while chanting, "I didn't see you; it wasn't me."

As they approached the wide plank doors of the monastery, Marku unleashed a maniacal laugh as he slipped inside without a backward glance.

When Travis and Sorinah entered, Marku stood riveted in front of a portrait of Christ with a severe yet serene expression of resignation while blood streamed from a convincingly graphic and oversized crown of thorns. His murmurs stopped, and they watched him pray, eyes closed and hands clasped in a sliver of light that pierced the thick stone wall through a narrow, stained-glass window. They crept up and stood behind him.

After a few moments, Sorinah placed her hand on his shoulder and gently pressed.

"Are you feeling better?" she asked.

Marku opened his eyes and turned. "Yes, it's safe here."

"Shall I walk you back?"

"I'd like to stay awhile."

The witches left him to find solace. It seemed to be working.

Marku shifted to face the portrait. He stood there, alone in the shadows of the chamber, praying aloud in a frenzied loop.

"Save me...I did see him...It was me...Forgive me...."

SIXTEEN

THE SETTING SUN STREAMED in the bay windows of the living room of Sorinah's villa in Cișmigiu, and a burnt-orange cast soaked the creamy masonry walls. A leather-bound manuscript lay open on a mahogany table, and Travis and Sorinah poured over it while seated together on wooden chairs. Travis scribbled on a notepad.

"It started well enough, from a purely functional standpoint." Travis exhaled deeply and pushed back against the cushion. "But I'm still shaken by his mania."

She swiveled to meet his gaze. "Marku shared a dark secret for the first time. On that level, the orb worked." She raised her eyebrows and took a drink from a tumbler of water. "His trauma certainly spun fuel. But where did the procession come from? It was not a memory."

"It was an intrusion that undermines everything." A shadow crossed his face. "The spell itself would not invite terror, and it struck before he shared his story." He closed his eyes and traced his parents' handwriting with his fingertips to coax an answer.

"His role in the massacre explains his guilt." Sorinah watched him. "It also explains his isolation. But the process convinced him he's marked. What would cause that?"

Travis blew out a slow breath and opened his eyes as he pulled up from the manuscript.

"There's another layer behind the magic. Something I can't isolate that's invading what was supposed to be benign."

Sorinah read silently for a moment. "It's strange there's nothing in the threads to make the connection."

Travis nudged the volume closer between them and shifted between the pages, tracing his finger over the script.

"There's an obscure root at the core of my parents' spells that bestows the power. Its origin remains hidden, and I've searched as far back as I can go. Without the ancestral root, each spell would be little more than a magician's trick, interesting to behold, but of no real consequence, no value in terms of replenishing the power we need to survive."

"The root is what empowered us from Marku?"

"Exactly. And it's every bit as potent as a kill. My bolts are charged. We could both immobilize a bear long enough to escape. Or with a smidgen of essence read and control any mortal."

"So what's next?"

"I will bypass the root in the next iteration. I have a patient in mind who would be ideal to test. Without the root I won't gain replenishment."

"So what's the value?"

"I want to uncover the source of his trauma. Then I can help him."

Travis strained to read a faded passage. He spoke quietly, almost a whisper.

"And I want to know if Marku's guilt prompted the intrusion. My patient is innocent. The test will shed light on the culprit: the magic or the sin."

SEVENTEEN

TRAVIS WATCHED HIS PATIENT settle onto the couch and push into the corner of the armrest.

"How are you?" he asked.

There was a pause, as if it were a trick question. "Fine."

The psychologist leaned back, smiled, and waited for more, but nothing came. "How are you doing with the daydreams?"

"Better. I always try to pay attention." Andrei pulled at the cuff of his sweater sleeve. He smiled and looked up at Travis. "It's hot now. I wore the wrong shirt."

"Summer surprised us. It hit all at once." Travis smiled back and folded his arms. "Are you riding your bike?"

"I will until it snows."

"That's a long way off." Travis leaned toward the boy.

Andrei smiled and nodded and exhaled slowly over a thick lower lip.

"Remember the tool I told you about, the crystal ball? Do you want to try it?"

Andrei's lips formed a tight line, and his eyes widened as he leaned back on the pillow expectantly. "Is it hard?"

Travis reached into his desk drawer and withdrew the orb. "Not at all. Just look into the center, and daydream out loud." He carefully passed the globe to the boy. "Roll it between your fingers. Let your mind wander like a daydream. Say anything that comes to mind. There is no right or wrong or bad or good or not allowed."

Andrei took the sphere and held it in front of his stomach as he rotated it gently, staring into its core. Travis felt a tingle as the boy's thoughts synched with the probing currents of the spell. It was just beginning to ignite.

His patient's lips trembled as his wide eyes fixed on a black light that glimmered within the balls' core and started to ricochet.

"Everything OK?" Travis asked and leaned in closer, his heart racing. "What do you see?"

Andrei breathed in sync with the pulses of ultraviolet light. As his patient struggled to find words, Travis felt trauma energy trickle to his core even before the boy started to whisper. Most curious because the root was truncated.

"There's flickering firelight and a headdress with coins dangling down. There's a bad feeling. I know my father is gone or dead. It's scary because it's night, and we're near the woods, and everyone knows we have to leave again. The big chief tells us the outsiders are marime and infect us."

Andrei gasped. "My mother wears the headdress. She is desperate to please the others and chants to atone, but it's too late. She is marime because the outsider did something bad, and my mother caused it."

"What is 'marime'?" Travis watched Andrei's eyes dart within the orb as he pulled it close to his face.

Andrei paused and bobbed his head between words: "Dirty. Dirty. Dirty."

A deep violet light shimmered against his cheeks and forehead.

"My mother knew the outsider was marime but read her fortune anyway because we need the money. She's a diviner, but can be infected by an outsider. My mother always tells the truth; it is marime to lie."

The boy trailed off, then came back. "But the outsider killed herself because she didn't like the fortune, and now it's my mother's fault. The chieftain is furious, and the outsiders want us out."

Perspiration beaded on his forehead as Andrei stared intently into the globe, which trembled in his grasp.

"Now the band is not welcome. Many have jobs and want to stay. The chieftain is expelling my mother because she is marime. They will put her in jail. Don't take her from me!"

Andrei sucked in a gasp, and tears pooled in his eyes, but his stare never faltered from the bolts within the orb.

Travis almost stopped the experiment when the fuel started to trickle in with tiny jolts of adrenaline, but it seduced and empowered like spun gold, and he wanted to learn more about the boy's Romani past. Plus he craved evidence to weigh against Marku.

"It's not my mother's fault, but she knows the name of the secret baby. The outsider slaps my mother and tells her husband, but he denies it and curses my mother. *That fucking Gypsy!*"

Travis stared at Andrei, transfixed and unable to move.

"The outsider finds the baby and also her husband's secret wife. The man screams and beats her for knowing." Andrei's nose crinkled as he strained for more.

"*Stay away from that fucking Gypsy!*"

The boy paused and then whispered, "They blame my mother for her suicide. They want us out and my mother in jail."

Travis hoisted himself from what felt like quicksand. "I'm so sorry, Andrei." He fought to catch his breath. Why was the infusion so forceful?

"You can stop now, that's a lot of good work for one day."

He recited the incantation, in full voice, to break Andrei's connection to the sphere, but the boy stammered on.

"No, no, no. What do you want? We are back by the fire and my mother screams because she sees you too. She fights and claws when the police drag her away, but her eyes are on someone in the shadows. He's pointing at me from behind their backs. He wants to take me, and the chieftain nods and offers me as sacrifice."

Andrei's cries grew louder, and Travis grabbed for the globe, but the boy swiveled and gripped it tight.

"Pass it to me, Andrei." He fought against the spell, but the influx of power surged.

"It's my story. You can't come in and change it!" The boy's face went ruddy and his forehead dripped sweat as he strained against an invisible force.

"The devil man has control."

Andrei seized up on the couch, and a deep voice, resonant and other-worldly, escaped his lips.

"*I'm going to kill your mother.*"

Andrei's head shook as he spasmed but still clutched the orb.

When he spoke again, the voice was his own.

"The story changed. That's not allowed. He's inside me, the Devil! Why me? Get out!"

Andrei shrieked as Travis lunged for the orb and wrested it from the boy's grip. It was oddly cold, and the light inside faded as he rolled it onto the rug and coaxed it under his desk like a croquet ball. The boy seized back against the sofa cushion and gasped for air.

"It's over now," Travis said. "Take a moment to relax. You shared a lot."

Andrei covered his face with his hand.

"Take a deep breath, hold it, and then exhale slowly."

Andrei did as he was told and peeked out.

"Again, several times."

The boy propped a pillow up behind the small of his back. He puckered his lips and blew out a soft whistle.

"What did you hear?"

Travis paused to watch him. "What do you remember?"

"I was telling my story, and then everything switched; a demon came in, and now he's inside me. You shouldn't have done that."

"I'm sorry. It's an illusion, just a bad feeling." Travis forced a smile and leaned forward in his chair. "Let's wait for the anxiety to pass. It always does."

Andrei pushed aside the bangs of his straight hair and dried his face. "I can't think right now."

"It's OK to just sit quietly."

The boy shuddered and took a moment to answer. "I'm worried the Devil found me. I feel different."

"Different how?"

Andrei stiffened and closed his eyes. "I feel a presence, cold; it's like he's inside me. He knows my name. I can hear it, just barely, that voice."

Travis didn't like the answer.

"We won't do it again. Forget about him, and your memories from the globe will fade soon after you leave this office. Just like hypnosis."

Andrei puzzled for a moment and then slowly peeled himself from the couch.

"Next time we can talk more about your mother if you want. Forget the rest."

When Andrei left, Travis closed the door to his office and collapsed in his chair.

Tinkering with the root had made things worse. He couldn't stop the orb and found himself oddly mesmerized. He grabbed the globe from under his desk and locked it in the bottom drawer.

Travis closed his eyes and waited for the infusion rush to subside.

EIGHTEEN

LATER THAT WEEK, RACHEL OPENED Old Gold for the morning shift. As usual, her boss, MK, would take over after lunch. The part-time work was perfect for the summer, at least until she found a real job. And yes, a boutique of her own would suit her just fine.

She set her phone and venti dark roast on the counter next to the register and stuck her salad in the mini-fridge on the floor in the back room. The nightmares had stopped, and she felt refreshed and energized. James had been sleeping over and hadn't reported as much as a whimper overnight. She was going with the narrative their trek to the woods near the reservoir had exorcised Sophia from her subconscious. Finding her body seemed to have doused the kindling for dreams.

A corpse a day keeps the nightmares at bay.

Rachel smirked at her dumb rhyme as she adjusted a formidable pile of women's argyle sweaters, scooted back to the counter for a swig of caffeine, and circled back to the display. Of course, the media had broken she was the "hiker" who'd "stumbled upon" Sophia's gravesite by chance. And yes, everyone thought she was crazy, or maybe even guilty. Recurring nightmares had compelled her to dig under the sign, after all.

Strangely, she wasn't the least bit concerned about the attention because she had nothing to hide. She was the victim here. First, her friends were taken from her, and then, four years later, the nightmares came. None of it was her fault, and if it sounded strange, she would point out that everything else did too. Mia's case still wasn't closed, and it was obvious Sophia would never have run away. Then, four years later, a skeleton turns up in the woods.

She'd figured as much all along. Perhaps she'd been divinely chosen to help Sophia rest in peace. That theory would shut them up.

About an hour passed before the door opened and two customers entered. Rachel looked up from the counter and smiled as they took tentative steps toward her.

"Good morning. Let me know if I can help you find something," Rachel said cheerily as she wandered back to the counter next to the register. "The men's section is thataway." Dancing fingers nudged them to the right.

The man nodded and steered his son in deeper.

"Thanks. Do you have denim jackets?"

"Yes, there's a bunch along the side." Rachel trotted over and showed them where. She took a step back and studied the teenager. "You look like a medium."

The boy smiled and stretched out his arms.

Rachel separated out the options and pushed away the others. "Give these a try."

He reached up to the rack. "Thank you."

"My pleasure." She detected an accent. "Are you visiting?"

The man answered. "Yes, we're new in town."

"That's great, welcome." Rachel leaned in to look at his son. "What's your name?"

He swiveled to face her. "Andrei," he said.

"Oh, that's a nice name. Where are you from?"

The man answered. "Try to guess."

Rachel's fingers tickled her chin. "I would say the UK."

He smiled and watched as his son pulled a jacket from the hanger. "A bit farther east than that, actually, we're from Romania. The English we learn is British. I'm Stefan."

"My name's Rachel." She thought about extending her hand but it felt forced, so she flashed a wide smile instead. "Let me know if I can help with anything. The mirror's in the corner." She pointed and then sauntered back to the register. "Nice to meet you."

"Thank you," they said in unison.

She turned and watched the pair pull a few jackets from the rack.

Rachel flipped through her phone, hoping to find a message from James, but she knew he was in the police station for another round of questioning, and her turn would follow in the afternoon.

A few more customers entered, and Rachel helped one of her regulars with a size exchange on a blouse and the purchase of a pair of 1970s-style bell-bottom overalls.

When Stefan and Andrei approached the register, she was pleased to see she'd made a sale.

"That jacket is just in," Rachel said. "We carry whatever's got a vintage look."

Andrei smiled. "I like Levi's; it's retro."

Stefan handed Rachel a Visa card. "No need for a bag; he'll wear it out."

"Perfect. Let me help you clip the tags." Rachel took the jacket and laid it flat on the counter while the register spat out a receipt. "Please just sign here." She handed a pen to Stefan and then snipped the plastic filament that secured the labels. She held up the jacket and passed it to Andrei. "All set."

Andrei smiled, reached up, and pulled the jacket over his slender frame.

"It looks great," Rachel said.

"Thanks for your help." Stefan grabbed the receipt and labels and stuffed them in his backpack. He smiled at Rachel and held out a hairbrush. "This was under the rack of coats."

She studied the shape and bristle length. "My paddle brush disappeared a few weeks ago; it's my favorite." She clasped the wooden handle. "Thanks for finding it."

"Sure thing," Stefan said as he followed Andrei toward the door. "Have a nice day." He turned and lit his face with a grin. "We'll see you again."

"I'll keep an eye out."

Rachel watched them leave and took the hairbrush to the back room, rinsed it, and placed it on a shelf in the corner where she always kept a stash of Kleenex, hand lotion, and lip balm. How it had ended up out on the sales floor under a coat rack she hadn't a clue.

"Hello? Does anyone work here?" The question wafted from the front.

Rachel rushed out and found herself at the mercy of a mother-daughter pair until past lunchtime when, happily, they settled on a vintage pearl necklace and left.

She eked out fifteen minutes for a salad in the back because MK didn't want her to eat in front of customers, only sips of coffee and water. The back room wasn't fancy. It was basically a storage area with a table, mini-fridge, sink, and a tucked-away toilet stall. She went to the mirror and tried out her newly recovered hairbrush for good measure and headed back out to the sales counter.

The afternoon started smoothly, and when MK breezed in around 2:30, Rachel had Old Gold fully under control with a decent stash of receipts to show for her efforts. The store owner wore a jean mini with a pair of navy Dr. Scholl's and a pink polo and rested her Ray Bans on the counter next to Rachel's phone.

"How did things go?" MK tossed her hair and smiled.

Rachel handed her a leather folder. "It was a brisk morning. Glad you came by early."

MK put her bag on the counter and surveyed the store. "I wouldn't forget your appointment."

"I hope it's the last one."

MK flipped open the folder. "They're meeting with James now?"

"Yes, it's a cross-examination to see if they can catch a discrepancy."

"Do they expect your story to change?"

"There's nothing to change. I was having bad dreams, and it seems Sophia was trying to reach me."

MK raised her eyebrows and nodded slowly to coax more.

"An old sign flashed in the dream, again and again. It pointed to the reservoir. And we found it tucked away in the woods not so far from the park entrance."

"What made you dig?"

Rachel rubbed her temples. "I hoped it would free my subconscious." She paused and had to look away. "I couldn't take another dream. I had to do something, anything, to get it out of my head. I figured it would help if I could uncover the sign. The cycle had to stop."

When she looked back, her eyes were teary.

"I get it." MK sighed. "But the dream makes your discovery all the stranger, especially for the police."

"I know. But it somehow makes sense, at least to me."

MK took Rachel's hand. "Did you know the sign was there all along? You can tell me."

"No, of course not, she never mentioned it. But someone impaled her there."

"What did you tell the police?"

"The same, like a broken record." She peeked at her phone. "I'd better get to the station now. Hopefully, James got through OK. They're going to compare our stories."

"Speak your truth, and you'll be fine. No lies, no holding back."

"That's why I'm not nervous. It's too bizarre to lie about. I had my dreams, and they led to Sophia's body. I mean, these things sometimes happen, right?"

MK smiled and squeezed Rachel's hand.

"Not really, Peaches, but after what you've been through, who's to judge?"

Rachel smiled and slowly released her hand.

"And I always bring up Mia. They hate it when I throw that in their face, how everyone thinks they bungled her case."

"Good, let me know how it goes tomorrow."

Rachel nodded and made her way to the backroom to gather her things. She used the bathroom, fixed her hair with the paddle brush, and blew a kiss to MK as she left.

NINETEEN

STEFAN KEPT HIS EYES on the road but shot glances at Andrei, who fiddled with the window button on the car door. The Vermont roads were unfamiliar, windy, and narrow with potholes and sloping crevices that required attention.

"It's very different here," Stefan said.

"I'm glad to get away from Bucharest." Andrei waited for the window to go up and looked at his father. "Maybe it will tire of tracking me."

"Is the distance helping?"

Andrei clamped his eyes shut for a moment. "I'm not so sure."

"Why didn't you tell me sooner?" Stefan shot his son an angry look. "Travis must have done it."

Andrei grew quiet and rubbed his forehead. "I hoped it would go away, and I knew you would get mad."

"Everything about him makes me mad." Stefan forced a smile and then softened his tone as he studied the road. "Let's see if the change of location weakens the effect. We'll focus on your training to reset your consciousness. You're ready for the new tools I was granted. Obviously, you've already mastered the disguising spell."

Andrei nodded and shot a baleful glance at his father. "You need to win, especially now."

Stefan reached over the console and smacked his son's thigh.

"The talented Doctor Coman is not the only one who's evolved."

"Thanks for including me."

Stefan's grip widened and squeezed the wheel tight. "Being back here makes it raw again." He signaled and turned left onto their street. "I am back to my old self, Radu, rejuvenated to make things right."

Andrei swiveled on the car seat toward his father. "Plus me, I'm no runt, not anymore."

"Yes, we both have roles to play. You are his weak patient, and I'm Stefan, the bad father, with magic stronger than his own. He can't smell us out."

Andrei studied the unfamiliar landscape until they pulled into the driveway. "Be careful with him. Travis is also strong; his magic is different. He said the orb would help, and I played along. But something infected me anyway; he didn't even plan it."

"You think the presence is still inside you?" Radu stiffened. "What exactly happened?"

"I don't remember well; his spell evaporates. I started with my Gypsy story as we planned, but a curse came in, the devil man." Andrei paused. "It happened again last night."

"Tell me more. You have to share these things." Radu's eyes narrowed and turned dark.

"It's new, and I still don't understand it. When the vision comes, the devil man says my name, I get cold and feel him behind my eyes, and he sniggers. Travis said I'm not supposed to remember anything. But the spell wasn't wiped away; something's still there."

Radu parked the car behind an old farmhouse in front of a large red shed. He turned off the engine, hesitated, and then punched the steering wheel. The horn blasted.

"That makes me burn. How could you let this happen?"

Andrei exhaled slowly. "You wanted me to spy. How could I know?"

They locked eyes.

"I'll be sending him quite a dream in return," Radu scoffed. "I took plenty of essence right out from under his nose in the restaurant. We've got the upper hand. He's oblivious. As a last resort I'll kill him, the spell might die with him. But I want him alive to fix this."

They climbed out of the car.

"Let's take a walk. I want to show you around," Radu said. "Don't fixate on the visions."

He tapped his son's shoulder and ushered him off the gravel driveway onto a lush lawn that abutted an untamed field. The grasses grew tall and tangled with reeds, weeds, and thickets. A trail skirting the overgrowth led them to a clearing at the edge of the woods. Radu pointed to football-sized rocks still arranged in a circle on the mudflats of a marsh.

"That's where Travis scorched my face, broke my will, and shamed me into exile."

Andrei knelt and pushed dandelions aside to examine the rocks. "The coven doesn't care now. You did your time, and they set you free. Why do you still hate him?"

"Travis has persuaded the elders to expand his experiments. But he's dangerous because he messes with forces he doesn't understand, as did his parents. He thinks he's elevated, somehow on a path to good, and needs to be corrected before he destroys us all. Our collective power built over centuries will weaken to the point we can no longer sustain ourselves beyond our mortal lifespans. The whole coven will die."

"Why would he do this?"

"He doesn't know, and I need to convince him before it's too late."

Andrei stood and joined his father near the edge of the woods. "And the elders?"

"I need to gather enough evidence. Elizabeta knows I have every reason to hold a grudge, so she won't heed my warnings. The best way is to convince *him* of the danger."

Andrei nodded. "What if he doesn't listen?"

"I'm betting he's smart enough to see for himself. And I need him to help you. If he can't, he dies."

Radu took a few strides onto a trail into the woods and waved to his son to join him. "This old road leads to another farmhouse; the family on the other side is part of the plan. They don't know me, but I know them. Travis does too, including the girl from the store." They started down the overgrown pathway. "I sent her dreams, and she's discovered a corpse. The trap is set, and all that remains is to ensnare Travis."

"I'll see him again next week." Andrei plucked a milkweed pod as they walked along the stagecoach road.

"Find out everything you can about what he did to you," Radu said as he wiped sweat from his brow, "and then lure him in."

"What do I tell him?" Andrei shot a quizzical look at his father.

"He'll want to know why you missed a session. Tell him we're moving for seasonal work in the states. Make sure he's listening when you tell him Vermont."

"That's it?"

"That will be enough."

TWENTY

JAMES WAITED BY THE KITCHEN DOOR for Rachel. Aaron set the table while Paula tended to a Thai curry chicken simmering on the stove. He wondered if he should help with preparations, but his nerves kept him frozen.

With the crackle of tires in the driveway, James jumped out to the kitchen steps. He watched as Rachel rolled into the spot he'd saved for her under the old maple near the door.

"Perfect timing," James said as she climbed out. "How did everything go?" He met her on the pavement, pulled her close, and nestled his face against her neck. "You smell nice."

They embraced for a long moment. "They let me leave, so I'm guessing that's good." She guided his head up, and they kissed. "I think they're scared of me, the troublesome clairvoyant."

He chuckled, took her hand, and led her up the steps. "Let them puzzle over it. The ball's in their court, now."

The screen door whisked shut as they entered the kitchen. Paula and Aaron turned to greet them, and Rachel flashed a smile as she followed James toward the table.

"It's great to see you." Paula beamed while wiping her hands with a dishtowel.

"I'm so happy to see you again, too." Rachel nodded with tight lips and flushed cheeks.

An awkward silence threatened to overshadow their entrance, so James stepped forward.

"It's been a crazy ride." He studied his parents' concerned faces across the table. "But we hope we're done. Now, it's up to the police."

Rachel chimed in, "They told me today would be it unless something changes."

Aaron smiled and pointed to their place settings. "That's great. Please, have a seat."

Paula put on oven gloves and carried the fragrant skillet to a trivet on the table. "Anything more?"

James pulled out Rachel's chair and then took his own. "Basically, we're still involved because we're the ones who discovered Sophia's body."

Aaron opened a bottle of merlot and carefully poured it. "The story's strange, especially given what happened to your friends." He finished the glasses and opened a second.

"Unfortunately, I'm still kerosene on a dumpster fire," Rachel said. "I was part of the so-called clique. And I had the nightmares that led to Sophia."

"The nightmares are understandable," Paula said as she started to serve.

Rachel paused to take a sip of wine. "The police think Sophia must have said something that stuck in my subconscious, something about the sign, some connection to the reservoir. I honestly don't remember anything. But I'm grateful James humored me enough to look."

"That's the strange part." Aaron raised his eyebrows as he sipped. "Because you were right."

"We didn't do anything wrong," James said. "We knew nothing, I swear. It's some kind of cosmic coincidence, something supernatural."

Rachel jumped in with, "I passed a lie detector test," as if she were now absolved of, well, everything.

"Of course you did," Paula said, finally taking her seat. "It's an important formality. This isn't the first mystery for the Sussex police."

"I've heard of psychic dreams before," Aaron said. "Some crimes are solved by psychics, at least in thriller novels."

"Right? That's exactly what I told them." Rachel smiled and cheered him across the table with her wine glass. "Just like in *Ink and Bone.*"

"Unfortunately, cops don't like dreams or coincidences that lead to skeletons," Aaron said. "Did they find any new clues?" He glanced at Paula. "This is delicious, by the way."

James and Rachel chimed in praises between bites.

"There's a murder weapon, the fence post, sharp as a stake." Rachel averted her eyes and got quiet. "But it was four years ago, and maybe the trail's gone cold."

"Where did they find it?" Paula asked and put her fork down.

"It was in the grave on top of Sophia." Rachel averted her eyes and turned rosy.

"I'm sorry about all the questions. We can stop now, but the whole thing is morbidly fascinating." Paula reached across the table and touched Rachel's arm. "You did the right thing, and I hope the nightmares stop. Maybe now Sophia's parents can get some closure. The police are on the case, thanks to you."

"Unfortunately you're popular again with the gossips in town." Aaron frowned and took another sip. "I heard from some guys at the lake; there's talk."

"I don't care what they think." James grew sullen and folded his hands in his lap. "The police seem to believe us, and they're studying evidence and testing for DNA. If we had something to do with it, why would we dig her up and then call the police?"

Aaron paused to finish a bite. "That's a great point to note. I'd feel a lot better if you weren't involved at all because I know how gossip burns. I've been a focus myself. But with the divorce, I deserved it. You two don't."

He shifted his gaze from James to Rachel. "I'm worried about the toll your friends' deaths have taken on both of you. Recurring dreams mean you're bothered by something, you can't fool your mind."

No one spoke for a moment, and Rachel rebounded enough to top off her glass.

"Have the dreams stopped?" Paula asked.

"Yes, so far, and James helps to monitor the situation." Rachel took a sip.

James squirmed in his chair and noticed his father's smirk.

Rachel noticed too and jumped back in. "He watches for signs of distress each night. He's a witness, and I need it. But all joking aside, the nightmares have stopped."

"Great, and we should change the topic," Aaron said. "You need a break."

"It's true." Paula put down her fork and looked at Rachel. "We're going to the lake Saturday to watch Aaron's boat race. Do you want to join?"

James felt a flash of guilt. It was an event he'd so far managed to avoid.

"I don't know with the gossips about," he quipped.

Aaron's face fell, so he quickly added, "Sounds fun. I'm in."

James glanced across the table to Rachel. "Should be off work, right?"

"Yes, and I haven't been to the lake since last September." Rachel surveyed their faces. "Only if it's not an imposition."

"We'd love to have you join." Aaron beamed and refilled his glass. "The race itself doesn't last long. But it's fun to get outside and play bumper cars in the water. At the end, you can take a ride yourselves, and we can go to dinner or barbecue, or whatever."

There wasn't another word about the dreams, the police, or Sophia's body.

TWENTY-ONE

IT WAS A WARM SATURDAY EVENING, and Radu descended the wooden steps to North Beach with the stealth of a hungry raptor. The sun was getting low enough to tint the clouds citrusy against a deep blue sky and to cast shifting shadows along a forested pathway that led from the stairs down a slope toward Lake Champlain.

At the water's edge, light shimmered on the surface, rippling and glowing in stark contrast to the darkness of the woods nearby. Radu followed a grassy walkway along the edge of the beach that wound toward a wooden dock lined with Walker Bay dinghies of white and gray, each with a single set of oars. One by one, a group of men boarded each single-size boat and pushed off from the dock. Radu scanned the scattered blankets and folding chairs spread out on the sand and spied Rachel and James with Paula.

The witch stooped under the cover of a large swamp oak near the shore with a good view of the dock. He watched Aaron wave to the trio on the beach as he rowed away to catch the other competitors.

The boats bobbed in the waves and jostled into a starting line. A whistle blew from the dock, and the men tore toward an orange buoy a mile out. Aaron's boat bashed two others as they pulled ahead and fought for position.

Flight and fear and pain and blood.

Radu disappeared behind the tree trunk and an instant later scurried to the top.

A large black hawk with a thick orange beak launched from the swamp oak and took flight with a powerful wingspan that soared into the brilliant sky. The raptor trailed the flotilla of rowboats that raced toward the orange buoy in a frenzy of enthusiastic taunts and splashes.

Aaron fought his way to the front of the pack and grinned as the next closest rower fell behind. If he spied the hawk, he didn't flinch and was focused on smoothing out his strokes to extend his lead. He rowed furiously and rounded the buoy to make his way back, but it seemed the bird was trailing him, trained on him, closing in. He took notice as it gained speed and then froze in disbelief as it swooped down to hammer the top of his head.

Aaron bellowed and dropped an oar as he tried to block at the last second.

"What the fuck was that?" Aaron shouted as he gripped his skull. Blood oozed into his eyes as his dinghy went into a directionless spin. The hawk sailed north and disappeared into the shadowy woods along the lake.

"It burns! What the fuck!"

He pressed down on the wound with both hands. Blood dribbled down his face and splattered on his chest. Aaron stood and tried to balance as he stepped toward the front to try for the life preserver he'd tossed there. He shook his head and clamped down harder.

The dinghy rocked as he thrashed with his eyes locked tight against the stinging pain. He stumbled and lurched to the side and everything pitched. He caught the outer edge and gripped it under his armpit, but the tiny boat tipped further and slipped away.

Spectators on the beach leaped up and ran toward the water, raising a ruckus.

Radu came down from the tree unnoticed and focused on Aaron. The witch's eyes grew dark as his lips moved in a silent chant, arms trembling, fingers stretched toward the lake.

Fear and pain and blood and water.

"I can't move!" Aaron shouted when he surfaced near the front of his rowboat, gasping for breath. He craned his neck to keep his face above the surface, but sank again, gurgling just below the waves.

Pain and blood and water and gyre.

Aaron popped up and gulped air as the rowers nearby shouted and threw red flotation cushions close enough to hit him. His arms lurched to grab one, but with wild eyes he bellowed and sunk again, fingers clinging to the cushion's strap.

A moment later, he surfaced.

"I'm caught in a whirlpool!" The cushion ducked under the waves with him.

One of the rowers dove in, and another extended an oar toward Aaron. "Grab it!"

Aaron popped up again and sucked for breath before disappearing below the swells. Bubbles stirred in his wake as the rescuer frantically scrambled in the roiling water.

The cushion launched from the depths and then smacked the surface to bob above the churn.

Blood and water and gyre and death.

A lifeguard in a motorboat sped from the dock toward the dinghies as Radu braced against the swamp oak to absorb the infusion.

TWENTY-TWO

TRAVIS LAY IN BED IN BLACK briefs, and his thoughts drifted to Geri. His hand passed over the ridges of his chest and rested on his abs. *Should I contact her?* No, he needed a clean break. The entanglement had left him bitter; it was still too raw. And there was no time for distractions. The malignancy lurking behind his magic demanded full attention.

He finally drifted asleep but woke up early, his mind fixated on his 10 a.m. meeting with Andrei. The boy had skipped his last session, and follow-up was critical. The orb could not be used before learning more, and the suspense was excruciating.

Worse, what if his patient didn't return?

Travis arrived at his office before anyone else and left his door open a crack. He scribbled notes while he waited, but he couldn't focus. His heart leaped when he heard a familiar light tap on the door and swiveled his chair to face Andrei, who lingered without a sound in the doorway until the doctor waved him in.

Andrei closed the door behind him and shuffled to the far corner of the couch near the window.

Travis waited for the boy to settle and smiled. "Nice to see you. How are you?"

Andrei exhaled and leaned back in the chair. "I'm nervous. It's been a little while since I've seen you."

Travis swiveled his chair a bit closer and took a closer look. Was Andrei bigger?

"You're looking fit, looking healthy," Travis managed in a flat, professional tone.

"I need to get stronger."

"Everything OK? Anything you want to talk about?"

Andrei's eyes darted as he strained to consider. "Something scary happened last time."

"Ah, yes, the crystal ball. How do you feel?"

The boy exhaled loudly. "I don't remember everything." He looked about the room. "But there's something bad inside."

Travis carefully took in his patient. "Bad how?"

Andrei paused to think. "Like a demon is waiting."

Travis raised his eyebrows and smiled, but his heart raced. "How can that be if you don't remember?"

Andrei squirmed in his chair. "I remember the crystal ball, and I wanted to try it. I don't remember much else, except for the demon, because that's how it ended, and it stuck. I feel like he's inside me." Andrei paused and stared at Travis. "What happened?"

Travis exhaled. "You told me about your mother."

"That's a secret," Andrei whispered and folded his arms.

"It's OK to share; that's why you come here. Over time, it will help to talk about it."

"Well, I won't." Andrei looked toward the window. "Everything is worse."

"What do you mean 'worse'?" Travis studied his patient, who didn't move.

"I get visions now," he whispered. "Scary ones."

Travis sat at attention. "Can you tell me about them?"

The boy's gaze didn't waver from the window. "I'm trying to ignore it so it goes away."

"Please, tell me."

"There's always the same dark feeling that comes with a nightmare."

Travis held his breath, raised his eyebrows, and waited. "What more, can you share?"

"My mother is trapped in a jail, crying near the window. She calls for me but can't see out. The devil man guards her cell. His eyes lock on mine, and he whispers my name. His voice is deep and scary when he talks to me. *I'm going to kill your mother.*"

Travis watched his patient hold himself tight as his face blanched.

"It's not just dreams. If I clench my eyes, I feel taps inside my forehead just above them, and his whisper floats in. My body freezes tight when he's there. *Andrei, I see you.*"

The boy drew in a shuddering breath and turned to face Travis.

"Twice I woke up screaming. My dad doesn't like it."

Travis rolled his chair close to his patient.

"That sounds horrible. I'm so sorry."

"My dad blames you for starting it."

Travis's spine stiffened. "What did he say?"

"He said you are traumatizing me and making me worse than before. That's why I skipped."

Travis couldn't find words. *Stefan might be right.*

"Anyway, it doesn't matter because we're moving for the summer before school starts."

Travis tried to recover. "That sounds very exciting, where?"

"The States."

"Why there?"

"My dad wants to try it and found something at a lake resort."

Travis gripped his jaw as he leaned in and furrowed his brow.

"There's a small state I've never heard of, but it's supposed to be nice. Workers go for the summer season." His patient stared straight at him and almost whispered. "Vermont."

Travis coughed, but just barely. "I know the place."

Andrei pressed back on the couch. "So I guess I won't see you for a while."

Travis's pulse rate surged. Now he wanted his patient to leave.

"It's a good time for a break. The change might shake the dream. We'll make a plan for the fall."

"Maybe," Andrei said as he looked at the clock on the wall. "Is it time?"

"Sure, good luck, have fun, and a great summer. Try to ignore the scary stuff. I really hope it stops. You have my cell. You can always call."

Andrei got up from the chair and walked to the door.

"Thank you." He turned with a dispirited look and left.

Travis closed the door behind him and went to his desk.

Stefan was taking his son to Vermont? Something wasn't right. He tapped at the computer keyboard and began to search for news out of Sussex.

TWENTY-THREE

THE GRAY MORNING LIGHT matched her mood. She recognized the gravity of the day, but even so, Sorinah was surprised Travis had already left as she poured steaming water over the coffee grounds. Since his arrival, they'd always shared breakfast in the kitchen before departing for work. But there was no sign of him, not even a dish or crumbs in the sink.

She figured he'd been anxious about his patient's follow-up session and had to get to it. A burning to check in with Marku consumed her as well. She filled a mug and made for the bedroom to finish dressing. Her part of this was also key to the spell's progression. Right now everything was stuck.

It looked like rain, so Sorinah pulled a beige Burberry trench over her chiffon pantsuit on her way out the door. She didn't want to hunt for parking near Floreasca Manor, so she hailed a taxi and took it to the corner adjacent to the nursing home near the monastery.

Sorinah passed the front desk with a nod to the security attendant and marched to the elevators. The air in the lobby was stuffy, so she took off her jacket, and folded it over her handbag. On the fifth floor, another wave of stale, warm air welcomed her as left the elevator. She cracked open the first window she came to and then did the same to each one she passed on the way to Marku's room. No one else would bother to do it. The workers were barely more alive than the residents.

She rapped on Marku's door three times and waited. Nothing came from within, so she knocked again and jiggled the doorknob. It wasn't locked, so she quietly pushed past.

The lights were off, but daylight filtered through the window's sheer, water-stained curtains that rippled like a ghost above an overturned fan. She stepped inside and immediately closed the door against the sweet, putrid smell of rot. Marku sat motionless in his rocking chair. A blanket covered his head and torso and left his thighs bare, thick, and spread on the wide hardwood seat. Wet white briefs clung to incongruously swollen genitals.

"Marku? Are you sleeping?" Sorinah rushed to the far side of the bed.

She touched his arm and recoiled from the cold. The blanket was soaked, and she gently tugged it from his body and let it drop to the floor. She stifled a scream and jumped away. Marku's neck was twisted, his face turned backward with a cheek pressed against the ornamental headrest. His agonized expression froze her breath; dark eyes were glazed and his tongue was elongated and curled beyond incisors that clamped down on it: leathery, purpled, and forked.

Sorinah's heart raced, and she collapsed on the side of the bed. What was happening? She tried to think. Should she call security? The horror in the chair would unleash pandemonium. The sight was diabolical, patently obscene. Nothing rational could explain it away. She'd witnessed Marku's hysteria and knew to her bones that the globe and Travis's spell were to blame, and so was she. A shiver ricocheted down her spine.

I didn't see you; it wasn't me.

Why was he so wet? She reached out to touch the arm that dangled close. It was icy. Yet only a few hours had passed; the fabrics were sour and dank.

Security had to be alerted. But first Travis had to know. He had to see Marku through her eyes before she softened the spectacle to make it more palatable.

I just found Marku, she transferred and sucked in a breath.

He's been savaged. It's the Devil's work.

She sat on the bed with eyes fixed on the former *Securitate* agent to send a clear vision.

La naiba! Travis cursed. *Are you OK?*

I need to dilute this, or chaos will erupt.

Do what you can, and then rush back home. There's trouble.

What more?

Andrei and his father are in Vermont.

Why of all places?

Nothing is clear, but I checked the news. Sophia's remains were mysteriously discovered in the woods in Sussex, and there's been a drowning, Paula's ex-husband.

I'll come as soon as I deal with this.

I know you'll handle it the best way. We'll see each other soon.

Sorinah was alone again and focused on Marku's head. It had to be turned. She stood and applied pressure to twist it back into place, carefully at first, but then with all the force she could muster. It snapped sideways, then a notch at a time with each thrust. Sorinah massaged his neck skin to redistribute it properly. She softened his gruesome expression with her fingertips and forced his mouth open to trap in his reptilian tongue before sealing it closed.

Nothing could assuage the protuberance in his briefs, so she covered it with the wet blanket draped from his shoulders and then paused to survey her work. The corpse remained a fright, but not like what had greeted her arrival. She hustled from his room to the elevators, and when the doors shuddered open, ran to the front desk.

"Marku Catargiu in Room 339 has passed. I just discovered him."

The attendant's face froze, and her eyes went wide. "Are you certain?"

Sorinah nodded twice with lips tight.

The attendant reached for the phone. "Thank you, Sorinah. Please wait outside his room. The patrol will meet you there."

"Of course." She stepped back from the desk and returned to the fifth floor. The rank odor permeated the hallway despite the open windows as she walked toward Marku's room. About ten minutes later a pair of security guards appeared and cupped their noses as they approached.

"Christ, that smell," the first one said when he arrived at the door. Close-cropped, peppery stubble covered his jawline. "You are Sorinah Petrascu?"

"Yes. Marku is inside. I found him just now."

A blond guard turned the doorknob. "Bodies don't normally stink up the place, not like this." He pushed the door open and stepped in. The window crack was useless against the stench. The overturned fan buzzed as it tried to swivel, and the blades grazed wire.

"Christ our savior," the blond said as they gathered near Marku's rocking chair.

"He looks like he was electrocuted," the stubbled guard stated. "Why's the fan knocked down?" He circled Marku and clicked off a series of photos.

"Got him?" The blond guard waited for a nod before tugging at the blanket. "It's soggy." He pulled the cover away and let it drop to the floor. "What the hell got in his shorts?"

The guards stared at Marku's remarkable groin.

"He pissed himself. Cover him back up." The first guard rubbed his stubble and looked at Sorinah. "Was he like this? Did you touch him?"

Sorinah helped the blond guard cover Marku with the blanket.

"I probed his neck to check for a pulse. And I had to close his lids, he looked pained."

"Pained? He looks like he's in a goddamn electric chair in the throes of cardiac arrest," the blond interjected. "He stinks like a rotten river fish, and what's with the horse cock?"

"I don't understand the wetness. Is it a suicide? Maybe he used the fan and that's where it landed, the power cord looks frayed." The guard stopped rubbing his stubble and stepped closer to photograph it.

"Can I go now?"

There was silence for a moment.

"Yes, thank you, Sorinah. We'll let you know if we have more questions."

Sorinah nodded and shot a last glance at Marku.

And that's when his mouth popped open.

The blond guard smacked the other. "His tongue's slithering out like a fucking eel! Get the coroner here fast, he must be bloating. I'm not touching this shit."

The guards were mesmerized by the sight and didn't notice as Sorinah slipped out. She tracked down her supervisor and was granted a leave of absence, given her discovery.

Her internal alarm finely attuned to danger sounded a high alert.

TWENTY-FOUR

TRAVIS LEANED AGAINST the armrest of the brown leather couch and tapped at his keyboard. News reports online confirmed dark trouble in Sussex. An unwelcome sense of vulnerability crept in. His eyes darted up from the screen when the front door burst open and Sorinah raced in.

"Whatever defiled Marku," Sorinah said as she pulled a Windsor chair close to Travis and clasped his forearm, "is lurking in the orb."

Travis set the laptop on the cushion and leaned into Sorinah, his face hard and tight.

"It left him a broken obscenity. I've seen the work of the Devil before, but only in pictures, hand-sketched in India ink by my grandmother. Marku's head was twisted backward, a scream frozen on his face. He was drenched and stinking and nude except for briefs, his genitals engorged, his tongue blackened and elongated like a lizard."

Travis held his breath and then exhaled slowly. "What did others make of the scene?"

"Before they arrived, I adjusted his head, and folded his tongue back into his mouth." Sorinah locked eyes with Travis. "But the sight was ghastly by any standard. The guards suspected a stroke or heart attack or an electric shock, and the coroner was on the way. There isn't much for them to go on, and now there isn't much point to our wondering."

Travis stared at her, brows furrowed. "Right, we've got bigger problems."

"Your magic does it." Sorinah stiffened against the chair slats.

Travis closed his eyes while he searched for words. Each *tick* from the swinging pendulum of the grandfather clock near the spiral staircase sounded like a hammer strike.

"And it's happened to Andrei," Travis said. "He says there's a demon inside, similar to what we heard from Marku. He's had recurring visions."

Sorinah pushed hair behind her shoulders. "You've got to save him."

Travis's lips were tight as he leaned toward her. "That's another layer of trouble."

Sorinah froze until he found words.

"Andrei told me he's moving to Vermont for the summer with Stefan, his father. It can't be a coincidence, and it can't be insignificant. I'm being goaded into something, and it's working. I don't know whether to fight for Andrei or against him."

Travis grabbed his laptop and scanned the screen.

"Sophia's corpse was discovered in the woods last week where I buried it in Sussex after Radu impaled her. And now there's been an alarming accident."

Sorinah craned her neck to look.

"Aaron, the father of the family in Sussex, is dead."

Sorinah's eyes narrowed and scanned the screen. "Dead how?"

"He fell from a boat and drowned, but details sound mysterious and implausible."

"We both don't believe in coincidences." Sorinah shifted her eyes away from the screen. "Did you ever detect a trace of witch on Andrei, or his father?"

Travis's expression soured. "Nothing."

Sorinah gripped the armrests with both hands. "It might be a potent disguising spell."

"I never had cause to probe deeply. I care for the boy. And his father could barely disguise his temper, let alone his witch essence."

Sorinah's voice was measured. "Yes, but someone is toying with you. And whether Andrei is innocent or not, he's submitted to your globe, so now he's in danger."

Travis leaned back and folded his arms. His lids drooped for a moment before going wide. "I spent a good part of the day arranging logistics. Tomorrow we depart for London with a connection to Boston, then to Burlington. I've taken leave from the hospital to attend to a personal crisis. The Malloy house is booked, but I found an Airbnb listing nearby."

Travis closed the laptop and took Sorinah's hand.

"I knew you would appreciate the urgency. Can you appease Floreasca Manor?"

She smiled and squeezed it. "They agree I need time after Marku."

The *tick* of the clock pendulum again dominated until Travis broke the silence.

"What's happening to me? My hope for an heir collapsed, and my family magic is unleashing Hell, literally." He choked up and paused as a wave of disappointment muddied his sharp features. He massaged his temples for a *tick* to two to steady himself.

"There's another detail."

Sorinah scooched closer and waited.

"I cut the spell's root to protect the boy, but the infusion surged anyway. I was powerless to stop the orb until the intruder got in."

He looked up and his expression hardened.

"I'm ready to fight, but we don't know what, or who."

TWENTY-FIVE

PAULA SAT IN THE UNNATURAL HUSH, staring at the open casket. Scenes from the evening at the beach rolled in an unwelcome, endless loop. Through binoculars, she'd watched a diver in scuba gear hoist Aaron's body from the murky depths while another hauled him over the side of the rescue boat. It had all happened so fast. Something swooped down and attacked him. *What the hell was that?* Why did he try to stand with blood streaming into his face? *My God, I'm blaming him.* An instant later the boat lurched, and he tumbled overboard.

He was a strong swimmer; how could he drown? She couldn't shake the question, and with no answer, it numbed her senses. She'd watched in shock as the rescuers motored back to the beach. Everyone ran to the shoreline. The lifeguards lifted Aaron, laid him on the sand, and frantically tried CPR for what seemed an eternity. Blood drained from the wound on his head and stained a patch of sand.

"Breathe, Dad! Come on!" Paula remembered James shouted as she watched one lifeguard pump Aaron's chest while the other alternated breaths into his mouth. But he didn't stir. She heard a siren, and moments later her ex-husband was loaded onto a stretcher and raced to the ambulance.

Paula closed her eyes, rubbed them gently, and then tried to focus. She stared at the casket and realized she still hadn't cried. It was the numbness. *Does that mean I don't love him?* She knew that wasn't true, but since the divorce, she'd kept her emotions under wraps and welcomed his return to Sussex more for their shared history than for any kind of romantic notion. Still, there was no denying something plugged her up.

She gently squeezed James's knee with one hand, and Katherine's with the other and maneuvered out of her seat to kneel in front of the casket. She studied Aaron's face that in death looked ghoulish yet handsome, an ashen Roman sculpture, displayed in cold clay for a few hours before the bridge cover locked forever.

She closed her eyes. *I liked having you back; I dared to dream things might all work out. James still worships you, and Katherine's coming around. She's had a tougher time with the divorce than anyone, maybe even me. I told her she doesn't have to forgive you because sometimes forgiveness isn't an option or even necessary. Just moving on is what's important and the hardest part. I learned that on my own, and your change of heart helped to get me there. It's too bad you had to rip our family apart before getting it right, but I suppose that's the way life works. And in the end, what good did any of it do? It would have been better if you'd stayed away. At least you'd be alive. Why couldn't you swim back to the boat? You couldn't grab on? Why the hell not? It makes no sense, killed by a goddamn blackbird. What do we do with that?*

Now, she felt tears coming so she clamped down to choke everything back. A buzz from the air conditioner below a curtained window kicked in and held her attention, and in a few moments, the numbness returned. She backed away from the kneeler and made her way to her spot in the first row between James and Katherine.

"It's all a blur. Thanks for dropping everything and coming so quickly," Paula whispered to Katherine and took her hand.

"Of course," she answered. "I had to see you."

Paula leaned closer. "And say goodbye to your dad."

"I'm still in shock; it's so surreal." Katherine wiped her face with a tissue. "I don't get it. He was always an athlete. How could he drown?"

"I've been asking myself that over and over." Paula exhaled slowly and squeezed her hand. "None of it makes sense, especially the bird."

James nudged his mother and angled himself toward Katherine. "It's unheard of, the hawk attack. I'm sure it's what killed Dad, shocked him enough to drown."

Katherine watched her brother's face. "Could you get any more information, like other incidents? The story freaks me out."

James shook his head. "No one knows anything. I read hawks rarely strike humans, so something's wrong with it, a sickness, right? I'm going to take it down. I'm buying a gun."

"That sounds crazy," Katherine whispered as she leaned closer and gave James a look. "You can't just pull out a gun on a public beach. Plus, you'd never find the same one."

"I'll know it when I see it, the attack is burned in." James raised his eyebrows as he whispered. "Want to come with me, tomorrow after the funeral? I'll show you exactly where. The gun won't come out unless there's just cause."

She glanced at Paula. "I'm going to hang with Mom. I feel guilty enough. I'm leaving Thursday. Wish I could stay longer, but I'm the newbie and not allowed a personal life."

Paula shook her head. "We already went through this. I'm handling it, and you need to focus on what's new and exciting and positive." She shifted her gaze to the casket and then back to Katherine. "You should spend some time with him. There won't be another chance."

Katherine sighed and blinked a few times. She squeezed her mother's shoulder before heading to the kneeler.

James watched her in front of the casket and took his mother's hand. "I know it sounds crazy, but I'm gonna find that hawk. It might be cathartic, right? No one else is going to help. Maybe I can get revenge, do it for Dad."

"I don't like the sound of this."

James scanned the mourners seated near them, and whispered.

"I need a focus, the same way Katherine has one. The rink

sucks and I can't just mope around. That beach is calling me be-cause my dad died there and the shock won't clear."

Paula's face got tight as she watched him continue.

"He was targeted, I saw it. Dad didn't just drown. The hawk caused it. That hawk's a killer even if the cops won't listen. I want to bring it down."

"Don't get worked up." Paula squeezed his hand.

James bit his lip and rocked gently against the chair's uphol-stery.

TWENTY-SIX

HARDWOOD TREES FLUSH WITH SUMMER girdled the parking lot and camouflaged a shortcut to Lake Champlain. Radu led Andrei down the steep, sloping path of mud and shale. An arched, wooden footbridge steered them toward the docks.

They found seats on a bench behind the beach with a view of mountains across the whitecaps and near the rowboats still off-limits since the fatal accident the previous weekend.

Radu squinted as he stared into the expanse.

"The misery and magic of existence flows like the waves, an interplay of darkness and light that reflects the fickleness of creation. Water captures it perfectly."

It was high noon but clouds filtered the sun and shifted while wind tossed the treetops.

"Do you know why I brought you here?"

Andrei looked hopeful. "For more training like you promised."

"That will indeed happen." Radu folded his arms and leaned back. "And you will be linked with a mortal before we're through. That is your incentive; expectations are high."

Andrei stiffened on the bench. "I want to make you proud."

Radu's eyes locked on the orange buoy bobbing in the waves near the spot his incarnation as the hawk attacked Aaron.

"And so we begin. You must focus and command the power that courses through your veins. The pressure is real now; the plan is in place."

Andrei looked out to the water. "Why did you drown him?"

"He has value to Travis."

"What value?"

Radu focused on his son. "He's part of the family Travis knows from before, and now his death serves as bait."

Andrei nodded and scooched closer. "Dr. Coman flinched when I said 'Vermont' as if it were a magic word."

"And presently he's arrived, and our trap is set."

Andrei folded his arms and leaned back to watch his father.

"Dreams I sent lured Rachel to the corpse in the woods; the first morsel. Then, this lake swallowed the neighbor; a second. And now his son, James, wants to kill the hawk he blames for the death. You will intercept him and move our plan to the next phase. Your lesson begins."

Andrei looked anxious. "I've never shifted."

"High stakes beget high performance; it's the best way to learn." Radu placed his hand on Andrei's shoulder and squeezed.

"Shifting and disguising are similar tools, except you will inhabit an animal and use its essence to inform future shifts."

He stood to scan the shadowy depths of the woods. "Your avatar will be drawn to you."

Radu led them away from the water and they hiked off-trail up an uninviting, overgrown slope for a few minutes in search of a secluded spot in deep cover.

"The black hawk found you?" Andrei asked.

Radu turned to catch his eyes. "The magic decides."

"Are you pleased with it?"

"It suits me perfectly, as will yours."

They settled on the forest floor in a glade shielded by brush and thick trunks. Andrei closed his eyes and whispered what he'd practiced, waited, and repeated. The wind rustled the branches and scattered shifting patches of sunlight. There was a stirring in the undergrowth, then silence, and then a soft crunch as a striped badger padded out from the shadows. It slunk low and snarled as it crouched near Andrei's leg, ready to pounce.

The boy locked eyes with the animal and then shot a glance to his father.

Radu nodded almost imperceptibly and transferred, *Project yourself with conviction and suffuse him. You must possess the beast; only then will you be able to shift. Absorb how he feels, how he hungers, how he fights, how he kills, and how he escapes. It will be a new weapon.*

Andrei stared down the badger and growled the incantation.

Radu watched as Andrei's muscles tensed, and his arms glistened with sweat. The young witch froze with fists clenched. The badger reared on its hind legs and snarled as it lurched toward him, eyes blazing. Andrei crouched and crept toward the animal until their faces almost touched. The badger hissed and dropped to all fours before rushing back to the undergrowth. With a bestial reflex, Andrei tore after him.

Radu listened to thrashes and heaves in the brush. He waited for the tempest to subside and heard leaves and branches crunch as Andrei emerged, muddied, scratched, and dazed.

"I think it worked."

"How do you feel?"

Andrei paused to consider. He looked at his father and then clamped his eyes tight.

"The same except everything's expanded."

His head tilted, and he pulled in a deep breath as his eyes shot wide. He did a slow turn, crunching fallen branches with his bare feet.

"Insects scream; water smells rich; the forest looks sharp, even in shadow."

He took another step and noticed mud smears on his limbs.

"Where are my clothes?"

Radu smirked. "When you shift you shrink, and they fall away. Go retrieve them."

Andrei nodded and scrambled back under the brush. He re-emerged with his t-shirt and shorts, pulled them on, then sat next to Radu to push into his sneakers.

"With practice, you will shift at will," his father said as he affectionately squeezed the back of his son's neck. "The avatar's heightened senses and instincts are at your disposal."

Radu waited for Andrei to finish before he jumped up and started down the slope toward the lake. "Shift to attack and replenish yourself with essence. It's another weapon, another means of infusion; it also grants control of your mortal. You choose the best way to strike, weighing the element of surprise."

Andrei caught up to his father. "I feel weak and a little dizzy."

"Shifting drains energy. You'll have to replenish it."

As they neared the lake, the sound of waves breaking began to overtake the brooding rustle of branches swaying on the breeze. They hiked to the bench where they'd started the day's lessons, but now voices from a scattering of beachgoers wafted across the sand.

"What's next with your plan?" Andrei asked as he took a seat.

Radu again fixed on the orange buoy as he stretched out his arm behind his son along the backrest. "Tonight I draw Travis in deeper, now that he's arrived."

"How?" Andrei leaned in closer.

"I will welcome him with a nightmare of his own, a taste of what he's offered you." He touched his son's shoulder. "Have they stopped, the visions, the whispers?"

Andrei gave his father a wary look and then extended his legs to wipe dried mud from his knees. "Right now the training blocks everything else. My mind is racing, I feel alive."

"Good. Focus on that," he said with a smile, "explore your new senses."

By the time the sun had shifted toward the mountains, a newcomer appeared on the beach with a black nylon sling bag over his shoulder. He paced the shoreline with a scowl and eyes trained on the treetops. The witches sat at attention.

That's James, Radu transferred silently, *the son of the drowned man. He's looking for me and questioning his senses. It's time to test the shift.*

What if I can't?

You must.

I'm weak. Andrei wiped sweat from his brow.

You'll replenish what's drained.

How?

Ingest his essence however you choose. You'll gain control of him. The plan demands it.

Andrei's heart raced with trepidation.

Radu inched to the bench edge. *It's a necessary next step.*

The boy closed his eyes and repeated the incantation. After a few moments, he opened them wide, huffed, and slumped back.

"It's not working."

"Take your time and focus on the pairing forged by the spell."

Radu pointed as James scanned the treetops with binoculars.

Andrei shivered, sat straight, and took a deep breath as he closed his eyes.

"Ah, my avatar is stealthy, but he's with me now."

Radu swiveled to watch Andrei as he stood from the bench and slipped into the forest. A moment passed before Radu heard a menacing growl and then crunches and snaps as his son slunk just out of sight near the edge of the woods toward his target.

James continued to wander the sand with his neck craned, binoculars combing the treetops. A rustling of branches near the shoreline caught his attention, and he crept toward the woods. He skulked forward, pausing as a shuffle and pop on a tree limb lured him off the beach into the forest.

Something leapt from an upper branch and then disappeared. James followed the shadows and crackles off-trail and paused to listen. A snarl started low and then overcame everything else. James froze and was slammed by a tempest of claws, fur, and tearing bites. He writhed in pain as he flailed to knock the beast off his back, using the binoculars as a club.

Radu bolted toward the action in the woods and watched as the badger held fast. It anchored itself behind the mortal's broad shoulders, licking and snorting and gorging on the feast of sweat, scent, and blood.

James bellowed and charged backward into a tree trunk. The badger clung to the top of his head and then leapt to the bushes as James tore for the parking lot.

Then the melee went quiet.

Radu followed a clothing trail to find Andrei on the forest floor under the cover of branches. He reached down and gently shook his son's shoulder.

Andrei's eyes shot open, and he bounced up, gasping for air, arms wrapping tight around his legs that folded to his chest.

"Don't gulp. Savor the infusion slowly," Radu said.

Andrei nodded as he drew in long, slow breaths.

"I can see through his eyes." The boy glanced at his father and then clamped his lids shut. "He's in the car, pressing the back of his neck. I feel his pulse racing."

Andrei shuddered as fresh, raw essence coursed through him. He clenched his fists, restraining the rush with long-held breaths while he tossed on the ground, every muscle taut.

"My heart's racing with his," he whispered. "There's a link, I can read him."

All at once, his grimace relaxed, and his whole body went slack. He sat up and his eyes darted about in wonder.

"Everything stopped. The pressure's gone, I thought my head might pop. I'm charged."

Radu smiled and extended his arm.

"See how fast? Sometimes the beast works best. No elaborate plan, no gathering of residues. You did great."

Andrei gripped his father's wrist and hoisted himself from the forest floor, wiping off dirt, sticks, and leaves that stuck to his skin. He blew out a deep breath.

"I gathered your clothes." Radu handed them to his son.

When they reached the parking lot, an ambulance already flanked James's car.

TWENTY-SEVEN

SOMEONE WATCHED HIM FROM above while he tossed, sprawled on his back with a bedsheet between his legs in the clammy, cramped bedroom. Travis felt the sticky wetness of the mattress under his neck and shoulders and came to realize it was his doppelgänger floating in darkness, somewhere near the ceiling, and he was in both bodies at once.

A sharp wail outside made him peer through a row of window panes. In the shadows of the mist-shrouded Vermont moonlight, a figure wavered near a row of hedges. With a strange certainty, he recognized the girl as she came into focus. A moan drew his attention back to the bed and held it as he watched himself kick and twitch in the tangle of sheets.

He was fascinated and torn between examining his naked body in the throes of a nightmare and marveling at the wraith who hovered above the manicured lawn of the rental house. The girl was dressed in tatters, and her eyes glowed within skeletal sockets through a straggle of matted hair. She extended a long, crooked finger that looked like bone and pointed at him. He knew with the certainty of dreams it was Carol Stilton who beckoned from beyond the grave in the warm night air.

She drifted closer, undulating in the mist, and when she grimaced, Travis felt terror seize his core as the window panes began to shudder within their loose, weathered, wooden frames until one cracked.

"You shouldn't have come back."

The voice was scratchy and halting as if each word required effort.

"You have much to account for."

Travis braced against the ceiling.

What the hell is happening?

He wasn't immune to fear. The specter of death cooked that into all creatures. He knew he was dreaming yet couldn't rouse himself as was usual when nightmares took hold. He glanced at the bed and watched the muscles of his clone struggle, shiny with sweat against invisible restraints.

The fissure in the windowpane feathered and expanded with a *crack* like the breaking ice over a pond. Travis clenched his eyes shut just as the glass shattered and blew into his face as he floated prone only inches away. Shards clattered as they hit the wooden floor. He refocused to watch Carol beckon him with wavering arms that stretched and billowed like tendrils under water.

He understood the open pane was a portal, and he effortlessly passed through and drifted to the grass beside the wraith. He steadied himself and stepped forward, nude as the moon.

She trembled as if she were crying, but no tears came, only agony etched deep.

"You did this." She shook her head and clutched at her breast as if she were corroding from within.

"Everything was resolved. Why are you here?" Travis asked warily. "I don't understand."

He studied the locket that hung from her neck on a sturdy, tarnished, silver chain.

She gripped it and thrust it toward him. "You stole it from my casket and cursed it with your magic. You marked me."

The water-stained, tattered gown she'd worn for decades underground billowed out around her as he reached for the chain.

"Your spell damned a stranger." Her sunken face quivered, almost imperceptibly, as burning orbs floating in oversized sockets locked his eyes. "This is the face of a stranger."

Travis held her gaze as he passed the heavy silver links between his fingers.

"What can I do?" he whispered.

The wraith's voice quavered.

"Come see what you've done already."

Carol grabbed Travis's forearm to pull it away from the chain. She shot straight up, leaving a translucent trail. Travis found himself following her into the wispy clouds of dawn. The Sussex rental house shrunk in the distance, and he realized he wasn't in control at all but somehow synced within the wraith's orbit and pulled along for the ride.

For how long they sailed, he didn't know. He watched Carol's legs kick slowly as if swimming with incongruous grace, skeletal toes pointed beyond her tattered, billowing dress. The white tower of a church steeple came into view, and she started their descent. Behind the neat clapboard structure were stone grave markers and a mound of fresh dirt.

Travis watched with horror as Carol dove slowly into an open pit, headfirst. If this were a nightmare, he wanted to wake up, and tried to picture himself in the bed that he'd studied from his ceiling perch. He'd always been able to stop nightmares. Witches could inflict them on others, and he was quick to halt his own. But Carol was in control.

"Where are you taking me?"

If she heard she conceded nothing, and then everything went black.

When he recovered awareness, his sweat stained the stone where he lay on a ledge overlooking an abyss. Roaring flames somewhere far below threw heat and wavering, orange-hued highlights up the towering walls of an enormous circular cavern. He sat and pushed back several meters from the edge, bracing himself against a boulder. The ledge snaked around the abyss at a steep pitch, like the spirals inside a tornado that extended up to infinity. Below, an inferno raged.

Travis pinched himself; his forearms were slick. He stood

and hiked up the slope to escape the blast furnace. Stalactites hung amid cavities along the outer walls that looked like hardened lava. He climbed two rotations from where he started before he heard a shriek. It echoed in the cavern for what seemed an eternity. The sound chilled him, and he froze in place with all senses attuned.

At first, there was nothing more, but before he dared to breathe, he heard sobs. They echoed eerily throughout the cavern despite their softness. The cries seemed to rise from the abyss above the flames, and Travis inched closer to the edge. Carol Stilton hovered in the center of the fiery expanse, elevating slowly, crying softly. When she was level with Travis's ridge, she glared.

"You did this." She trembled, and her taut skin was shriveling to the bone.

"It's impossible. You were free!"

"You were wrong," Carol continued, her voice quavering. "You damned me."

Travis held his breath.

I did nothing to you. Her words carried soundlessly, and he flinched.

"It was not my intention to hurt you," he said. "How can I fix it?"

Carol's eyes glowed red in the sockets. She drifted close, fingers curved like claws. One talon trailed down his forearm. Skin sizzled but he couldn't pull away.

"Your magic does this. Now the Devil counts me as his own."

Travis felt her despair radiate in waves like the scorch of her touch.

"You ripped my soul from heaven. I did nothing to you."

She was weeping with no tears, and reached out with brittle, gnarled hands before a savage suction sucked her down. Her screams echoed as she disappeared, and he strained against the blowback behind her descent, but helplessly plunged over the ledge after her.

Travis shouted, and when he opened his eyes, Sorinah was

kneeling on the edge of the bed beside him. He sprang up and gasped for air, his skin slick.

Sorinah adjusted the sheets to cover him. "You're back; it's over."

Travis studied Sorinah's face for a moment. "How did you know?"

"I heard a window shatter."

"How long was I out?" Travis tried to gauge the light streaming in.

"I shook you for the longest time. No one could sleep through that, so I slapped you." She caressed his cheek. "Hard. At least that worked."

"I deserve it," he said, finding a smile and wiping his brow.

"You were entranced; it was a spell." She paused and gently probed the swellings of red and white on his forearm. "You're burned. I watched the flesh sear as the blisters spread."

Travis flinched as he probed it himself. "It was part of the dream."

"Tell me about it while it's fresh."

Travis exhaled slowly, then closed his eyes. When he opened them, he scooched back to prop himself up against a pillow. "Carol Stilton, the first of the wraiths I conjured, paid me a visit. My magic damned her."

Sorinah looked for more burn marks. "How?"

"She killed Mia by mistake, and my spell sent her to Hell," he said, locking her eyes. "Her soul switched sides."

"Eternal rest, disrupted by black magic," Sorinah said, stony-faced.

Travis furrowed his brow, and a shadow crossed his features. "She's in agony."

Sorinah looked about the room as she considered. "Someone sent a welcome gift. It's our first night in Sussex, and you know there are no coincidences." Sorinah went toward the window and jostled shattered glass on the floor with her foot.

"What happened here?"

Travis leaned over the edge of the bed. "A windowpane blew in when the dream started."

Sorinah walked to his side of the bed and sat next to him.

"The trance, plus the burn, plus the glass. It's the work of a witch." She watched him poke at the blisters on his arm. "Who could have done it?"

Travis's lips pulled tight as he pushed back against the head-board. "My patient Andrei is the only lead I've got. His father's sudden move to Sussex, that's why we're here."

Her eyes narrowed. "Could Andrei have your essence?"

"No, I took *his* for use in the orb. And I've never detected a smidgen of witch essence."

"What about his father?"

Travis closed his eyes to think. A cooling breeze wafted in the broken window.

"That looks bad now. I met Stefan once at his restaurant. I wasn't on the lookout for a witch." Travis propped his pillow up and leaned back. "He had access to everything over the course of my dinner."

"They must be powerful, or you wouldn't be fooled." Sorinah frowned and stared down his scowl. "And you wouldn't have burns."

Travis stroked the stubble on his jaw, then met her gaze. "I care about Andrei, and I'm not ready to believe he's an enemy. I want to help him. I've placed him in danger. But his father...."

Sorinah considered. "Why would Stefan want us here?"

Travis shook his head. "Somehow he knows my past and is taunting me."

"He has the upper hand, and now the dream power." Sorinah gently touched his cheek. Redness from the slap was faded. "Your nightmare was only a prelude."

Travis stiffened. "I have a good idea where to track them down."

Sorinah raised her eyebrows.

"The Malloy house, just to fuck with me."

"Yes, where we stayed the last time." Sorinah's lips were tight as she shot up from the bed. "Meet you downstairs for coffee before we go?"

He nodded as she turned and then closed the bedroom door behind her.

Travis shifted toward the broken window, and a whisper found its way in.

I did nothing to you.

TWENTY-EIGHT

RACHEL SKIDDED INTO James's driveway. She wanted to come sooner but had promised MK she'd finish her shift. Why did the horrors never stop? It was so depressing. She'd joined James at Aaron's burial the previous morning, but had to take a shift in the afternoon. James was headed for the lake. What could go wrong? Apparently, a lot. Thankfully, he looked steady waiting for her planted on the top kitchen step, and she waved as she jumped out of the driver's seat.

"What the hell?" She hustled over and found a spot beside him.

"It doesn't hurt unless I bump it." James reached behind and tapped the bandage stuck to the back of his neck, sticking up above his t-shirt.

She caressed the bare skin around it. "It sounded wicked crazy on the phone. At first, I couldn't believe it, but given everything else, why not?"

"It scared me shitless."

"Did they find the werewolf?" She fought back a grin.

"I haven't heard anything, but I got a rabies shot." James swiveled as he lifted his t-shirt sleeve. "They're on the lookout for a rabid raccoon or badger or whatever it was. I'm lucky, the damage isn't bad, but that fucker attacked me."

She leaned in and kissed his shoulder. "Thank God it isn't worse."

"I can't even." He rolled his sleeve down.

Rachel stretched out next to him and saffron rays of sunlight felt just toasty enough to lavish a moment's comfort and serenity. But it didn't take long for her hypervigilance to ruin things. She couldn't relax, not these days, anyway.

"What about the hawk?"

James shook his head with a disgusted look.

"I could help you spy around the lake again if you want." Rachel pushed her Ray-Bans up into her hair. "I feel bad you went alone."

His muscles tensed. "I'm never going back."

She took in his sullen face and felt herself choke up. "I don't blame you." She put her arm around him, careful not to jar the bandage.

"The police think we're toxic," he said as they locked eyes. "And I don't blame them. Trouble finds us. First Sophia, then my dad, and now I'm attacked by a wild animal. I need to disappear for a while."

Rachel squeezed him a little. "So do I." She felt him press closer. "They know we're a couple, and I'm not exactly their favorite."

James smirked. "Yeah, and now we're pretty much even."

"Thanks for keeping up." Rachel took his hand. "How's your mom doing?"

"OK, all things considered. She's mostly quiet." James wormed his fingers between hers. "Katherine left this morning for California. My mom seems fine with it, and so am I. We need normal and positive right now. My mom's going back to work next week."

"What about you?"

He stiffened, and his lips pulled into a frown. "I'll do my thing at the rink until school starts. I'll master Zamboni loops while I'm obsessing about my dad's accident. But that's normal, right?"

She nodded and tightened her fingers on his. "How are you handling it?"

James leaned in. "My feelings flip-flop."

Rachel felt him swivel for a better grip, and their eyes met.

"I can't figure it out. He was an alpha and wouldn't just drown. And that hawk? It happened so fast. So bizarro. It must have struck a brain nerve, or he wouldn't have seized up. I Googled hawk attacks, and it's super rare. His sinking in the water keeps replaying in slow motion. I can't turn it off."

Rachel watched as his hand cupped the top of hers and pressed. "People try to rationalize horrible things every day; that I know for sure. Don't even try."

She felt James ease closer.

"Like a lightning strike or an aneurysm, there's not a damn thing anyone can do when fate comes calling." Rachel snuck her hand out from under his and took hold of his forearm. "What happened to your dad was an act of God—"

"Or the Devil," James interrupted. "He didn't deserve it."

He was touching her face now, and Rachel's pulse rate doubled.

Is this bad timing? She raised her chin and smiled as their eyes met. She scooched sideways and steered her arm around the waistband of his shorts.

Rachel, your timing isn't the best. He's vulnerable.

Their faces came close, and a deep kiss happened.

But maybe this will help.

She swiveled to allow space for his arm around her shoulder and felt his stubble against her cheek as she sucked in a breath, then nuzzled his face.

"This is one nice thing." She exhaled and ruffled his spiky hair.

"It helps to be with you." He smiled and his eyes signaled he meant it.

She paused to take in his scent, his taste, the sunshine, and the moment. "Maybe fate wants us together. Something good out of all this death."

"We should go with it, right?" He smiled and kissed her cheek. "I'm not sure I said it out loud, but I'm thankful we stayed in touch. Things could have gone the other way."

Rachel put a finger over his lips and then leaned in to kiss him again.

When she pulled back, she took in his hazel eyes. "Things are so fucked up again: your dad, the nightmares, Sophia's body, the animal attacks." She leaned her head on his shoulder. "We should get out of here; we could escape for a long weekend. I'm sure MK would understand and probably encourage it. She knows about everything, including the police."

James's eyebrows pitched as he pondered the possibility. "Not a bad idea, depends if my mom would be OK on her own. Where should we go?"

"I don't know. Camping?" She snickered and hoped he knew it was a joke.

He smiled and shook his head. "No way I'm staying in the woods."

"Fair," Rachel said and rested her hand on his thigh. "What about the ocean? We could road trip to Massachusetts. You could show me your school on the way."

James perked up and took her hand. "That sounds like a plan."

Their fingers intertwined, and Rachel leaned back again. A breeze rustled the upper branches of the maple behind the driveway. Beyond it, the lawn expanded to the forested path of the stagecoach road, and as she gazed a black pair of wings sailing on the wind caught her attention.

She sat straighter as she stared; her eyes narrow slits as she watched.

"What the hell is that?"

James turned, studied where she was looking, and then jumped up. "It's the hawk."

Rachel joined him on the top step. The raptor circled the backyard level with the treetops, gliding low and then beating back up.

"Shit me. It's the one from the lake." He held his breath to take it in. "It has to be."

James slowly released her hand and dashed to the edge of the driveway.

"The motherfucker came here." His neck craned up as he lumbered to the garden. "I'm sure it's the one. I *feel* something."

Rachel caught up to him. "It can't be the same, that's impossible."

The upper branch of an oak near the edge of the forest bobbed under the black hawk's weight as it landed, and a screech echoed across the meadow.

"Keep your eye on him. I'll be right back."

Rachel turned. "Where are you going?" she asked as James raced back to the house.

"My pistol is downstairs."

Rachel stepped beyond the garden toward the field that led to the woods. A moment later, James came up beside her with a Glock 19 in his right hand.

She eyed it warily. "Is that legal?"

"I'm not hunting; it's self-protection." James marched toward the forest. "I'm going after a public menace," he said over his shoulder, "for the sake of my dad."

With another screech, the hawk launched from the tree and looped the meadow before soaring over the woods.

"It seems like he's watching us," Rachel said as she followed a pace behind.

James stopped to plant his legs and took aim with both hands. "I gotta get closer," he said and then gave up the shot to carry on.

Rachel scoured the treetops. "Maybe we should call the cops."

The raptor unleashed another screech, this one with a lingering echo on the breeze. They slowed to a jog and strained to listen when they got close to the woods.

"Why does it sound like that?" Rachel asked as they entered the tree cover and the stagecoach road at once looked dark and uninviting.

"It's like we're in a movie."

The overgrown pathway curved left and deep. They navigated past clumps of milkweed and tree roots pocking the knee-high grasses that carved through the woods. About halfway, everything went eerily silent, and they strained to hear anything at all until a loud *crack* sounded somewhere in the shadows.

"The hell was that?" Rachel whispered as her eyes darted about.

James raised his pistol with one hand, and his index finger

with the other to signal quiet. Sweat trailed down the back of his t-shirt below his bandage.

They trudged forward as quietly as possible. A sudden, violent rustle in the branches just overhead broke the stillness, and the black predator launched above the treetops.

James gripped the pistol with both hands and fired off two rounds. "It's not right. I can't get a good shot." He glanced at Rachel and started to run. "Follow me."

They sprinted along the trail, eyes trained on the black target that glided on wings spread wide, soaring over breaks in the tree cover.

"We're losing him," Rachel said as she caught up to James, and they jogged side by side.

"It opens up once we're out of the woods." His right hand gripped the pistol. "I'll get another chance."

They slowed to catch their breath once they cleared the trees.

James pointed to a farmhouse beyond the meadow. "We call it the Malloy house. I'm not sure if anyone even lives there now."

They crept onto the property, all senses on high alert.

"Wait, what if someone still does?" Rachel whispered.

They scoured the sky and listened for anything beyond birdsong and the chirrups of crickets. A screech in the distance soon grabbed their attention, and powerful black wings sailed on the wind.

"It's heading straight for us," Rachel said, and grabbed James's arm.

He planted his legs and aimed the pistol. "I'll take it out."

He popped off three shots, which in three second's time confirmed he'd missed.

The black hawk circled wide and shrieked as it bore down on them.

Rachel's whole body tingled with adrenaline and she was panting. "It's coming for us!"

TWENTY-NINE

MORNING SHIFTED INTO EARLY AFTERNOON before Travis and Sorinah finished setting up their Airbnb near the park in Sussex and grimly set out to discover why they'd been lured here.

As they drove across town in a compact Nissan SUV, Travis couldn't shake off the dream, an ominous and unwelcome stain on his first night back in Vermont. With eyes peeled and all senses trained on the new surroundings, neither of them spoke. Things looked familiar but menacing given the circumstances. They passed Paula's house on the way to the curve onto Shaker Lane just ahead. If the Malloy house was clear, she was next to visit.

They came to a wide shoulder on the side of the road and pulled over to park.

"Give me a second," Travis said to Sorinah, and shot her a tight smile before climbing out of the driver's seat. He stepped onto the gravel driveway to probe for a witch barrier. When he wasn't shocked or shoved backward, he signaled to Sorinah.

Their steps crunched the stones as they headed toward the house.

"Nothing so far, but be ready for anything." Travis said as he sucked down a deep breath

"Let's expose the witch." Sorinah's eyes got wide as she scanned the premises for any clue that might signal a trap.

"Whoever lured me would likely stay here, close to the family I knew." Travis stepped from the gravel and tested for a barrier on the old brick sidewalk to the front door. "It's a show of power and mocks me."

Sorinah's face tightened. "I don't like being back. Last time wasn't a joy."

Travis tapped his fingers on the rail up the steps: no tingle or burn.

"This visit won't be either, I'm afraid." He looked up toward the buzzer as he mounted the steps, and a dark flicker overhead caught his eye against the brilliant blue sky. He scanned and froze as a large black bird of prey swooped low over the lawn on the side of the house.

"There we are," he whispered, and motioned toward it. "A witch's calling card."

Sorinah stepped backward to follow the raptor's trajectory as it gained altitude and circled overhead. "That didn't take long."

It screeched as it soared over the roof of the house.

"Someone is expecting us." Travis hesitated before pressing the doorbell.

Sorinah came up behind him. "Let's take it as a warning."

There wasn't a sound except for a breeze in the treetops and the grinding of crickets, which sounded like a hundred little screams. Travis tried again and waited. In due time, the knob joggled, the seal broke, and the door creaked open.

Andrei appeared behind the mesh screen. His eyes bulged wide as he sucked in a breath and then smiled. "Dr. Coman, what are you doing here?"

Travis braced himself with one arm on the iron railing and smiled back.

"You mentioned you were spending the summer in Vermont. Turns out, I had to come straight away because a family I know that lives here has suffered a loss." He inhaled deeply and scanned the boy for the essence of witch, something he'd never even considered during their sessions in Bucharest. He picked up minty soap and licorice with no hint of an aura.

"It's quite a coincidence you're staying here," Travis continued. "Sussex is small."

Andrei averted his eyes and whispered, "I didn't know exactly where."

"I stayed in this house four years ago; that's the coincidence." Travis swiveled sideways and put his hand on Sorinah's shoulder. "This is Sorinah. We're partners in Bucharest."

She smiled and pushed her sunglasses up into her hair. "Nice to meet you."

Andrei nodded and smiled.

"Is your dad home?" Travis asked.

Andrei took a step back from the screen. He clenched his jaw and shook his head.

An awkward moment passed with Travis's eyes trained on the boy.

Andrei dropped his gaze. "He goes to work."

Travis jumped in quickly. "And leaves you alone? Are you safe?"

Andrei nodded and held himself tight. "There's not much choice. He just started. He needs the job, and I can't drive anyway."

He jumped in again. "Do you know anyone if something happens?"

"No," Andrei whispered, and his fingers pressed into his biceps enough to indent.

Travis stooped lower to speak face to face. "Do you know why he picked Sussex?"

Their eyes locked as Andrei considered. "This town is near the lake resort, but cheaper, he told me. He can make more money because Bucharest is slow in the summer. Plus, I've never seen the States."

Travis transferred to Sorinah, *Do you detect anything?*

No, let's check inside. She shot him a look.

Travis straightened and sidled backward. "I don't like you're alone in a strange country."

"It's just for right now." Andrei shrunk back and squeezed even tighter.

Travis hated feeling helpless and fought to hide a scowl. How did he end up standing on the front steps of a house he'd hoped never to see again? Meanwhile, his patient bobbed on the highly suspicious side of the screen. He needed answers fast. Plus there was the omen: the black raptor that greeted them.

"Is there anything you'd like to talk about?" It was the best he could manage. "Since I'm here anyway, we could chat. I'm worried you're alone."

Andrei crinkled his nose and exhaled through his teeth. "The voice."

Travis shot Sorinah a look, his lips tight, then looked back to Andrei. "Can we talk?"

Andrei flicked his eyes to Sorinah and then back to Travis and nodded. He fiddled with the lock on the screen door. "It's what I told you in your office."

Travis smiled broadly. "Sorinah can give us some time alone."

"I'll wait in the kitchen or in back. I know the house, too," Sorinah said quickly.

The metal latch made a *click* as Andrei pressed the lever. "It's funny it's the same house." He pulled the door open and ushered them in.

"Yes, strange indeed," Travis said as he entered and Sorinah followed, securing it shut.

"Did you tell my dad about it?" Andrei asked as he led them into the living room. "That time you met in his restaurant? Maybe that's how he knew."

"No, it never came up."

"I'll ask him later how he found it." Andrei shrugged as he made his way to a dark brown leather armchair and motioned his doctor toward the couch.

"I'll go anywhere you want, so you guys can talk." Sorinah smiled and stood politely in the corner, both hands clasped on the chain of her bag.

Travis settled on one side of the couch. "Maybe the kitchen is good or the backyard?"

"The kitchen works. Is that OK, Andrei?" Sorinah took a step toward the hallway. "I know the way if you want me to find it myself."

Andrei smiled and nodded. "Sure, help yourself to water or whatever." He looked at Travis. "Are you thirsty?"

Travis folded his arms and shook his head. "I'm fine."

"Come get me when you guys are ready." Sorinah disappeared down the hallway.

Probe as much as you can. You know the layout, Travis transferred.

He leaned against the thick armrest of the couch and swiveled close to Andrei. "So, tell me what's been going on."

"We've only been here a week or two." Andrei looked toward Travis and then out the picture window. "I thought it would be more fun. It gets lonely by myself."

"Did you tell your father?"

Andrei hesitated before answering. "He knows. But there's nothing we can do."

Travis narrowed his eyes. "Why?"

"He needs the money."

Travis kept steady and exhaled slowly. "Maybe there are activities like swimming lessons or bike rides. Did you bring yours?"

"We couldn't, and it doesn't make sense to get one for just a few months."

Travis watched as Andrei fidgeted in the chair. "You can't just sit home by yourself."

Andrei's lips were tight as he nodded. "The quiet makes the voice get louder." He folded his arms and exhaled slowly. "I thought I could escape here."

Travis held his breath and focused intently on his patient.

"I still get the bad feeling when he whispers." Andrei stiffened in the chair and his eyes blazed at Travis. "You don't remember?"

"I do, I do. I'm sorry." Travis leaned in close. "I was really hoping that had passed."

There was the tinge of panic in the boy's wide eyes. "It hasn't. He followed me."

Travis watched him twist in the leather chair. His words came slow and quiet.

"The demon comes to my window. He can get in, he told me so. There's a tap on the glass. And then there's scary silence, and I can't resist peeking, and his face is there. *Andrei*, he tells me, *I'll take you when it hurts the most.*"

Andrei's lower lip trembled, and he hid his face. "What did you do to me?"

Travis studied the boy, and if he were faking, it was mighty convincing.

"I'm so sorry, and I'm going to fix it," Travis said quietly as he gripped the armrest. "It was never supposed to happen. I wanted to expose what hurt you so I could help you get past it."

Andrei looked up and sat quietly, his eyes locked on his doctor. "It set off something worse, and you have to stop it. It's not a game—"

A volley of gunshots from outside shattered the conversation in the living room.

"What the hell was that?"

Travis jumped up to cover the boy.

"It came from out back," Andrei said and gripped Travis's forearm where the blisters had been, but had mostly healed into a leathery, hairless patch.

They raced through the hallway to the kitchen where Sorinah was already standing at the bay window facing the meadow behind the house.

"They're coming this way," Sorinah said as they rushed to her side. "James has a gun."

Travis surveyed the scene. "Rachel is with him, the neighbor."

"Are they dangerous?" Andrei asked, and tucked himself below Travis's arm that was braced on the window frame.

"No, not at all, but they shouldn't be here. I don't want them to find us, not yet. There are too many variables." Travis threw a nervous glance at Sorinah.

The three of them watched as the pair marched toward the house.

"Andrei, come with us. I can't leave you here alone. I will bring you back later when your dad gets home. He'll understand. I won't leave you in the line of gunfire."

Andrei nodded and followed Travis and Sorinah through the kitchen. They rushed out the front door and locked it behind them. A moment later they were on the gravel driveway moving toward the SUV parked on the side of the road.

"What's wrong with that guy?" Andrei asked as he waited for the locks to pop.

"His father just died in an accident, and he's distraught. I can't get involved until I find out more, like, why you're in this house. I need to see your father, and soon."

As they climbed into the car, Travis again glimpsed the hawk in the sky, and another shot cracked as they sped away, wheels spinning a dust cloud.

THIRTY

JAMES FIRED BUT MISSED AGAIN, and the black hawk swooped down on them like rats.

"Watch out!" Rachel shouted from a defensive crouch behind the thick trunk of an old birch tree. "Get over here!" The words forced past her clenched teeth like a stage whisper.

James lowered his pistol and bolted toward Rachel as the predator screeched and sailed toward him like a missile, wings tight against its core and eyes trained on him over the curved, flaming beak. James dove and rolled to escape the strike, and ran toward Rachel as the hawk whizzed past and disappeared into the treetops behind them.

"Let's run for it. We're pinned down." James pointed toward the Malloy house and they sprinted. He glanced over his shoulder. "It's coming again!"

Rachel looked backward and screamed as the raptor barreled toward them, and in a flash it clipped James's head.

James cursed and swung the gun uselessly in the hawk's back-draft. "Go for the shed!"

Rachel followed his lead as another screech echoed from across the meadow.

"We provoked it. Sprint, I'll catch you!"

James threw a thumbs up and kept his focus on the weathered, red-stained shelter behind the house. He reached it first and wiped sweat and blood from this forehead as he surveyed the sky.

He toyed with the metal latch and kicked the door open just as Rachel came up behind him.

They jumped in and slammed the door before doubling over and sucking down air. Light streamed in through horizontal single-pane windows near the ceiling beams. The air was stale and heavy with mold from damp straw that lay scattered about the plywood floor.

"Let me check your head," Rachel said between breaths. James bent down, and she probed his hair with two fingers. "There's a gash, but it doesn't look deep." She reached into her shoulder bag and pulled out a travel-size pack of Kleenex. With a few wadded, she pressed down on the pooling trail of blood. "Does it hurt?"

He flinched and a groan escaped.

"I've got to reload. I can't believe we're—"

A *bang* on the roof shut him up. They listened closely and held their breath, eyes darting about the cramped space. Footfalls followed, and the roof beams creaked as something heavy crossed the sloped shingles and then flashed past the window in the far corner as it dropped.

"What the hell was that?" James's heart pounded as he craned to look out a window.

Then there was a crackling outside. Branches? Gravel?

"Someone's heading for the house," James whispered.

They held their breath and waited.

"Should we hide?" Rachel asked finally and sidled toward a storage cabinet against the far wall.

A moment later they heard a door close, not a slam, but a solid *click*, followed by the unmistakable crunch of footsteps on gravel.

Before James could answer, the door to the shed squeaked open on rusted hinges. A fit 40-something guy with black, straight hair and sharp features appeared in the doorway.

"What's going on here?" His voice was deep and accented.

"Sorry, man. I know it sounds crazy, but we had to run from a hawk that attacked us." James swiveled to show the top of his head and some blood on his t-shirt.

"I heard gunshots." His dark eyes focused on the pistol James held at his side. "Why are you in my yard?"

"We live nearby; we're neighbors just across a path through the woods." James pointed in the general direction of the stagecoach road.

The man took a step inside. "Let me see the wound." He approached slowly and eyeballed it while James bent forward. "Heads bleed a lot. Doesn't look so bad, but it's wise to clean it. Let's get you inside." He stepped aside and noticed the bandage peeking above the neck of his t-shirt. The fit was tight enough to show the outline.

"What happened there?"

"Another animal attack yesterday," James said. "I must look like meat."

The man hesitated and eyed the neighbor's build. "You might. I'm Stefan, by the way."

Rachel smiled and noticeably exhaled. "Wow, I think we've already met. I helped you with denim jackets at my store. I remember your accent." She held out her hand. "I'm Rachel. Sorry for the intrusion, but the hawk forced us inside. I'm still shaking."

Stefan tightened his lips and studied her for a moment. "Of course, I remember. It's nice to see you again." He took her hand. "Though I didn't quite expect to find you in my shed."

James unzipped his shoulder pack and put away the pistol. He followed Rachel and Stefan out onto the gravel driveway, and held out his hand. "I'm James."

Stefan grabbed it and smiled. "Hello, neighbor. Where do you live?"

James pointed toward the woods behind the meadow. "There's an old road through the trees. We're not far away. It's closer on foot than by car."

Stefan motioned across the driveway, then started toward the back door to the house. "Follow me to the kitchen for some antiseptic and a bandage."

The trio crossed the gravel, and Stefan led them up the wooden steps. He held the door open and motioned to the empty seats around the table.

Rachel took one at the far end, nearest the hallway. James sat next to her with his back to the sink. Stefan opened a cabinet, pulled out peroxide and a washcloth, and dampened it under the faucet.

He came up behind James. "Mind if I take over?"

James nodded and left the wad matted in his hair.

Stefan dabbed around to free the Kleenex and tossed it to the counter. He pressed on the small gash and followed with peroxide, and then wiped the trail that streamed to James's t-shirt.

"A bird, you say?" Stefan blotted James's scalp, took a peek, and then dabbed again.

James swiveled in his chair to shoot him a glance. "Yes, a giant, black hawk."

"I wasn't aware they attack mortals." Stefan folded the washcloth into a small square. "Humans, rather."

"They don't; that's why it's so bizarre." For a split second, James considered sharing his suspicion it was the same hawk that'd struck his father a week earlier but thought better of it. "Even stranger, it seemed to lure us here. We didn't plan to trespass. I swear."

Rachel nodded. "It wanted us to follow, but then turned on us."

"I see." Stefan stepped back still applying pressure to James's wound. "You're safe now."

"But the hawk is still out there." James swiveled again to lock eyes with the neighbor. "It's a public menace, and I tried to kill it."

"I bet that's what riled it."

Stefan firmly took James's wrist and guided his hand. "Hold this while I get a bandage. I'll be right back." He disappeared into the hallway.

"Do you think it's safe to walk home?" Rachel whispered.

James frowned. "I'll reload before we go, just in case."

"You weren't much of a shot, by the way." Rachel smiled and took his other hand.

"It's hard to hit a moving target." James squeezed back. "I was shaky. That hawk freaks me out, especially after my dad."

"How could it find you?" Rachel's lips tightened, and she shook her head. She could see the turmoil in his eyes.

Stefan returned without a sound and placed a sealed bandage on the table.

James moved his hand to his lap, and Stefan tossed the washcloth to the counter. He gently dabbed again. He hummed and murmured in Romanian while he unwrapped the bandage, smoothed the hair down, and pressed it on his scalp.

"That should do the trick." Stefan took a seat across from Rachel. "Try not to rile anything else." He raised his sharp black eyebrows, and a curious smile formed dimples. "What happened yesterday?"

"Something jumped me at the lake." James straightened in his chair and reached behind his neck to probe the bandage. "I think it was a badger. I know it sounds crazy."

"It's been a strange time for both of us." Rachel folded her arms and leaned back.

Stefan studied both of their faces. "Your auras must be out of alignment."

"What does that mean?" James watched him and for the first time fixed on his good looks.

"We all send out energy that attracts good or evil. It's a continual, unconscious process." Stefan ran one hand through his thick hair and again murmured softly. "The aura can be healed."

"That accent, your whispers," Rachel said as she adjusted the shoulder strap of her bag, "I forget where you said you're from, Europe?"

Stefan smiled and a shadow crossed his face as he answered, "Yes, Romania."

James felt a twinge as if for an instant he were outside his body looking down at the kitchen table, but then it passed and dissipated like a flash of déjà vu.

"Do you want to soak the stain so the blood doesn't set in your shirt?"

"I don't think that's necessary." James's eyes were drawn to the crevices under Stefan's cheekbones as his lips formed syllables.

"A shot of seltzer water, and we can dry it quickly like a wine spill in a restaurant." The neighbor's expression hardened. "Bloodstains are often seen by others as unclean. *Marime.*"

James puzzled over the word as he watched the neighbor's lips continue to pulse, silent, thick, and lush. He leaned forward and carefully pulled the t-shirt over his head. He folded over the sweat stains and blood and held it out. "Only if it's not a problem."

Stefan stood and smiled. "It's no problem at all."

He took the shirt and collected the soiled Kleenex and washcloth from the countertop. In the corner of the kitchen was a door to the basement. He bowed to excuse himself before creaking down the wooden stairs.

"Does it look OK?" James stooped to bend the top of his head toward Rachel.

She touched it delicately. "Looks like nothing now, so that's good." She leaned in and pecked his cheek. "Does it hurt?"

"There's a tingle." He took her hand as she sat back down. "It throbs with each heartbeat. I actually feel discombobulated."

Rachel forced a tight smile and squeezed his fingers.

For a long moment, there was nothing but the hum of the refrigerator and birdsong outside until the sound of a washing machine kicked on in the basement. They listened to the water pipes roil and flow as it filled.

The sound was soothing until a voice wafted up the basement stairs.

"Help me, son."

There was a pause, and then the whisper came louder.

"Help me, James. I'm down here."

James's face blanched, and he froze against a bout of dizziness. *What the fuck is going on?*

He tried to stand, but his legs had apparently fused to the chair. "Did you hear that?"

Rachel sat stiff as cast iron. "It sounded like your dad."

With eyes wide, James craned his neck toward the door to the basement.

"Someone help me, I'm drowning!" Aaron's voice strangely echoed as if from far away and mixed with bubbles. "There's a whirlpool pulling me down!"

James searched Rachel's face for a reaction, but now she was rigid with eyelids fluttering and lips trembling.

James jumped up and grabbed her.

"Wake up! What's happening?" He shook her shoulders, but her blank expression didn't budge. He couldn't wake her, and if she felt anything, she didn't respond.

I've gone insane.

"I can't hold on. Please help!" the voice moaned through bubbles below.

"Dad?" James swiveled toward the basement.

The response was immediate. "Yes, where are you, James?"

He charged for the door. At the top of the stairs, James fumbled for the light switch and flicked it on. Feeble pools of light on the concrete floor below only diluted what looked like a thick, inky abyss. Each heartbeat inflamed the wound on his head as he descended, and he stopped halfway to steel himself against what felt like jabs on his skull from a soldering iron.

At the bottom of the stairs, he froze to listen and then found his voice.

"Dad? Are you down here? Stefan?"

He felt for the gun in his shoulder pack as he turned from the stairwell to survey the basement. The slosh of the washing machine came from the near wall. He crept toward the glow of the washer's window portal and knelt to look inside. His t-shirt swashed in suds.

Why in the world did he think his father had called him?

Three overhead bulbs with exposed wires flickered, and he fought to steady himself. Water gushed into the washer and packed a wallop that almost toppled him. But then a scream overtook the roar in the basin. James looked up and Aaron's stricken face filled the portal. His father's eyes were wild as he struggled in the churn.

"Help me, James! What are you waiting for?" Aaron's voice

echoed around the basement, muffled and bubbly in an other-worldly slow motion.

James shouted and tugged on the handle. He braced his foot against the front of the machine and pulled at the portal latch until his arms trembled.

Aaron's head went under, and when it popped up again, his mouth gaped for air above the roiling water. His face was pressed to the glass with enough force to flatten his cheeks.

"Don't let me die. Please, James. Do something!"

James dropped to his knees and pounded both fists against the white steel door.

He didn't hear Rachel's screams upstairs.

THIRTY-ONE

TRAVIS AND SORINAH STUDIED the boy as he picked at the string beans on the side of his plate.

"That's all you eat?" Travis raised his eyebrows and smiled. "You're growing fast and need more."

Andrei took a half-hearted bite from his grilled cheese sandwich. "I'm slow."

Sorinah topped off their water glasses. "Take your time."

Andrei swallowed and took another bite. "I'm nervous."

"That's understandable," Travis said. "We all are."

Andrei's phone pinged as it lay on the table and his eyes darted to the screen. "It's my dad." Andrei wiped his buttery hands on his napkin and tapped the phone with one finger to answer on speaker.

"Hello?"

"Where the hell are you?" Stefan asked in Romanian, and the tone wasn't gentle.

"I already texted you. I'm with Dr. Coman."

"What in hell is he doing here?"

"Visiting someone."

There was breathing. "I want you home. Now."

Andrei eyed his sandwich. "I'm finishing dinner."

"I came home to make your dinner. Tell him to bring you back."

Andrei looked warily at Travis and moved to pick up the phone, but Travis shook his head.

"Are you there?" Stefan barked.

"Yes."

"Then answer me."

Andrei hesitated a moment. "You sound drunk."

"It's a work party for staff. I'm allowed some fun." Stefan coughed and his voice got raspy. He switched to accented English. "I left early because of you."

Travis stiffened and couldn't restrain a response. "Stefan? Hi, it's Travis. Nice to hear your voice. We haven't spoken since that night in Caru' Cu Bere."

"He had me on speaker?"

"We all have greasy hands from the grilled cheese. It's easier."

"I can't believe this." Something slammed in the background.

"I think it's better if Andrei stays here tonight."

"Bring me my son. Where the fuck are you?"

"We're in a comfortable Airbnb nearby. I'll be happy to bring him tomorrow."

The room went quiet except for more panting from the phone.

"That might work. I could go back to the party." Stefan's voice softened markedly. "Are you OK, Andrei?"

"Yes, I'm fine. It's fun to see a different house." Andrei's lips tightened.

A long, slow breathy whistle came through. "You have to make do on your own right now."

Travis jumped in. "I'll bring him back tomorrow. And then we need to talk." His eyes narrowed on the screen as he waited for a response.

"That might work, but not for breakfast. Lunch would be better." Stefan cleared his throat.

"He'll be there for lunch," Travis locked eyes with Andrei. "No worries."

"The party is apparently a tradition that kicks off the season. I'm meeting people for the first time since we got here. And we traveled all this way. Can you see it's for the best?"

"Yes, Dad." Andrei reached to tap the screen. "Bye. I'll see you tomorrow."

"Bye. I love you. Tell him to fix the nightmares he gave you." All eyes were on the phone. "I know about that, Dr. Coman. Yeah, we have lots to talk about." He ended the call.

Travis exhaled and shifted his eyes from Sorinah to Andrei.

"I'm going to help you. In the meantime, you need friends too. Connections keep our minds occupied." He smiled at the boy. "I know just the place. There's a park with a big pool, and you can get a pass or something."

Andrei's face brightened as he considered.

"We can take bikes in the morning; there's a pair in the garage," Sorinah said as she eyed his plate. "Let's get back to dinner."

Andrei grabbed the grilled cheese with both hands.

"It's better you stay the night." Travis motioned to the string beans and French fries on the table. "There's more of everything."

Andrei nodded and dug in.

Travis quietly pushed his chair back. "I'm going to straighten the kitchen. We can go out for ice cream later. I noticed a shack nearby."

Sorinah and Andrei continued with dinner as Travis passed through the archway to the kitchen. Two skillets and a sheet pan were waiting, and he moved them to the sink. He opened the tap to set the cover of running water against the stillness.

It burned him that Andrei and Stefan were here, and he needed to know why. He'd hoped to avoid probing his patient, but it was the quickest way to get answers.

Travis closed his eyes and shifted his focus from the warm water to Andrei. He could hear the boy's breaths and feel his blood pump again with the tingle of mint and licorice.

Where are you, Andrei?

Travis dove in forcefully, all at once.

Ah, there.

He waded past the usual random emotions and memories to the sweet spot where thoughts and motives roamed. Travis pressed hard, and an unexpected rush of horror bolted through him like a lightning strike.

Get away! Get away! Get away! You can't follow me here.

Travis held back a groan as he braced himself against the sink. Did Andrei know he was in his head? Warm water streamed from the faucet.

You don't have my mother, so you can't kill her. Stop lying.

Travis closed his eyes to sharpen his focus and regain control. He exhaled slowly, realizing Andrei's panic wasn't directed at him. But who was the boy fighting?

I didn't see you; it wasn't me.

He remembered the words clearly from Marku.

Everything clamped shut, and Travis was forced out. He dropped the skillet.

It took a moment to parse the sense of dread he felt. The boy's dominant aura pulsed barely contained terror and not a trace of witch. Something was inside him.

He turned off the faucet, dried his hands, and returned to his seat in the dining room.

"We agreed to take bikes to the park tomorrow," Sorinah said.

"I'll tell my dad about it at lunch," Andrei added.

"Sounds like a plan." Travis shifted in his seat toward Andrei. "Outside activities will do you good. I'm very concerned about the visions." He shot a look at Sorinah, and then back to the boy. "Sorinah had a patient with nightmares. Do you mind if we all talk?"

Andrei's eyes shifted between them. "I don't mind. I need help."

"When the intruder comes, what happens?" Travis asked.

Andrei put down his fork as he considered. "There's nausea and chills."

They both stared at the boy.

"And then?" Sorinah asked softly.

"He gets inside me, the demon from Dr. Coman's globe."

"How do you know he's there?" Travis asked.

"I hear a whisper and feel a presence. There's a tingle behind my eyelids."

"When?"

"Sometimes in dreams at night, sometimes it just happens. Like right now, he was here. But it all shut down in a second. I push him away, try not to panic, try to ignore and deny I'm who he wants."

"What does he tell you?" Sorinah reached out for his hand.

Andrei held his lips tight and stared at the ceiling. "He has my mother, and he's coming for me."

"Even here, across an ocean?" Travis carefully watched the boy's breathing.

"Wherever he wants," Andrei whispered.

We can't leave him alone, Sorinah transferred to Travis. *It's just like Marku.*

I know, I need to protect him. I'll do whatever it takes.

"I get nightmares, too," Travis said to Andrei. "Last night was bad."

"From your globe?" Andrei's voice was flat but firm.

Travis exhaled slowly. "No, something different." He locked eyes with Andrei. "I need you to know I never meant any harm. I hoped the orb would help our connection."

"How can I trust you now?" Andrei whispered. "You did it to me."

"I don't blame you for feeling that, and I want to fix it while we're both in Sussex." Travis leaned in. "We can focus on it. We're free to experiment and stop whatever's happening."

Andrei seemed to brighten.

THIRTY-TWO

RACHEL WOKE UP ALONE and under a wooden table. Why on earth was she on the floor? She climbed to a chair and surveyed the kitchen. Where was James, and what the hell was happening?

She remembered hiding in the shed outside the window after running from a hawk. The owner of the house found them and brought them inside. But where was everyone?

"Anybody here?" she called out.

She listened for a response and focused on the hum of the refrigerator but realized there was something else: water sloshing in a washer and coming from the basement. The door was ajar, and she crept toward it, peering down the stairs. If the lights were on, they didn't much help.

"James?"

She felt a shift, like a subtle spin of vertigo, and shook her head to clear it. When she opened her eyes, the stairs had morphed into a dirt road pitched straight down, bounded by trees, not walls. A soft glow of moonlight illuminated the scene, and she took a few steps down.

Moonlight? I'm indoors. What's happening?

After a few more steps she heard panicked breathing and a whimper that she immediately recognized as Sophia's, exactly the same as in the nightmares that had led her to the reservoir.

I'm dreaming. That's it. I'll wake up soon; just go with it.

The slope leveled off and veered sharply around a curve and

into a clearing. The trees retreated to the outer edges of a glade, and she spied James nearby, kneeling in the middle of a dirt road in front of a whirling washing machine and pressed against the window portal.

Why is a washing machine in the middle of the road? How does it plug in?

"James? I'm over here. When's your load ready?"

He didn't answer, and Sophia's cries grew louder so she stepped backward. Through a cloak of mist, she found Sophia cowering just down the road. And a dark shape was sneaking up behind her with a spear. Rachel moved closer and could make out the features of a man who hoisted the sharpened slat of a picket fence.

Rachel screamed and rushed toward Sophia.

"He's coming! Hurry! I'll get you out!"

Sophia scrambled to her feet, and together they rushed for cover behind a large hot water heater, humming and warm, also abandoned in the road. Rachel stooped low and held her breath as the predator came into view.

I know that man. It's Stefan, I remember now, we're in his basement!

Rachel wasn't sure if she spoke the words aloud. But any time to parse her thoughts vanished as the man spotted them and moved in to strike.

Sophia screamed, and Rachel crawled away on all fours, frantic, knees and palms prickling on the unfinished concrete floor.

THIRTY-THREE

WHATEVER HOPES TRAVIS HELD for reversing the globe spell evaporated by midnight. He sat on the hardwood floor in the hallway outside of Andrei's room, ears pricked up for trouble while he scrutinized a copy of the incantation he'd brought from Bucharest. There was nothing ambiguous, no loose thread he could identify and snip. He still felt the boy's visceral fear at the dinner table and now it pressed him against the wall, useless as a miswired power socket.

Whatever evil stalked Andrei got in despite Travis's best attempt to block it. And the infusion of power that followed the orb session was more alarming than nourishing. He felt tainted by it the same way late-summer nectar seduces yellowjackets but leaves them dull and vulnerable.

He probed the leathery patch on his forearm. The pain was gone now, thanks to the nectar that had oozed from the globe. His bolts were primed, his immobilizing powers sharp, but who was he fighting? And what was the point of it all if his magic harmed someone he cared about?

Through his jet lag he dreamed of a hawk screeching as it bore down on him, and hours later woke to find himself sprawled on the hallway floor, morning light streaming from the kitchen, quiet snores wafting from beyond the crack in Andrei's door.

He roused himself and made for his bedroom where he'd wedged a patch of cardboard into the broken window pane. He surveyed the sun-drenched lawn and the shadows cast by trees, swollen and verdant. What time was it, was his phone even charged? At least Carol Stilton had left him alone for the night, and he felt rested despite the hardwood mattress and no pillow.

By the time he got himself showered and ready, Sorinah was waiting in the kitchen.

"Good morning," Sorinah said as he entered. "You look much better than yesterday." She placed a K-Cup in the Keurig and pressed the button. "How's your arm?"

Travis shot a tight smile and held it up. "It seems your protection spell worked."

Sorinah waited for the brewer to stop and then passed Travis a mug. "Or your hallway outpost gave Carol Stilton the slip. Today we root out the witch."

Travis took a seat at the table and grabbed a banana from the fruit basket before filling a bowl with granola. "I'm on tenterhooks waiting to see Stefan, but I'm going to Paula's first."

"When?"

"Right now. You and Andrei can do the park yourselves before lunch." Travis cut a few banana slices. "Aaron's dead, and we watched James and Rachel storm the neighbor's house with a pistol. I've got to get over there."

"The Malloy house was his deliberate choice." Sorinah took a sip from her mug and locked his eyes. "Stefan wants to be discovered. That makes me nervous. I'll find out what I can while I've got Andrei. If there's a disguising spell at play, it's a powerful one. I've detected nothing."

"The black hawk appeared so on cue that it's comical, but I'm not amused. It takes a witch to provoke a witch."

Travis poked at the bowl with his spoon. "He's luring us in, even using his son as bait, but I don't know why or how. Prepare for a fight."

"Of course. Meanwhile, Andrei is in trouble *and* troubling. We're stuck."

Sorinah joined him at the table as he forced down a bite. He took another swig of coffee just as the hallway floorboards started to creak, and then Andrei padded into the kitchen.

"*Buna dimineata*," the boy said shyly as he inched his way along the wall.

"Good morning to you, Andrei. How did you sleep?" Sorinah asked with a warm smile.

He rubbed one eye. "Good, better than usual."

"Very glad to hear it." Travis smiled and motioned to an empty chair at the table. "Take a seat, and we'll fix you breakfast."

Andrei nodded and slid into it.

"I've got to run an errand," Travis said as he watched him. "While I'm gone you two can relax and check out the park."

"What do you want for breakfast?" Sorinah asked.

Andrei surveyed the counter. "Cereal's fine."

"What about eggs? Or pancakes?" Sorinah poured a glass of orange juice.

"Maybe pancakes if it's OK."

"Coming right up." Sorinah smiled and made for the kitchen. "When you're ready, we'll head for the swimming pool. You can text your dad, and then we'll bring you there for lunch, or earlier if he wants."

Andrei eyed his phone. "He's not awake yet. I already tried."

"We're going whether he answers or not." Travis started to make his way to the hallway. "Have fun at the park and plan on lunchtime like he said."

Travis headed for the stairs and into the bathroom on the second floor. He brushed his teeth and checked the weather app against his outfit: khaki shorts, a Lacoste fitted polo shirt, and scuffed-up white Adidas sneakers, no-show socks. A favorite outfit was a form of armor.

Quiet chatter in the kitchen filtered into the hallway as he made his way outside to the rental car.

He lowered the windows to take in the morning sun and a crisp breeze. But unease crept in as he rolled toward the rural part of town. *What to say to Paula? 'Surprise!'* He'd vowed to leave her and her family in peace, but someone was interfering. Aaron's death rattled him because he felt responsible. And from the looks of James and Rachel, things were getting worse.

He hit the accelerator and relished the wind. There wasn't much traffic so fifteen minutes later he was already pulling into Paula's driveway. He parked near the street so he could calmly stroll to the kitchen entrance. But Paula came running just as he closed the door. He hurried from behind the hood and intercepted her between the car and the house.

"Oh, hello, Travis," Paula said as they nearly collided. "You're not whom I expected."

"Sorry to just drop by without notice." He watched as her eyes darted nervously about.

"I'm afraid this isn't a good time." Paula looked strained and her chest heaved. "I thought you were James, my son. He's missing."

Travis froze. "For how long?"

"Since yesterday afternoon; he never came home last night." Paula pointed to the car parked near the kitchen door. "That's Rachel's, she's gone too, his girlfriend. They're always together. Something's terribly wrong. I feel it."

Travis's pulse rate surged. *Should I tell her I saw them yesterday?* He decided to stall to learn more. "Can I help you look? What can I do?"

"The police told me to search and hold tight, at least until three. I've been in touch with Rachel's parents, and I monitor my phone." She glanced at the screen and put it back down. "What are you doing here? I thought you'd moved back to Europe."

"I did move. I'm here for only a brief visit. But I saw the news about Aaron and wanted to pay my respects and see how you're doing."

Paula glanced toward the house. "That's kind of you. Would you like to come inside?"

His brow furrowed as he surveyed the yard. "I can keep you company outside so we can scan the grounds, if you like, while we catch up."

Paula nodded, and they started up the slope of the driveway. "That works. You're looking well. It's been a while. Now that you're here it seems time just evaporated."

"I'm sorry life is rough right now."

Her expression went dark as she pulled in a deep breath. "A week ago everything was fine." She backed up the kitchen stairs and took a seat on the top step while Travis leaned against the wall of the house. "And then Aaron drowned."

"I'm very sorry." Travis exhaled slowly. "Can you tell me what happened?"

Her lips were tight, but she nodded. "He had a freak accident on the lake. The whole thing was very strange. I still don't understand it." Paula covered her face as tears pooled.

Travis waited and spoke softly.

"Take as much time as you need."

"He was an athlete and a strong swimmer."

She found her composure. "And even more bizarre, a large black hawk dived and attacked him on the water in his row boat. He fell overboard, and for some reason couldn't float or grab onto the side. His friends say something pulled him under like a whirlpool. I know it sounds crazy."

Travis's mind shot to the omen that greeted them at the Malloy house. "Did they find the hawk or have an explanation?"

"No, nothing. It disappeared into the trees, and some swear they never even saw it." Paula peeked at her phone and then balanced it screen-up in her lap. "And then something awful happened to James after the burial."

Travis took in a sharp breath, locked eyes with Paula, and leaned in closer.

"An animal attacked him just a few days later."

He froze to listen and his nostrils flared. "I hate to hear this. Is he OK? Where did it happen?"

"In the woods near the lake. He went back to look." Paula closed her eyes and whispered, "It's like a bad dream except it's real, and I can't wake up, and it keeps getting worse."

Travis exhaled audibly and shook his head. This family had been targeted because of him. Only another witch would know he'd enchanted them before. "Tell me more about James."

"An animal jumped on his back out of nowhere. He did nothing to provoke it, so maybe it was a rabid raccoon. He managed to knock it off and escape with scratches and a bite."

"I'm so sorry."

Paula wiped her eyes and then continued. "I can't take much more. First Aaron drowns, then James gets attacked, and now he's missing along with Rachel. They're dating again. I love her to death, but trouble finds her." She held his gaze despite the tears. "I don't even know why I'm telling you all this. I forgot all about you, but here you are. It's like you never left, and now I feel completely open, which for me is odd in itself."

Travis watched as Paula's face went tight, and he felt shame for the pain he'd unleashed, however indirectly. "You need support right now, someone to listen. I'm glad you feel open enough to talk."

She nodded slowly.

"I'm trembling; my nerves have taken over. With everything that's happened, I started shaking the instant it was clear they were late for dinner. Then I called Rachel's parents, and they have no clue where she is either. Her apartment is in Burlington, but her car's still parked here in my driveway. I know they are together, but where? James wouldn't let me hang; something's very wrong."

Travis looked beyond Rachel's car.

"There's still time for an explanation, time for them to come home." A stiff breeze rustled the treetops as he scanned the back meadow toward the stagecoach road. The woods made him think of the skeleton.

"Why do you say trouble finds Rachel?"

Paula pulled back her hair and gathered her thoughts. "She survived the death of two friends in high school. You probably don't remember."

Travis held his breath. "I do, but I thought that was all in the past."

"It was until a month ago. She and James discovered the missing body of one of her friends. Now it's back in the news. The tragedy was something the whole town wanted to move on from, but it just won't go away."

Travis swiveled toward Paula. "How did they find the body?"

"James told me that Rachel kept dreaming about it."

Travis coughed and took a moment. "What do you mean, 'dream?'"

"She had a recurring nightmare, very specific, that turned out to be real."

Travis clenched his teeth. Whoever had sent him his own nightmare had been mighty busy. Stefan's generically handsome face flashed like a beacon on his alarm switchboard. It was time to confront the mystery man and quash the ruse.

He had to get to the Malloy house. James and Rachel were more bait. *I involved them in the first place. I owe them.*

He glanced at his phone.

"I should get going. I'm sure there's an explanation, and James will turn up."

Paula's eyes met his.

"Sophia turned up, four years later, underground." Her focus shifted to the driveway and she shook her head. "I know that sounds harsh, but I'm bitter now."

Travis took a step back and frowned with his lips pulled tight.

"I'm very sorry for all you're going through but glad I got to see you. I will check in again later, if that's OK. In the meantime I'll do a search of my own. I know these grounds."

He took a few backward steps toward his car.

Paula stood and stepped down to the driveway.

"Thanks. I'm not sure there's much anyone can do except hope." She looked weary as she held his gaze. "But that's in short supply these days."

Travis nodded slowly and backed toward his car with his palm raised. She held up hers and a listless wave followed when his door slammed shut.

THIRTY-FOUR

THE QUICK DRIVE TO THE Malloy house wasn't nearly long enough to devise a plan, but there wasn't time to spare. James and Rachel had stormed the place the day before, and he instinctively blamed Stefan: guilty until proven innocent. Whatever disguising spell had worked so well when last they'd met in Caru' Cu Bere was now a dangerous defense Travis had to strike down.

Is he so powerful a witch that I can't detect him?

The possibility stung. But now was not the time for self-doubt. He needed to find James and Rachel for Paula's sake if it weren't already too late, given Stefan's wildcard status.

A part of him wanted to believe the Vermont connection was all coincidence because Andrei was a favorite patient. But now it seemed clear that his father had orchestrated everything.

I can't detect witch in either of them. How can they hide it? Are they superior?

If father and son teamed up things could get ugly fast, given the past week's events. But right now nothing mattered except saving the neighbors. And it would force the witches out.

Travis turned left onto a narrow gravel road that wound past pastures and forest.

I'm almost at the Malloy house, he transferred to Sorinah.

Why so soon? I thought we were going for lunch.

There's trouble. James and Rachel never came home last night. We saw them last. Paula filled in some gaps, and I've got to find them.

Be careful with Stefan. I'll probe Andrei.

Travis settled on a pretense for his visit. As Andrei's doctor, he needed to ensure the safety of his patient before bringing him for lunch. He neared the Malloy house and parked in the same spot as before on the dusty shoulder on the side of the road near the entrance to the driveway.

A gray sedan was parked on the side of the house.

Good, Stefan must be home.

He followed the gravel drive as it wound to the back, and Travis spied the old clapboard shed behind the house.

Do I dare take a look?

He knew at once it would be impossible to resist. He'd used it to store remains from the grave for his experiments four years earlier.

Travis made it to the weathered, red-stained door planks. He glanced about, darted inside, and closed the door behind him. It took a moment for his eyes to adjust, even as light filtered in through horizontal windows that were murky with residue from rainstorms. He crept toward the wooden platform on the hay-strewn floor, the exact spot where he'd conjured Carol Stilton.

Four years later and everything is worse.

A shiver ran down his spine and he flinched. His eyes shot wide, and he felt woozy as the floor seemed to warp and the walls swelled and contracted as if they could breathe.

He needed to get out and bolted for the door. He shoved it with his shoulder and squinted against a flare as he staggered a few steps and tried to clear his head.

He steeled himself against whatever force was trying to invade. He knew exactly what was happening because he entered others the same way. A rage took hold as he found himself on the receiving end as someone else probed for control.

You won't get in, witch.

Travis planted both feet on the gravel driveway and strained against the cold pressure on his forehead that felt like jabs from an icicle. He looked up in time to spot Stefan as he emerged from the kitchen with both arms folded and stationed himself on the top wooden step.

"What a nice surprise," Stefan said with a broad smile. "Did you bring Andrei early?"

Travis felt the pressure lessen, at least enough to regain composure. "I wanted to check out the premises first. I'm his doctor, remember?" He studied Stefan from head to toe.

"Why start in the shed? There's nothing much in there, not anymore."

The icy stab on his forehead resumed, and instead of immediately resisting, Travis pounced behind Stefan's defense and bristled at the piney aroma.

Caught you, witch.

When he redirected his energy to block the icicle drill, the scent died with it, so Travis dropped his guard to pounce again, and again detected witch.

"I broke your disguising spell," Travis spat through gritted teeth.

Stefan scoffed. "It took you long enough."

Fury and fear coursed through Travis's core, and he instinctively fired a warning bolt at Stefan's spine. The weapon found its mark, and the man groaned and fell back against the door.

Travis marched toward him. "Explain, witch."

Stefan steadied himself and grimaced as pain ricocheted down his back. Nonetheless, he rallied and strode down the steps. "Explain what? You have my son."

"Why are you here?" Travis held his ground on the driveway and glared. "State your business. We met in Caru' Cu Bere in good faith to discuss Andrei. And you used my concern against me. I ought to kill you right here for the trouble you've caused, especially to Paula and her family. They are under my protection."

"You wouldn't kill your patient's father, now, would you?" Stefan clenched his fists and met Travis's dark, brooding eyes. "What kind of a doctor are you anyway, witch?"

"Cut the disguise, Stefan. Stop the ruse. It's only draining your energy, along with my patience." Travis tingled with adrenaline, his chest heaving.

"I suppose hiding no longer serves any purpose." Stefan took a step back and caught his breath. "You blocked my entry, for now. But I have your essence and a way in. I fancy sending you another visit from Carol Stilton, perhaps tonight."

He's goading you; stay calm.

Travis raised his eyebrows. "What's your grievance?"

"Aside from the fact that you're using my son as fuel?"

"I did that only once. No harm was intended and it won't happen again."

"But harmless it's not." Stefan's jaw went rigid.

"How would you know?" Travis's nostrils flared, and his heart raced.

"It changed him. Put something dangerous inside him. He's targeted."

"He told you?"

"Of course, I'm his father." Stefan spat and kicked gravel with the tip of his boot. "It was only fitting to send your wraith as a welcome present."

"How do you even know about her?"

"There was a time you were monitored very closely by the coven. Your brand of magic was something new, a possible path to the future, something that replenished power without leaving behind a corpse." Stefan locked eyes with Travis. "But it was never as simple as that. Some of us suspected it, but couldn't prove it, until now."

"Who are you?" Travis cast a cold gaze at the witch. "Drop the disguise."

"As you wish, orphan." Stefan edged backward, and stooped low as if about to pounce. He covered his face with his hands, and as he rose, he pulled them away, and his features shifted.

"Radu."

Travis shook his head, almost imperceptibly, with teeth bared in disgust. He studied the man's face: angular and square like Stefan's, but with a scar on his cheekbone and just different enough to be obvious after the fact. Character had returned to the generic mask. "Why would you go through the trouble?"

Travis held his gaze while he transferred to Sorinah: *Radu was disguised as Stefan.*

Are you safe?

For now, yes. Stay close.

"Did you think my humiliation would go unanswered?" Radu's voice was measured.

"You got what you deserved. Obviously, I didn't go far enough."

The two witches sized each other up, in a slow, face-to-face rotation. Travis felt the icy probing at his temple resume. He blocked it.

"I spent two years in isolation, but I used the time wisely. I studied and dedicated myself to advancing my ancestral spells, the same as you."

"I'm flattered," Travis scoffed.

"You should be; you beat me using mutant magic. But I've mastered new tools of my own." Radu fixed his gaze on Travis's forehead.

"Control is nothing new." Travis felt the pressure increase.

"I was granted more, as you will learn. The disguise, the hawk, gyre power; we both have new tricks. And what of that orb that you used on my son?"

Travis flinched and struggled to retain his focus. "Is Andrei a witch?"

"He's adopted, a mortal innocent. He provides good cover against prying neighbors."

"You've enslaved him?" Travis felt a jab and winced.

Radu raised his voice. "I needed to get you here."

Travis staggered back a step. "Why?"

"To complete the cycle you started so that you might learn from it."

As the sun beat down both men circled and glistened with sweat.

Travis found it harder to focus. "Learn what?"

Radu's eyebrows popped up. "The danger unleashed by your magic."

The words echoed heavily while Travis's fighting stance morphed into a confused shuffle. The woozy whirl he felt inside the shed wormed in and took hold. A few seconds passed before he could steady himself, and with it came a voice:

I'm inside you, Travis. Your attempt to block was impressive, but not enough. Your essence grants me all the access I need. Do you like the feeling? Body and mind pulsating, aroused, and activated. You invaded Paula this way. I know she was quite taken with you. I was forced to follow suit to turn her against you. It's unexpectedly erotic, as I'm sure you noticed when you took her son and also her husband. Some might call that risqué, but I'm intrigued. I recognize the allure, or at least the convenience. They're waiting, just downstairs.

He responded effortlessly, soundlessly, as if it were Sorinah: *Stay away from them!*

In a spasm of rage, Travis threw a punch, but it wobbled in slow motion while Radu smirked and stepped aside. Travis felt like he was underwater, but his wits were sharp enough to recognize his connection to Sorinah was severed and rerouted to Radu.

"What do you want?" Travis said aloud as he tried to calm himself enough to think.

Deep, rapid breaths volleyed between them as Radu studied his foe. "I want you to forswear your magic."

Travis's lips tightened, and he shook his head. "Why would I ever accede to that?"

"You will when I prove the danger you pose to the coven." Radu motioned to the kitchen stairs. "Your lesson begins in the basement."

Travis trudged toward the house despite his best efforts to resist. His sneakers left a trail in the gravel as beads of sweat trailed down the sides of his face.

Save your energy. You'll need it if you want to be of any use to anyone.

Travis struggled to find words. "What have you done?"

One day you will thank me.

Radu held the door open as Travis lurched through with a grimace. He scanned the kitchen and crashed into the corner of the large wooden table as he passed, eyes fixed on the open door to the basement. At the top of the stairs came muffled cries and the sloshing of water from the darkness below.

THIRTY-FIVE

SORINAH KNEW TRAVIS WAS IN DANGER when their transference went dead. She tried to resume contact from a shady, wooden park bench while Andrei searched out classes posted on the activities board in the pool pavilion.

Front of mind, at all times, we are one.

She pulsed him the message so that if he gained an instant of lucidity, he'd grab it. A plan was needed, and quickly. If Radu was actually Andrei's father, she was also in danger and couldn't be sure of Andrei's role in any of this.

She switched her focus from Travis to the boy. Why didn't he smell of witch? She studied Andrei as he waited in the sign-up line, no more threatening than the other teenage boys who seemed about the same age. Was it possible he was a mortal enslaved as cover for Radu? Perhaps, but it was equally possible his disguising spell was simply beyond her ability to crack, a different, even stronger, strain of magic.

Sorinah closed her eyes and probed him for a crack she might be able to penetrate. It was easy to get in, essence from pancake crumbles inside a used napkin was all it took, but she tensed when she discovered she wasn't in control. Where was he taking her?

She found herself transported to the Malloy house, the same first floor bedroom she'd used four years earlier. She didn't know how she knew it was Andrei's now, but it came with the certainty of dreams.

An old halogen lamp threw warm, muted light from the far corner. The window was open wide, and the sheer, pale curtain wavered as a breeze wafted in from the darkness outside. She watched Andrei in bed near the window and realized her perspective came from above as if she were suspended below the ceiling, looking down. The boy tossed beneath a single sheet and then kicked his bare legs free. He looked anguished and vulnerable as he squirmed on the mattress wearing only briefs.

Sorinah watched his head tilt back and strain toward the window as a whisper floated on the wind and broke the silence. The boy scrambled to hide below the top sheet.

"*Soon you will ripen.*" The voice was deep, slow, and quiet. "*Know you are marked.*"

The sheet pulled free of the bed, flew up toward the ceiling, and then floated down to the hardwood floor. Andrei curled into a tight ball and closed his eyes.

"*Youthful souls are most potent.*"

A gnarled, dark claw slashed through the window screen, and Andrei shrieked. A strong gust smashed Sorinah's back against the ceiling, and then she went slack. She felt herself drop, and when she opened her eyes, Andrei was standing in front of her as she collapsed on a wooden bench in Maple Street Park. She shook her head to clear it and forced herself to a sitting position.

The boy stared at her with wide eyes. "What happened?"

Sorinah took in a few quick breaths and studied him. "I'm still jet-lagged." She fought to rally and retain a shred of composure.

"You were dreaming. I tried to wake you."

"For how long?"

"Just a few minutes," he whispered, "but it wasn't peaceful. I was nervous."

"I didn't sleep well last night." She brightened and moved toward the armrest. "I was worried about you and Travis." There was a pause as her pulse slowed. "Did you find something?"

"Yes, I can join a class Tuesdays and Thursdays at 10."

Sorinah smiled. "That will be fun for you."

His lips got tight. "I'll have to ask my dad."

"We'll see him at lunchtime."

Andrei eyed the screen of his phone. "He still isn't answering."

"Neither is Travis. We'll have to find them both."

Sorinah stood, and they headed for the bicycle rack. She didn't know exactly what to make of the vision, but she was left shaken and wary.

Did he know she probed him? She didn't think so. But something certainly knew, sucked her in, and then spat her out.

A feeling of dread seized her gut, and her thoughts shot to Marku.

All she could do for now was watch the boy and hope he didn't ripen soon.

THIRTY-SIX

TRAVIS FOUND JAMES ON THE FLOOR transfixed and kneeling in front of the washing machine. The back of his head was silhouetted against a phosphorescent emerald glow beaming out of the window portal across the shadowy expanse of the basement.

He crept from behind to investigate and froze when he glimpsed what looked like Aaron's head inside, fighting for breath in the churning water, his coughs and cries for help amplified and bubbly and echoing as if miles away. Travis squeezed James's shoulder, but nothing.

A chuckle rose from the inky void behind him, and he turned to glare at Radu.

It was hard to find words. "What have you done?"

"I baited the hook, and you bit." Radu swiveled and motioned across the room. "It's harmless enough, a subconscious loop to occupy them until you finally got here."

Travis peered into the murky gloom on the other side, and a movement low to the ground caught his eye in the far corner before it disappeared behind a shadow. His eyes adjusted, and he watched as a young woman emerged, and he realized it was Rachel, crawling on all fours, out of breath and whimpering, hair tangles sticking to her face.

Travis stepped toward her as she circled the water heater. Then a pounding on the washer portal grabbed his attention, and he pivoted back to James.

His fury forced words. "Now you've got me. Leave them out of this."

"You plucked them from obscurity in the first place." Radu folded his arms and took in his handiwork in the basement. "You can't put the genie back in the bottle."

"You're mad!" Travis glared at Radu, and attempted to strike, but found himself frozen.

"Let me explain something now that you're listening." Radu strode toward Travis and stopped just short of touching him. He reached up and squeezed Travis's broad jaw.

"You have no idea what you've unleashed." He locked eyes with his foe, and spoke in a slow whisper. "The 'elevated' ancestral magic of yours is anything but."

Travis smelled him easily now: full witch, acrid pine. "Spells take generations to evolve." He couldn't move but was fully aware he trembled with rage.

"You have a blind spot to your own work."

"Show me."

"I sent the vision to enlighten you."

Travis held in a deep breath. "Carol Stilton? How would you know?"

"My eyes were opened to the urgency."

"Opened by whom?"

Sweat trailed down Radu's temples as he released his grip and stepped back. "A powerful visitor took interest while I languished in isolation."

Travis's nostrils flared and he again filled his lungs. "Who?"

Radu's face tightened. "The Devil himself; I knew it without asking, and he didn't offer. I was nothing next to him, a feeling I'll never forget."

The sloshing water and Rachel's incessant crawling were the only sounds amid the muted pools of light cast by bare, dangling bulbs.

Radu broke the silence. "In exchange for new powers of my own—shifting, gyre, and disguise—I agreed to give you a message."

Travis felt a tingling. "What message?"

"You posit your family's magic as elevated and plan to expand it, but already your spells dilute the coven's collective cords."

Travis held his lips tight and shook his head. "You can't know this. That is your theory."

James and Rachel were panting now, in chorus with the churn of the washer.

Radu exhaled slowly. "Coven magic follows edicts stemming from the Devil's fall to Christ and constancy concentrates our power. Inevitably, mutant strains of magic emerge, as championed by your parents, and thus they were banished. Their methods weakened core threads the coven took centuries to weave."

Travis scoffed. "That is a convenient narrative for you."

"Is it? Carol Stilton had long since died and gone to the side of God. Your conjuring pulled her away, and a mortal sin damned her. She is captive on a circle of hell, and her presence presents a spiritual wrinkle. The Devil cannot justify the victory but nonetheless is loath to concede her soul. This quandary will ultimately require resolution."

Travis studied his face. "Why would one so powerful share this with you?"

Radu blew out his breath quickly. "Because you've only just started, but if your magic is adopted by the coven, the wrinkles will multiply and force a confrontation."

Travis shook his head. "I need more evidence."

Radu licked his lips. "Shall I explain Marku?"

The man's name jolted Travis, and his eyes widened.

"Whatever your intentions, your orb draws its power from black magic. Marku repented in the monastery and maintained his right to a final judgment. But your interference served him directly to the Devil who was enticed to intervene and claim him. Do you know this?"

Travis stood stone-faced and trembling in a stew of fear, dread, and rage.

Radu smirked before he continued. "In some ways, you are correct. Your ancestral magic is supremely powerful and taps into a most potent fount. The pity is neither you nor your parents had any idea what you were doing. Your work arouses the attention of the Devil and compels him to act."

Travis's eyes shifted to James, who tapped at the portal, but Radu relocked his hold on his jaw.

"Your globe removed Marku's chance of redemption and incites a spiritual imbalance that had been resolved more than two millennia ago. Were you remotely aware of this?"

"No."

"You created the conditions for Marku's agony as the Devil collected his soul. And while it bestowed great power, you and Sorinah were the only benefactors. Spells from other witches are woven to shore up coven threads. Are you starting to understand the dilution?"

"I've used the globe only twice. The incantation will be developed."

"But you have made it personal. You did it to my son," Radu squeezed before he released his grip and glared at Travis, his voice hard like steel nails. "He's an object of attention, your globe channels it. Your tainted magic has marked him as fodder for the Devil."

Travis wet his lips and jumped in quickly. "Andrei is innocent. The Devil has no claim to him, not like Marku, who was already marked from past acts of pure evil."

A whimper from Rachel wafted across the shadowy basement as she resumed her crawl around the water heater.

"Are you willing to live or die by that supposition? My son has to, regardless."

Travis pulled in a long, slow breath. "I will find a way to fix things."

"That's what's keeping you alive."

The words hung in the air, and Travis averted his eyes. He didn't know if he could fix anything. He was certain only of his own confusion. Radu's new powers had come from somewhere and verified that part of his story.

A clammy sweat coated his arms, and the wooziness he'd felt outside resurged to warp his vision. He closed his eyes and stumbled backward, surprised to find his footing. Was he free to move again? His eyes shot open and he steadied his stance until his vision cleared, and he surveyed the basement.

Radu was gone.

Light streaming from the washer portal lured him closer. James pounded at the control panel and then ducked below the window, and Travis caught a glimpse of Aaron's gaping mouth, gasping for air amid the churn, sideways, and then lost again in the swirl.

Travis rushed behind James, crouched beside him, and gripped his shoulder. The washer began to shake and rumble as if spinning an unbalanced load.

"It isn't real. It's an illusion. You can fight it!"

James pulled at the window handle with both hands as if Travis weren't there.

"Let him go!" Travis shouted toward the stairs over the rumblings of the washer.

James didn't seem to hear, and gripped the sides of the washer, staring into the portal.

"Dad, I'm here. I'm coming for you." His voice was hoarse and quiet.

Travis heard sobs from behind and turned as Rachel rounded the backside of the water heater on all fours, eyes wide and lips trembling.

He crept toward her and scanned the shadows for Radu. With each step, a wave of dizziness rose and fell and fog enveloped him that smelled like sulfur. The cellar floor pitched like a ship on typhoon seas, and Travis dropped to his knees. He struggled to focus and couldn't shout. He clenched his eyes and tried to stand against a whirlwind that pressed down.

And then it all went quiet.

THIRTY-SEVEN

SOMETIME AFTER LUNCH, PAULA'S unease blossomed into a panic. She was sick of waiting around like a helpless hatchling. It was clear something was wrong, and before confirming James's disappearance with the police, she went to the garden to scan around another time.

Why did bad things keep happening? It wasn't fair. She wasn't one to wallow in self-pity, but she was quickly learning how people became broken and embittered. Getting old wasn't for the weak, and now she felt both. Aaron hadn't been the perfect husband. They'd been divorced, after all. But even so, the shock of his loss was staggering and had cast a pall over everything. And now with James missing, despair was about to swallow her whole.

She pictured James and Rachel meandering near the marshy edge of the forest, but her fantasy succumbed to reality, so she turned to go back into the house.

That's when she heard a screech and saw a black blur swoop low over the meadow.

My God, it's the hawk.

James had been obsessed with finding it, and here it was. All at once, she knew it was the one from the lake that had attacked Aaron. The certainty consumed her, and she marched toward its perch on a branch above the stagecoach road. There was nothing else to focus on, no other lead. She had to get closer.

Paula realized she was jogging and had covered half the meadow when the black hawk flew from the branch, circled low, and then entered the trail through the woods. It crossed her mind it might strike her as it had Aaron, but something told her she was fine and she followed. It screeched again and seemed to linger when she entered the stagecoach road, then skittered to new perches ever deeper in the woods.

She slowed to a sustainable pace, comfortable with the certainty the raptor knew she was following because it watched her. It even seemed to like her. Why she thought that didn't matter.

It had been a few years since she'd walked the stagecoach road. There was no reason to after the handsome neighbor had moved away. What was his name? Oh yes, Travis, the man who'd visited only a few hours ago. Funny how things worked.

She was still familiar with the winding curves of the overgrown pathway and trailed the screeches that now sounded more like a mating call, savage and alluring. And it was so timely the hawk had led her here because she could hunt for James and Rachel along the way.

At the end of the trail, there was still no sign of them, but the black hawk soared up and over the Malloy house in the distance. Obviously, she had to follow. Who even lived there now?

Paula took the trail that skirted the edge of the meadow, and saw the backdoor open as a brawny man not unlike Aaron rushed out. He waved as she got closer, and she picked up her pace. Did she know him? He was fit and barefoot and wore camouflage shorts with no shirt.

When she got near the red shed behind the house, he was waiting for her, beaming.

"Paula? It's been a long time."

She narrowed her eyes to study his face. "I know you from somewhere, let me think." She tried to cut past the cobwebs but couldn't hazard a guess.

"The hospital when Katherine was sick. I was one of her teachers, Radu." He extended his hand and they shook.

"Of course, I remember now." Paula smiled and folded her arms. "Do you live here?"

"Just for the summer while I work a seasonal job. What brings you by?"

"I'm looking for my son."

Radu's eyes got wide. "You're in luck, guess what? He's right downstairs." He smiled and motioned toward the backdoor to the kitchen. "Go right in, you know the way."

Paula's heart raced with excitement. "Sounds too good to be true." Nonetheless, she marched toward the steps and then stopped. "Can you show me?"

"I'm running late for lunch plans. The door to the basement is in the far corner of the kitchen. Grab a steak knife from the drawer before you go down. Help yourself, it's easy."

Paula smiled and nodded and made for the back door. "Thanks for your kindness."

As she entered the kitchen, it looked strangely familiar, shellacked with a dream-like varnish left by the passage of time. Without a thought, she pulled open the drawer of utensils and selected a sharp blade with a wooden handle. She pushed it closed and noticed the door in the corner was open, and she stopped to listen at the top of the stairs.

"James?" she called out into the shadows. She flicked the lights to discover they were already on. "Is anyone there?"

On the way down, Paula gripped the banister with one hand and the knife with the other, aware of the churn of a washing machine that grew louder with each step.

THIRTY-EIGHT

AT FIRST, THE THROBBING IN his temple felt like the icicle was boring back in, but it morphed into a stabbing pain strong enough to wake him. Travis opened his eyes to find himself sprawled and sweaty in the middle of the basement floor. It took another instant for him to recognize Paula crouched above, a knifepoint pricking his forehead. Was he still dreaming?

He tried to swivel away. "Paula? What the hell?"

She repositioned the tip and prodded some more.

Her eyes were wide, her face tight. "I need to protect myself."

Travis managed to slide into a sitting position and held up his palms in surrender.

"Paula, no, you shouldn't be here. It's dangerous."

Travis used his arms and legs to crab-walk backward as he scanned the cellar for any sign of Radu. He could move freely—that was one thing in his favor.

"How did you get in here?"

Paula's eyes darted about as she considered. "Radu let me in."

Travis sat stiffly and watched as Paula stooped in front of him on the cellar floor.

"He sent me to summon you." The knife swayed by her side.

Travis tilted his head as he focused on her. "Why would he do that?"

"He wants you to listen to reason and relent. I am just his helper." Her words came steady and with the conviction of a nun.

"He's tricking you." Travis stood and pointed to James at the washer, and Rachel at the water heater. "He did this, you're all under his control."

Paula's eyes darted about as she warily followed his gestures. "You're tricking me. Why didn't I notice them before?"

Travis sidled away slowly. "You were focused on me. Your senses are playing tricks. Try to keep calm because it will pass. I'm going to stop it now."

Paula surveyed the basement and honed in on the washer. "What does anything matter? We'll all be dead soon, anyway."

Travis felt his adrenaline surge but kept his voice calm. "Don't talk like that."

Paula stepped toward the churning machine and pointed the knife. She looked downcast and broken and perplexed by the scratches around the bandage on her son's bare back.

"Stay quiet and cool, and put down the knife." Travis spoke softly as he approached her. He held out his palm, and she surrendered the blade. He smiled with tight lips and whisked it away. "I'll be back soon to get you home. Your job is done here. Thanks for waking me."

All at once she sucked down a series of shuddering gasps and crouched to fight for balance. "A twister," she whispered.

Travis grabbed her and eased toward the wall opposite James, where she slumped and then folded to the floor. Her breathing was steady, so he nestled her head into an elbow, and surrendered her to Radu's whirlwind. There was nothing left to do but stop him.

Travis bolted up the stairs. He crashed through the kitchen with no sign of the witch. A stiff breeze through the screen door beckoned him outside.

Vibrant color in the sky and muted light signaled dusk was near. How long had he been captive? Travis stopped in front of the shed and tried to sniff out any trace of his foe. Why would Radu set him free? Was it overconfidence or a trick? He tossed Paula's knife into the grass with a flourish of defiance.

A shrill caw in the sky broke the silence, and Travis craned his neck. The sky was aflame with orange and violet as the black silhouette of an enormous hawk streaked across sharp clouds.

There you are. Travis strode onto the lawn beyond the shed and pretended to make for the stagecoach road as though unaware of the predator flying overhead. *Come and get me.*

He jogged toward the forest as if attempting an escape with his peripheral vision fixed on the shadow as it swooped lower. But then it disappeared, so Travis picked up his pace.

Like a projectile, the hawk launched at its prey in a savage, silent attack, beak and talons slashing at hair, bone, and flesh. Travis bellowed as what felt like bullets hammered into his skull in rapid-fire succession. He swiped at the raptor as he dove to evade it. Blood was already streaming down his right temple. He rolled on the grass, wiped his face, and fixed on the powerful black wings that thrust the animal skyward to circle for another attack.

Wounds on his head burned like acid as he scrambled to devise a plan. Radu's ploy was in play, so now what?

Travis jumped up from the grass and bolted toward the shed. About halfway there, the raptor stuck again, talons gripping his ears as the beak battered his skull with what felt like stabs from an ice pick.

It swiveled and went for his eye, but instead grazed his temple while talons dug into his skull anchored in thick hair. Travis struck at the hawk with his fist, and it adeptly took to the sky and spattered him with his own gore as it launched from his head.

Blood streamed into his face, and he swiped it aside with his forearm long enough to continue his sprint toward the house. He spied the raptor's trajectory as it angled for position, and frantic breaths betrayed his fear. After a few more strides, Travis dove to the grass. He rolled to his side and narrowed his eyes to slits, focused on the hawk. The predator descended and circled as it prepared to dive.

As Radu plunged toward him, Travis recalled his father and the lesson long ago of the weathercock. A stirring in his gut coiled and throbbed as he primed his weapon. Through his forehead he launched a bolt at the raptor, sending it into a tailspin as it drew closer, wings beating wildly to no effect as it plummeted upside-down. Travis veered at the last second, and the hawk smashed to the ground full force.

Travis sprang to grip its talons with both hands, forcing its flailing wings into the grass. The creature thrashed until it was clear Travis was in control. Then the animal calmed and slowly morphed into a human form.

Radu lay nude on his back in the grass and glared as Travis gripped his legs by the ankles, and thrust them up. Blood dripped from Travis's face and dribbled over his captive. Radu struggled to move, but immobilized, he could only spit.

"You were a fool to underestimate me again." Travis locked eyes with his nemesis. "Your attack was unprovoked, and I am free by coven law to slay you."

"I was only toying with you, showing off the hawk. I could have killed you here or in the basement. You are smart enough to recognize that." Radu winced as he forced the words.

"Then why didn't you?"

"You are needed to protect the coven and to save my son."

"I've already vowed to help him."

Travis dropped Radu's legs, and the fallen witch groaned as they hit the grass, heavy and lifeless as logs.

"And we can return to Bucharest to meet with the elders to find a solution."

Travis released his captive, and Radu moaned as he struggled to rise.

"They might not have one." He grimaced as his elbows wobbled to prop up his shoulders, and his muscular legs spasmed. "My back, you broke it. You can't leave me here."

Travis shook his head and scowled. "It isn't lethal, you'll heal soon enough. You're still juiced from Aaron's slaughter and fresh essence of my own. You're lucky." He took a step backward and wiped blood, hair, and sweat from his face. "I'm freeing the mortals from your basement. Leave us alone and focus on your back."

"Wait!" Radu shouted as Travis started toward the Malloy house. "What about my son?"

Travis turned and pondered the question. "I'm keeping him until you prove it's safe to return him to you."

Radu's breaths were rapid and shallow. "I love him and would never harm him."

"Is he human or witch?" Travis stepped closer as Radu craned his neck to lock eyes.

"I told you he's human. He's harmless. I adopted him as cover, but now I'm attached."

Travis's face was as unmoved as stone. "He's not your pet. You abandon him for hours, and there are clear signs of abuse." Travis planted himself alongside his foe.

"It's a ruse, all of it." Radu winced as he pulled in a deep breath and held it. "I needed you to take the bait, as a civilian doctor. It was the best way to reestablish contact with you and, in turn, study your techniques. The demon foretold your danger to the coven. I needed time to investigate."

Radu struggled to spit out words as Travis glared down.

Shadows grew long as the light drained from the sky.

"Your work with Andrei is proof of your magic's menace. Something haunts my son." Radu's tone was desperate but measured. "I tracked your movements and your work with Sorinah. I was inside you and watched sessions. And then you tried it on him. Only later was it clear your orb slaughtered Marku. I read what came out of Floreasca Manor."

Travis prodded Radu with the tip of his sneaker. "I'm listening. You've made your point in a most circuitous way. It's a matter for the elders, and I will bring it up myself. See you back in Bucharest."

Radu's eyes were wide.

"You have to save my son."

Travis stopped and stared down. "With you restrained, that will be my focus. None of this had to happen. You've wasted time. It's over."

"You have to fix him." The witch looked despondent. "I could have killed you, just now, in a gambit to free my son. I almost did, but held back. It's not certain your spell dies with you."

"If you'd killed me, you'd already have your answer." Travis turned away. "I don't think you'd like it. Your arrogance saved you." He raised his voice as he started toward the house. "The hawk was never battle-tested."

"It's not like that. Please, help Andrei! I purposely let you live to give you that chance. You need your eyes to save him. I could have savaged them. You would be oozing on the lawn in death throes. All the essence in the world wouldn't heal you in time."

Travis gingerly probed the open, bleeding gashes on his temple and his legs kept moving.

"Wait!" Radu called out and attempted to rise. "There's one thing more."

Travis didn't falter and resumed his march across the grass that was wet with dew as darkness fell under a pale moon. He watched as a figure rounded the side of the Malloy house. As it drew closer, he stopped and made out a female form draping fabric.

Travis tensed himself to defend, priming a bolt within his core.

"There's nothing to fear." Radu's voice was hoarse but carried across the yard.

Travis backtracked toward him, eyes on the stranger clutching a bundle who'd crossed onto the lawn and slowly approached. Radu had managed to prop himself up on one elbow, and Travis skulked a few feet away as shapes came into focus.

"What are you doing here?" Travis asked the woman and then glared at Radu. "What have you done?"

Radu watched her approach and his voice was firm.

"I need you to listen."

Travis tensed and clenched both fists. "I'll kill you both."

"It may be best to hear from Geri before you do."

Radu collapsed on the grass but swiveled his head to watch. "There's more to this cycle. You think you are virtuous, but your magic isn't. At least I am true to my dark nature, without delusions. I know who I am."

An uncomfortable stillness lingered.

Geri offered a tight smile that strained like bending steel.

"Hello, Travis."

Travis's chest heaved as he stood livid, trembling, and unable to respond.

She gently hoisted the bundle with both hands.

"Behold your daughter, Lulia."

THIRTY-NINE

THE SUN HAD ALL BUT SET and the sky radiated purple with wispy gray clouds diffusing an amber moon rising that made the white bundle appear to glow.

Travis staggered and struggled to process the gut punch of betrayal.

Control yourself and show them nothing.

They'd blindsided him, and he knew he was emotionally ill-equipped to deal with it. He fought the instinct to mow them both down. Already the wriggling bundle limited his options to retaliate. He wasn't sure how much time he'd spent staring as Geri held his daughter aloft.

He stifled himself and probed for weapons churning in either witch. Their auras of hostility read neutral. He moved to the next step, the formation of words.

"You faked the miscarriage," he managed.

Geri flinched and drew the bundle close.

"It was the best option."

Adrenaline coursed through his veins, and he shot her a baleful glance. "Best for whom?"

Geri whispered, "For the coven."

Travis exhaled slowly and shook his head. He waited for more.

"There's a bigger picture."

Travis couldn't restrain himself. "I believed you killed our baby."

Geri continued softly.

"It was explained to me the danger you pose to the coven."

"Explained by whom?" Travis turned and glared at Radu.

Radu spoke slowly and craned his neck toward Travis.

"I knew of your contract, the same as most coven members. I approached Geri as a confidant, with a shared ancestral cord, in order to better study you. I'd sworn to deliver you this message as prescribed by the demon during my isolation. But Geri herself felt powerless to influence you. Already you were meeting with my son, planning your test on him. The danger was personal, and Geri confirmed my suspicions."

"Suspicions of what?" Travis flicked his eyes at Geri and then locked them on Radu.

"Your disregard for the coven's shared cords. Your work unbinds them."

Travis was reeling and struggled to keep calm. He wanted to vanish and buy time to think, but before he could, he blurted, "You spied on me for months."

He paused, looked skyward, and realized it fit for both of them.

"You infiltrated my house." This was directed at Geri, who nodded solemnly.

He shifted his gaze to Radu. "You planted your son in my office."

Radu summoned more strength. "I did it in the spirit of discovery. I needed to reach you, to help you understand what you would never recognize on your own. There is a bigger picture behind your family magic that actually undermines everything after centuries."

Travis folded his arms, clamped onto both biceps, and closed his eyes.

Geri took a step toward him. "He convinced me of the danger, the dilution of our communal power, and the Devil's own displeasure. I always knew you would be reunited with your daughter later. I understood a time would come when the leverage would be needed."

Travis jumped to attention, eyes wide. "Leverage?"

Geri raised her eyebrows and whispered, "To force you to listen, if all else failed." She paused and repositioned Lulia in her arms. "We understand that it goes against nature to renounce ancestral magic."

"Is that what you're asking?" He turned to Radu.

Radu held his gaze and unapologetically nodded. "It's necessary for the coven's survival, and for your daughter."

Travis swiveled toward Geri as she took a step forward, and extended Lulia.

"Here, hold her."

Travis hesitated before taking backward steps. His mind raced, and in his confusion, he shot a message to the only one he could trust:

Geri has arrived with my daughter. She lied about the miscarriage. I've disabled Radu.

Sorinah responded immediately. *Get out of there. Andrei has disappeared.*

An alarm siren wailed inside Travis's skull, and he abruptly stopped the transfer.

His words came sharp and cold as his eyes blazed at Geri. "I want nothing to do with you. If that is my daughter and not another deception, you can rest assured I'll come for her."

Geri looked stricken as she pulled Lulia close and rocked her. "There is no deception. We need you to listen and absorb. Take as long as you need."

A clamor from the Malloy house drew their attention as the screen door slammed and Paula, James, and Rachel climbed down the kitchen steps onto the driveway.

"Leave us alone." He glared at Radu. "Any interference, and I'll finish you off. There's a knife in the grass by the shed. Or my bare hands will do; magic won't fix fatal."

Then he locked eyes with Geri. "Watch yourself, or I'll pluck Lulia from your corpse."

Travis rushed toward the house, intent on steering clear of the witches. He intercepted them halfway to the house, and they smiled politely without faltering. The trio's nonchalance was both expected and revolting, his eyes were open to both sides now.

"What are you doing here?" Travis asked, testing the vibe, addressing the group but focused on Paula. He didn't slow and shifted direction to keep pace with them toward the woods.

Paula's brows furrowed and she spoke quickly and quietly. "James and Rachel found me downstairs." She eyed the bloody spectacle of his face and hair. "What happened to you?"

"I had an accident. There's danger here. You need to get home."

"It's been a while. I forgot about you," James said as if they'd just toasted at a fraternity party. "Do you still live here?" He turned to Rachel. "He dated my mom after the divorce."

Travis shuffled on and couldn't muster an excuse. "Yes, and you shouldn't be here."

"A hawk lured us," James answered. "The same one that killed my dad."

Travis arched his eyebrows. "What do you mean, 'lured'?"

"It just seemed obvious. He flew low and waited and called out. He watched us. I fired a few shots but missed." James adjusted his shoulder pack, and felt for the pistol.

"We know it sounds strange," Rachel piped in. "We had to follow, especially after the lake."

"Same thing for me, it's lucky. I wouldn't have found you otherwise," Paula said.

They kept pace toward the forest for several strides without speaking, then James tapped Rachel's arm.

"Your knees looked scraped, like rug burns."

Rachel reached down and winced.

"Yikes! I must have tripped."

Paula flinched and stopped. "Now I remember you were missing. That was the whole point of my search. Why were you at the Malloy house, and why were you gone for so long? Something's out of whack. My memory is so sketchy. Who let me inside?"

"We didn't go in," James answered.

"No! Your mom is right; we were all inside," Rachel insisted, "I remember the kitchen table, and that man cleaned your head and gave you a bandage." She touched James's hair.

"What happened?" Travis asked.

"The hawk attacked me. I remember now. The one that got my dad."

They started walking again, skirting the edge of the meadow on a trail toward the woods, the urgent chirrups of crickets cutting the silence.

Rachel caught up to Travis with a confused shuffle. "You live here, so you must know him. Stefan, that's the man's name. I remember him from Old Gold. He's a customer."

"I do, and he'll be leaving soon," Travis answered as they approached the entrance to the stagecoach road. "Do not visit here again—I think it's haunted. Please stay away."

Paula turned and stopped. "Somehow that makes sense."

Travis frowned, and his jaw was tight. "I'm new here but it's clearly sinister, old grounds stowing malevolent spirits and unresolved trespasses. Get home safely and lie low for a week. Do you want me to walk you back?"

"No thanks, you've got to get yourself to a doctor," Paula said and started along the trail.

Travis watched as they picked up the pace and marched deeper into the woods.

Amber moonlight broke through tree branches as the wind shifted. He lingered a moment, studying the shadows that swallowed them, but had to get back to Sorinah.

FORTY

PAULA FELT DRAINED AND EMPTY as they walked along the moonlit trail. What the hell had happened and why wasn't she frantic? The better part of an afternoon had passed with no clear recollection of, well, anything. But she felt helpless to act. Confusion and anxiety were constants following Aaron's drowning. At least she'd found James and Rachel; that was something good and she had to get them home.

It's better to just keep quiet and melt into inevitable sadness.

Where did that come from? She didn't disagree, but it wasn't exactly empowering.

James and Rachel trailed just behind, and, oddly, no one spoke until the trees thinned and they reached Paula's property line. They navigated the coarse grass and thickets of the meadow and then the tidy, mowed lawn behind her house with still not a word.

Paula found her voice as they approached the driveway just past the garden.

"It's strange no one's talking, and everything's foggy. What's real and what's a dream?"

"I keep thinking that," Rachel said. "But I can't get words out of my head. You know that feeling where something's on the tip of your tongue, and it takes a while to suss it out? I have that, except nothing comes."

They exchanged nervous glances and headed for the blacktop.

"I keep obsessing about the hawk like it's branded on my brain, even when I close my eyes," James said. "It was taunting me, daring me to chase it, I feel it inside me still."

"I would think you were exaggerating except I saw it, too," Paula said.

"And I know it's the same one that got Dad. That's the obsessive part, I want revenge." James probed the bandage on his head, and then reached for Rachel's hand. "I'm not done yet."

"That's how I feel about Stefan," Rachel said. "He's what I remember; he's on my brain."

"Who's that?" Paula asked.

Rachel swiveled to answer. "He lives there. I met him once in the store. His son got a jean jacket."

There was silence again, filled by the rustle of branches and more crickets. "It's strange there are three men living there. I only know about Travis and Radu," Paula said.

"Three grown men, all middle-aged, all living together?" James asked.

"And all hot. I guess they're gay," Rachel said. "Not sure how the teenage son factors in."

"I can assure you that Travis isn't," Paula said. "We're jumping to conclusions."

"I'm going to find out more from Stefan." Rachel squeezed James's hand. "We've met formally, so it's not strange for me to ask him what happened and find out what's going on. Were we drugged? Why can't we remember anything? I'm wicked scared and want answers."

"I beg you to stay away," Paula said.

"Beg?" James asked.

"There's been too much going on, too much to handle so soon after Aaron."

Paula gripped their shoulders. "Travis thinks the place is haunted, and who's to say he's wrong? We've got nothing else to go on. If we were drugged, that's a matter for the police."

"I'm open to anything," James said, "except more police, we sound crazy, right?"

They sidled next to Rachel's car in the driveway, and she pulled keys and her phone out through a zipper in her backpack.

"I've suspected dark forces ever since Mia and Sophia, and then came my nightmares, and that freaky hawk that struck your dad shows up here, and we just left some kind of time warp. I don't even know what day it is."

She glanced at the screen and tapped out a message. "My parents are freaking out. I'm shaking and can barely type."

"What can we do?" Paula asked. "I hate this helpless feeling."

Rachel looked up from the screen. "First, I need to calm them down. I'll come up with something. Tomorrow my plan starts with Stefan, and we'll take it from there when he fills in some blanks."

She pushed stray hairs out of her face. "We need rest to get our heads straight. Right now involving the police sounds crazy, and that's saying something, coming from me. I mean, what's our complaint? I can't even verbalize it."

James's upper body rocked in agreement. "We'll go together to your parents and figure things out on the way. We'll all get some rest, and regroup in the morning." He flicked his eyes between them. "Things'll look brighter, right?"

Paula pursed her lips and didn't look convinced. "Would you like to come inside?" She motioned to the kitchen steps. "I'm sure everyone's as hungry as I am."

"We need to crisis-manage, Mom," James said, and pecked Rachel on the cheek. "It's been a long, confusing day, and all I want is for it to end. We all need time to think."

"My knees ache, and I need a bath," Rachel added as she moved toward the driver's side. "But first I need to manage my parents."

James hugged his mother. "Will you be OK?"

"Do I have a choice?" Paula asked and squeezed him tight. "I feel the rush of calm after a bad scare. But I'd feel a lot better if you were staying." She took a step back, and cupped his elbows with her palms. "It terrifies me that you don't know where you were. Rack your brains and get a grip on things. Did a party go late and you passed out somewhere? You can tell me."

James smiled and gripped her forearms. "That would make me feel better, too. It's just right now I can't think straight. I need rest and a cold one. You do, too."

"The Gradys brought over a casserole I can pop in the oven and open a bottle of wine."

"That's a start. We'd love to share it with you, but Rachel's parents are pissed. Not that you're not, but now you're in cahoots with us. I feel that same calm and it makes me want to rest and hide. Tomorrow we'll be better with clearer heads." James shuffled toward Rachel's car and opened the passenger side. "See you before noon, right after we meet with Stefan."

"Maybe there was a party and you stayed over, but no one admits it because now it sounds weird. I'll tell myself that to feel better. I'd really rather you don't go back there," Paula called out as he closed the door. "Get some rest. I'll follow you down to get the mail."

She walked in Rachel's headlights as the car reversed down the driveway. It backed onto the road, and Paula waved until the taillights disappeared. She pulled open the mailbox, happy to find it empty, and turned up the slope of the driveway.

A low, guttural growl made her jump as she passed a row of hedges.

Her heart raced, and she froze to focus on a stirring in the laurel. Instinct took control, and she burst toward the house.

A beast gave chase, and she glanced backward long enough to glimpse snarling jaws and tiny black eyes burning behind bristling fur. She sprinted as fast as she could, while sharp claws skittered on the pavement. Pain flared on the back of her calf, and she yelped as she mounted the stairs. She gripped the screen door handle and threw it open to toggle the doorknob.

"Fuck!" She sobbed as she fumbled for the keys in her front pocket. She stared as the creature snarled at the edge of the steps. "Get away!"

The badger reared onto its hind legs and drooled bloody saliva. It lurched up the stairs.

Paula froze in disbelief as it morphed and stood erect with coarse, black hair yielding to smooth skin as a human form took shape and grew tall. She drove in the key and pushed the door open even as a hand behind her gripped the screen.

"Get away from me!" Paula shouted as she slammed the door, but the intruder shimmied through. She took backward steps, facing him, stopping in a patch of moonlight on the floor that spilled in under the window sash.

A strapping young man stood before her, nude, and close in age to her son.

"What's happening?" she whispered.

He closed the door behind him and smoothed away blood from his lips.

"My name is Andrei. I apologize for the intrusion, and for my nakedness, but neither can be avoided." His dark eyes fixed on hers as he moved closer. "My father is injured nearby and I'm forced to bring him here to recover. You're his helper and I'm afraid he needs your assistance."

Paula gasped and took a backward step. "Helper?"

She panted and eyed the knife drawer.

"You need to rest and be strong before he arrives." Andrei clicked on the kitchen lights. "A dream will help, no hunger, no confusion." He paused and folded his arms.

Paula's eyes grew wild, and she inched toward the counter.

"Something happened right here, in the closet. I'm sure you remember; a mother doesn't forget."

He glided in front of it and pulled it open while Paula raced to the drawer, scrambled inside, and grasped a carving knife. An instant later she sprang and plunged the blade at his chest, but he swiveled and grabbed her wrist.

For how long he squeezed, Paula didn't know, but she dropped the knife. And then came dizziness, and she realized she didn't want anything. In fact, the closet looked quite cozy.

Andrei backed away from the door.

"Because you are my father's helper, he's sending a dream that will make everything better. You'll feel it now, a welcome rest. You'll learn what happened to Katherine; why she cowered in the corner."

Paula looked at her hands and marveled at their petite smoothness. Her breasts were flat, hips and thighs tapered. She knew at once she was in Katherine's body, in Katherine's head, and wanted to burrow into Katherine's hidden spot in the back corner of the closet.

She covered herself with jackets and boots and closed her eyes.

It's better to just keep quiet and melt into inevitable sadness.

She agreed. She wanted to. But something dreadful was inside with her, hidden in shadow, hissing, clutching at her. Then she saw its face. Hauntings were real, she knew now.

Paula screamed, and Andrei clicked the closet door shut.

FORTY-ONE

TRAVIS GRIPPED THE WHEEL LOW and tight as he raced to join Sorinah. He had a daughter. The reality pressed on him like the darkness beyond the headlights. But now it was clear the family magic he hoped would empower her was malevolent. Could he trust Radu's account? Betrayal all around gutted him, and he struggled against the speed limit as his adrenaline surged.

He opened the garage door to the rental house to find two bikes blocking the way, so he wheeled them aside to park. The kitchen was quiet and dark when he entered, but light streamed from Andrei's bedroom.

When Travis slipped through the doorway, Sorinah flew past the corner of the bed and traced the blood trails down his face with her fingers.

"At least you outed the witch," she said as she gently probed his thick black hair. "Now let's clean you up. How bad does it hurt?"

"It's tolerable; he held back. Tell me about Andrei."

Sorinah's lips tightened as she continued her exam. "You first."

Travis relaxed with her touch. "Radu planned everything, he baited us here using his son. Shifting is a new weapon and enables his turns as a hawk."

She wiped his cheek, and they locked eyes. "Those threads don't bind our coven."

His face went hard. "He was granted new powers in exchange for stopping me." He guided Sorinah's finger to gouges on his scalp.

"Granted by whom?"

"A demon or the Devil himself visited his isolation cell and intervened."

Sorinah studied his face and waited for him to continue.

"Radu says my mutant magic dilutes the coven's shared threads, drawing energy from pooled reserves, without streaming it back. It stays with whoever summons it, full potency. That's why we're still juiced from the orb."

Sorinah pulled hair back to expose deep gashes on his scalp. "Where is Radu now?"

"I hurt him, but nothing lethal. His back is fractured and needs time to heal. He will be weakened for a few days. He wants me to forswear my magic. That's his mission."

Sorinah pursed her lips. "And Geri?"

"She's in league with him. I have a daughter named Lulia." His eyes grew dark as his eyebrows arched. "They're using her as leverage; it was his plan all along."

Sorinah ushered Travis into the shadowy hallway toward the bathroom.

"I understand my magic's tainted, as we learned from Marku and Andrei. But the deceit of Radu and Geri doesn't exactly engender cooperation," Travis stated.

"I probed Andrei at the swimming pool." She maneuvered Travis to the edge of the tub. "I was sniffing for witch essence but got something else entirely."

She wet a washcloth under the faucet. "His aura was blocked as a demon outside his window taunted and terrorized him. I was not in control and was violently thrust out. Next thing I knew I was sprawled on a park bench."

Travis flinched as she dabbed at his temple.

"I had a similar jolt when I tried him last night."

"What does Radu say about him?"

"He insists the boy is a mortal." Travis exhaled slowly. "He's lying."

"But something is after Andrei. I felt it." Sorinah rinsed the towel under the warm water. "The fear, the dread, the Devil's eye is too precise to be faked. Witch or not, he's marked."

Travis's jaw tightened, and he nodded. "Point taken; so how did he get away?"

"I was focused on contacting you. When I went to check his room he was gone. If he's one of us, he's powerful, I detected nothing during the probe before I got shoved out." Sorinah dabbed the towel on the top of his head. "And now he's gone without a trace. I was checking for fragments when you arrived."

"I've got to view Andrei as an adversary aligned with his father, not my patient, unless proven otherwise. It fits Radu would share his new weapons with his gifted son. The disguising spell is advanced, not the coven's own. It was difficult sneaking behind it."

Travis wiped his face with the wet, warm cotton. The gore and bloodstains were gone, and color returned to his face. Essence-primed rejuvenation was kicking in.

Sorinah examined her work. "So what is our plan?"

"I need to load the sphere."

Travis gently probed the wound on his head, and the gash on his temple no longer burned.

"There's the pillowcase, and crumbles in the kitchen bin. I'll recalibrate the orb to wield in defense if Andrei attacks. I have to face that possibility."

He balled up the towel and tossed it into the tub.

"Tomorrow we return for Lulia."

"Slow down," Sorinah said as she gently pressed his hair with a dry towel. "Radu's wounded, but Andrei and Geri will help him. We can't fight them all."

For a moment there was only the drip of the bath spout.

"I'll agree to renounce my family magic," Travis said as he rose and made for the door. "At least long enough to reclaim my daughter. Radu and Andrei had us fooled, but not anymore. Once Lulia's safe with you, I'll focus on Andrei. There still might be a way out of this."

"A happy ending?"

His obsidian eyes locked on hers. "With the intruder banished? I'd like to hope. Does that make me weak? Radu says I'm delusional, a dark witch chasing virtue."

"It makes you strong. You want to redeem your magic and save the boy, witch or not. It's about *you* more than Andrei; there are degrees of evil for all creatures, and degrees of good."

When Sorinah finished dressing his wounds, Travis set out to collect traces of the boy's essence. Then he reset the orb, bypassing the spell's dark root, retooling the incantation as a freeze defense to buy time.

A newfound raison d'être inspired him as he plunged into the incantation: he vowed to take control of his own magic; he would even expel the demon himself.

If he couldn't, Andrei would turn out like Marku.

It was on him.

Radu's words cut deep and more painfully than he would ever share.

Maybe he was delusional. There was no virtue in any of this.

FORTY-TWO

A DREARY AFTERNOON DRIZZLE KEPT the wipers flapping as Rachel and James drove toward Sussex. The patter of raindrops and the soothing, repetitive *slosh* on the windshield dominated the rumble of the engine like a hypnotic metronome.

Rachel still felt blank and struggled to make sense of a warped reality that had untethered from terra firma. All she could do this second was squeeze the steering wheel. She scoured the depths of her recollections and strained to clear away the murkiness that choked like seaweed. Incisors clamped down on her lower lip as she tried to force a tangible fact, anything, to break through. And then she had one: the nightmares had stopped. She could be grateful for that. But were they really gone, or was it just because James watched over her? The hint of a smile formed at the edges of her lips as she drove; she'd sussed out something nice. She loved the way he always clung to her hard before she could rouse him out of bed to face the day.

"Should we stop in on your mom?" Rachel asked as they approached the turn, her pinky on the signal.

"Better we go after," James replied. "We'll tell her what we find out, right?"

She nodded and resumed a firm grip on the wheel. It took a moment to choose her words. "I still can't remember details. It almost hurts to focus. And right now it's like we weren't even there. I feel OK if I don't think about it, but when I do I freak."

"I remember the walk home very clearly and also chasing the hawk. But we lost a full night somewhere, Rachel. That's insane." James cracked the window and wiped away a few raindrops that splattered onto his forearm. "Are we going crazy, like Alzheimer's?"

"We may have been drugged. We have to be careful." Rachel's fingers pulsed the wheel.

"I'll try to find Travis, maybe he can help. I trust him." His hair ruffled in the breeze and today the wound was fine without a bandage.

Rachel's eyes got wide. "What are those men doing in that house together?"

"I'm definitely curious." James buzzed the window shut. "Maybe they're not alone."

"True, let's look for women." She pulled in a deep breath and held it. "My mom is still pissy; she didn't love the excuse."

James grinned with his jaw clenched. "You can blame my mom for the idea: a party went late, and you couldn't drive drunk, so we stayed over."

"Are we sure that didn't happen? I've been so foggy since your dad. I think we're still in shock. Maybe this is all completely normal." Rachel glanced at James as he grimly stared through the windshield. "I'm still in shock since the skeleton. Meanwhile, there's nothing new there, except confirmation it's a murder and not a missing person's case. No shit."

James brushed Rachel's cheek. "We're on our own. They don't even care about the hawk, or whatever jumped me."

Her face tightened. "I'm implicated, just like before, guilt by association. I'm hiding what I know about Sophia's murder, the dream story's a lie. And now you're tainted by the uncanny death of your dad. We're outcasts to avoid. We need to get away from here."

"I agree, the sooner the better."

"We'll plan the move." Rachel raised her eyebrows and glanced over for his reaction.

"We've decided, somewhere near Boston." James's face turned hopeful. He reached up to probe the scab on his scalp.

Rachel broke eye contact and stared straight. "Travis said the Malloy house was haunted. Well, my nightmares came true and now I believe in ghosts; Sophia reached me."

There was a pause, and then James whispered, "Since the hawk, I believe in forces of evil."

Rachel shot him another look. "It can't be the same hawk that killed your dad. *That* would push me over the edge."

"I'm sure it's the same. Anything's possible and everything's scary again the closer we get to the house." James focused on her as she signaled a turn. "Let's find shit out and go."

"I'll be quick with Stefan. I pray, just this once, it all makes sense." Rachel shuddered and then pulled in a breath. "He calmed us with an elixir from his homeland, Romania. It was strangely potent because it's a secret, herbal remedy. We fell asleep and he let us stay over because the hawk was after us and we didn't dare go home....I tell myself this...."

James watched her trail off. "That damn hawk, how could I keep missing?"

Rachel smiled and touched his arm. "Your aim wasn't great."

James sniggered and took her hand. "We'll find shit out, then we'll check on my mom, and then plan to check out for good." His gaze pierced the streaky windshield. "You'll get set up first. I'll be ready in ten months, and then, bam!"

Rachel clicked the wipers faster against the rain.

FORTY-THREE

THE CLOSET DOOR CREAKED OPENED, and Paula peered up from her nest in the back corner. What looked like the silhouette of a giant leaned against the frame. Gray light filtered in from the window above the sink, and she struggled to make out the man's features. As her eyes adjusted his angular face and sturdy build came into focus and triggered a memory. Was it yesterday? Now he wore black boots.

The hospital, yes, when Katherine was sick.

She sat up and cleared a path through fallen jackets.

What am I doing in here?

Paula lurched up in the cramped space and realized she was trembling. She grabbed James's sweatshirt to cover herself as she stumbled out. She knew she was wet.

"Excuse me, but what the hell are you doing here?"

She watched the man slink backward toward the kitchen table and pull out a chair. A steady drizzle tapped at the window in the dreary morning light.

"I need your help," he said quietly.

The stranger didn't seem threatening, but that didn't excuse a thing. His eyes were dark and piercing, his face square and incongruously handsome, given the intrusion.

"You have no business here. Get out." She tapped her pockets for her cell phone, but it wasn't there so she bluffed.

"Explain yourself, quick, or I'm calling 911."

The man studied her and again spoke quietly. "You've helped me before."

His voice was deep and accented like someone else she knew, but couldn't immediately place. Snippets of memories whirled in a blur. Front of mind was Katherine, frantic in the woods, fleeing from a witch, but now black boots and the man with the accent flashed in from the Malloy house, from when, last night? Years ago? Serenity seeped in as she came to realize she somehow liked this stranger. She was his helper; it was coming back now, she could trust him.

"To do what?"

You don't need to speak, Paula, or be alarmed. My name is Radu. You've helped me in the past though your recollections are spotty. Last night's dream was an awakening. You had to see why Katherine hid in the closet. She survived an attack in the woods by the horror sent by Travis. There is much more to show you.

"Why can I hear you?" Paula inched forward, away from the closet because now it seemed menacing, inhabited by ghosts from the past, and the rescuer arrived just in time.

"We are connected inside, like mind reading." Radu's voice was deep and soothing. He sucked in a breath and held it for a moment, pain etched on his face. He winced as he straightened in the chair and fixed his gaze on her.

"Your mind will be expanded. You are no longer Travis's pawn left blank by his magic."

Paula felt a gale press down, and she fought to stand. The floor seemed to tilt, and she floundered toward the counter and held tight. She heard rain patter against the window and then peeked out as the storm inside and out crescendoed into the roar of a whirlwind, but then subsided all at once. And in its wake came the sobs of her daughter, a wavering reflection in the center of the window. A letter—a confession, a script—popped into her head.

Katherine,

I was wrong to doubt you. Everything you said is true. The wraith in the woods is as real as the fire that burns

her soul. Travis conjured her. This I learned in the closet, and it's entirely my fault. I brought him into our lives. I was vulnerable then and fell for his powers of seduction. God save me from the witches all around us. They've embedded themselves nearby, lurking in plain sight. But my death will set us free, a mother's greatest gift, the one thing that will deliver my children from evil. For none of this would have happened if it weren't for my weakness and my mistakes. I feel so guilty because he tried to kill you and four years later hunted down Aaron.
My heart aches and there is only one escape.
Your mother

"Well done, Paula." Radu's deep voice penetrated from somewhere distant, murky at first like a foghorn, then clear. "Katherine needs you to do this. You can break the calamitous cycle plaguing your family. It's in your power to make things right."

Paula nodded and opened her eyes as she sucked in a lungful of air. Why was she so discombobulated? At least the tornado in the kitchen had leapt somewhere else, and she shuffled away from the window.

"Things are starting to clear. It feels better."

She raised her eyebrows and focused on Radu with wide eyes. She noticed a scar on his cheekbone.

"Like a haze has lifted."

"You deserve your memories back." Radu held her gaze. "Travis took them."

"I didn't know." She trembled but was scarcely aware.

"It's not your fault, but you can help me stop him. All creatures have essence to share."

Paula shook her head slowly. "I'm lost again."

Radu's smile accentuated the angles of his face. "Essence fuels the universe. We all consume other organisms to survive, thankful for the sacrifice of animals and plants on plates for dinner. In turn we become energy ourselves, ultimately feeding bacteria and worms. Every living thing needs fuel for energy and growth. I need it to escape an unpleasant eternity."

Paula pondered it all for a moment and settled on a word. "Eternity?"

"Because of my origin, the end is something to avoid for as long as possible." Radu grimaced and then managed to recover his charm. "That's not important now. It's morning, and you may be hungry."

"Actually I am. I feel weak. It must be time for breakfast." She noticed the way he pressed himself against the back of the chair. "Why the pain?"

"I injured my back."

"I hope you're OK." Paula ambled to the counter and switched on the Keurig. "Coffee?" She took down two mugs and set them near a box of K-cups. "It takes just a minute to brew."

Radu watched quietly as she worked but then sighed and stopped. She looked down and there were stains on her shorts.

"If you'll excuse me, I need a shower, and then I'll join you." James's sweatshirt lay on the floor near the sink. She gathered it and her face got tight. "I'm all over the place."

"Just take it slow." His voice was soothing, the accent alluring as he stared at her.

She wasn't sure if the punch list that posted like magic was mental or verbal.

"They'll need an explanation. And I want to look my best, all things considered. My favorite dress, at least."

When she surveyed the kitchen, their eyes met. The list went on.

"We'll bring this chair to the basement where the beams are exposed. There's nylon rope in the shed. Aaron was good at slipknots. He showed me how."

In a flurry, she darted across the kitchen and grabbed a pen and notepad from the stash in the corner near the refrigerator. She flipped to a clean page, took a seat at the table, and popped the pen in her mouth as she paused to think. When the words came, she read aloud.

"Katherine, I was wrong to doubt you. Everything you say is true. The wraith in the woods is real." She stopped and looked up. "There's more, I need time to get it right."

The pen trembled in her grip.

"The wraith in the woods is as real as...."

Water steaming in the Keurig stole her attention. When it stopped, she drifted to the machine deep in thought, inserted a coffee pod, and pressed the button.

"...as real as the fire that burns her soul," Radu suggested.

"Yes," Paula said as hot coffee streamed. "Exactly that."

Her eyes narrowed as she dug deep for more and gently placed the mug in front of Radu. She pivoted to the notepad and completed the phrase in her most careful cursive.

"I'm blank again," she said, and then her eyes locked with Radu's. "What's wrong?"

It's better to just keep quiet and melt into inevitable sadness.

"That's the best advice I've ever heard," she whispered. "Where does it come from?"

I've been with you for a while, now.

Paula smiled and then drifted into the hallway to pad up the stairs, silent as a ghost.

FORTY-FOUR

RACHEL AND JAMES ROLLED INTO the driveway of the Malloy house to park.

"Shit me. I should have packed the pistol," James said, stiff in his seat, pulse pounding.

"It's a quick fact-finding mission, not a hunt," she answered.

James clenched his jaw and nodded. He hoped to never see the hawk again, truth be told. His escape from Sussex with Rachel was a much better focus. A web search would start as soon as they got back to her place, away from this dank, creepy old house.

"Do we need umbrellas?" Rachel asked as she stashed the keys in her pack.

"Nah, it's just a drizzle." James climbed out and scanned around.

They started toward the front door, but a motor sputtering out back caught their attention.

"Let's check it out," James whispered, and pointed toward the curve of the gravel driveway around the side of the house. "I hope he likes having neighbors. We're allowed to visit, right?"

Rachel nodded and shadowed his advance as they side-stepped puddles and crept along. A mist clung to low rain clouds drifting north over the acreage behind the farmhouse toward the mountains. Water streamed off the pitched roof of the red shed. They'd hidden there, he remembered now, but it seemed like weeks ago.

In the distance, a tractor rumbled deep in the meadow. The motor whined as the driver extracted a large drill from the ground, spraying soggy, tilled earth above tall, wavering grasses.

"I know that rig." James stood perfectly still as he stared across the field. "It's a tree planter. I'd forgotten all about it until just now. Travis used to have it."

"What for?" Rachel asked as she shielded her eyes from drizzle with her hand.

James squinted and held his breath. "No clue. Let's get closer. Sorry it's so wet."

They crossed from the driveway onto the lawn abutting the meadow. The guy on the tractor didn't seem to notice as they approached from behind. He wore jeans and tan work boots with a black t-shirt that clung in the rain.

"It's not Stefan," Rachel said as they drew near, "I think it's his son. He was with his father in the store. But he looks different now, a little older, bigger."

The motor whined as the auger spun dirt into a mound around the hole. The insistent rumble started to relax when the driver extracted the drill, then died altogether when he shut it down. He dismounted and confusion washed his face as he turned toward James and Rachel, but then he brightened.

Rachel held up her hand and stepped forward. "Hi there, we didn't mean to startle you. I'm Rachel, and this is James."

"I know you from somewhere." The worker narrowed his eyes and took in the pair.

Rachel wiped raindrops from her face. "I think we met in Old Gold. You were in the store with your father, but I thought you were younger."

"My hair's shorter now, and I'm working out, trying to get bigger."

Rachel shuffled in the wet, tall grass as she checked him out. "That must be it."

"I'm Andrei." A broad grin produced dimples in his deep cheeks.

"Nice to meet you," James said and extended his hand. Andrei clasped it, and their eyes locked. James felt a charge that made him flinch but also tighten on the damp, firm grasp.

"What brings you by?" Andrei asked as he released his grip.

"We were hoping to talk to your dad. It wouldn't take long." Rachel edged closer.

"About?"

"We came by yesterday, a hawk attacked us," James interjected, "I know it sounds crazy."

"Trouble is, we don't remember much," Rachel said. "But we met your dad in the afternoon. He brought us inside to help."

Andrei puckered his lips and jounced a bit as he folded his arms. "He works Fridays. I'm pretty sure he wasn't home."

Rachel shot James a worried glance. "Really? He remembered me from Old Gold. His name is Stefan, we chatted a while."

"We're neighbors," James said as he pointed in the direction of the stagecoach road, "the nearest house if you cut through the woods. Yesterday we walked here."

Andrei looked confused and blew out a slow breath. "My dad's name is Radu."

"Wait, my mom mentioned him. Can we talk to him?" James's eyes went wide.

"He's not here right now." His eyes shifted toward the woods. "He took that same trail a few hours ago to visit a neighbor's house."

James grabbed Rachel's arm. "My mom—"

Rachel's face blanched. "We should go." She turned to Andrei. "I'm sorry, I know this is an odd intrusion."

"No harm done." Andrei fixed a piercing gaze on James. "Tell me about the hawk."

James couldn't look away. "It's black as night and huge and lured us here, at least that's how it seemed. It's cunning. I blame it for killing my dad. Somehow I know it's the same one."

"I'm sorry; here in the woods?" Raindrops beaded on Andrei's forehead before dripping down his face.

"No, at the lake. The hawk dive bombed him." James's eyes

were wide and he didn't blink. "It's scary and has a will of its own, I mean, it plots against its prey; it's aggressive."

"I've read about animal attacks." Andrei raised his eyebrows as he scanned the treetops flanking the meadow. "Strange indeed. Faced with extinction, it seems a fight for survival has already started."

James felt an urge to share more. He liked the neighbor. "I was also attacked."

By a badger?

The question popped into James's head and resonated like a bell. His heart rate doubled and goosebumps erupted on his arms.

"By a badger?" Andrei asked.

James nodded slowly with his whole upper body. "How did you know?"

"There was something on the news, a rabies outbreak." Their eyes locked again.

The drizzle was beginning to disperse into mist, drifting on a stiffening breeze toward low, plump clouds hugging the mountain.

I met you at the lake. We fought. It was the only way to bond.

James flinched and shook his head to try to clear it.

Rachel watched him and touched his arm. "Is everything OK?"

I'm already inside you. That's how you can hear me. Just wait, it gets better.

The words intrigued and repelled him in equal, forceful waves. But the reverberations were electric and tantalizing. James shielded his face with his hand and smoothed away raindrops.

"What is it?" Rachel asked, and steadied him with her arm. "What's happening?"

James bent forward to hide his distress as his breathing grew weak and rapid.

"You're hyperventilating. What's wrong?" Rachel asked sharply.

An instant later James crouched and planted himself against an invisible onslaught. His eyes darted wildly as he listened for the voice.

"I thought I heard something," he whispered.

A breeze rustled the grasses as he struggled to comprehend the situation. Then came a flash of clarity.

"Not everyone gets a casket; just look at Sophia."

He stared up into the mist, his neck craned backward, his face locked in a grimace.

"James, look at me! Let's get out of here," Rachel urged, her heart racing. She grabbed his hand and tried to pull.

"A hole in the ground is where we all end up," James stated with a baleful expression. He shook her off and stepped toward the tractor. "I need to drill mine. It's all that's left."

Rachel's eyes were wild now. "You're scaring me. Stop it!" She retook his arm and tried to yank him toward the house.

Yes, there is important work to do.

The voice was back, and James felt a rush of excitement like the first plunge of a rollercoaster. He pulled free and climbed the tractor to take the controls.

Andrei jumped up behind him and grabbed for a lever, but James threw an elbow and sent him tumbling into the grass. The motor roared to life and the auger began to rotate.

As the rig lurched forward, Andrei sprang up with eyes trained on his captive. His gaze blazed a trail to an imaginary target about fifty feet closer to the woods. James headed straight for it, stopping when the auger whirled just above the bull's eye.

We are here for a purpose. We are the only sons of our fathers.

James nodded with his jaw clenched tight as Rachel trailed behind in frightened disbelief.

"James, stop," she shouted. "What are you doing?"

"I tried to get him down," Andrei offered. "He's gone crazy."

Without a word, James lowered the drill, and the tractor bucked at the point of contact then steadied. Wet earth spewed from the hole as the auger plunged deeper and straight down.

"What are you doing?" Her eyes pooled tears as she stood frozen in the sodden grass, helpless, impotent. Her limbs trembled. "Get down! We need to check on your mother!"

A father and son become one, absorbed as essence to endure forever.

The voice was commanding yet comforting, at once convincing and convivial.

He had a role to play, something big, something important. James worked the controls like magic, shimmying the auger just right to widen the hole to two feet thick.

"My father wants me to do this," James announced from rig.

As does mine.

When the voice came, James turned his head and smiled at Andrei. Now he recognized the source.

"Why do I feel you?" James asked aloud and then refocused on the levers.

It happened at the lake. We're conjoined like twins now, the closest bond.

James licked his lips and nodded, not understanding yet unconcerned, intrigued and mystified by unexpected yet not unwelcome stirrings of arousal that just made everything fascinating.

Rachel pulled out her phone to call the police. Clearly whatever was happening had gone on long enough. When it told her to enter the passcode, the device slipped from her clammy fingers and dropped into the meadow grass. She pushed a matted clump aside, and a thistle pricked her hand. She cursed but immediately thrust back in, and the phone flipped under a slick of canary grass.

"What the fuck?" Rachel got on all fours and plowed through reeds and weeds to try to grasp her phone from the wet tangle.

The motor groaned as James plunged the full depth of the auger into the earth and widened the hole. The mound of wet soil around the opening rose and spread like a volcano.

Our fathers compel us forward, and united we will endure forever.

The voice thundered like a Marines ad during the Super Bowl.

James knew when he was finished and switched off the drill as he backed the rig away from his work. He killed the motor and jumped down.

"The hole is ready," James called out and wiped sweat and beads of mist from his arms as he clomped through the grass toward Rachel. "Sorry it took so long."

She was hunched over and looked up. She frowned, soggy and exasperated.

"I was calling the police. I dropped my phone, and now it's disappeared."

James caught up and stooped down to help. "We'll find it, can't just disappear."

She shook the rain from her hair and droplets dripped down her temples as she watched him with a panicked look on her face, pulling in deep breaths with her mouth open wide.

James massaged the tangle with both hands, feeling his way, pushing aside thick swaths of matted grass. He sprang up when a phone chimed behind them.

"That's mine!" Rachel dashed toward the xylophone tones and stopped near the mud hole to hone in. When it started again she climbed the mound that encircled it, and peered down.

"My God, it's there on the bottom."

She turned toward James and pointed.

"How'd it get down there?" he asked.

She froze in place, and her face crunched as tears came. She swiveled to peek again just as the cheerful marimba chimed out from the muddy depths.

That's when James crept from behind and shoved her in without making a sound.

Rachel screamed as she slid down and found herself shoulder-deep in the hole.

"What the fuck?" came out as a screech. Her eyes darted as she struggled to shimmy her arms out from the tight squeeze of sodden, cold earth. "James! What the hell are you doing?"

James bent and heaved armfuls of dirt from the mound into the crevice as she squirmed.

Andrei by now had moved closer and stood with fists clenched, his body soaked, taut, and trembling as his eyes locked on James.

Shifting around the mound, James used his whole upper body as a plow to shove more dirt down to immobilize Rachel's limbs.

Her cries mixed with screams and spasmodic gasps for air.

"It's just a holding pit," James whispered and was fine with it. "We have a purpose."

Veins in his neck and arms popped as he strained against an invisible force, but he remained steadfast in his charge to pack her in up to her neck.

Rachel shrieked and spat dirt. "Please! Stop!"

She snapped at his forearm with her teeth and caught some skin.

James trembled as he pressed down the soil, and filled in gaps. Soon the hole that held her was level with the grassy floor of the meadow.

Then he collapsed on his back beside her, panting to catch his breath.

Rachel sobbed and struggled to move, but could only swivel her neck.

Grasses towered all around, yielding to the wind, spraying raindrops in her face.

"Why are you doing this?" Rachel managed, tears leaving trails down her cheeks.

This he heard, and James rolled in front of her, then leaned in close.

"It started with the hawk; it got my father, and now me. The other hole is mine. I won't be far."

Rachel screamed and clamped her eyes shut. "What are you talking about?"

She could only whimper in defense, and when she dared to peek, he was gone.

"James? My God, where are you?"

By then James had passed behind Rachel's head, out of the matted patch hiding her, and into the tall grass in the thick of the meadow. Andrei waited for him in front of the tree planter, arms folded, lips pulled tight above his square jaw.

Let's finish this.

James silently plodded toward the witch and stood at the ready, awaiting further instruction. When he got close, Andrei reached out and carefully wiped dirt from his face. James leaned closer, eyes wide and hazel gone green.

Follow me.

Andrei slowly turned and marched toward the hole James himself had bored with the tree planter. He waited for James to catch up.

And when he did, Andrei released control.

James felt like the falls spewing over Niagara suddenly stopped. He gulped down air, relishing the withdrawal of pounds of pressure. He scanned for Rachel, but her head was below the billowing grass line.

James tensed and locked eyes with Andrei. "I'm free now."

Your essence needs to be primed.

"I know it was you. I'm going to kick your ass."

Arrogance shifting to fear will do it.

James charged with everything he had, but Andrei swiveled and sent him stumbling with an elbow to the ribs. James groaned, jumped up, and pounced again. He was sailing into a perfect full-body tackle, but felt his momentum shift and catapult him over the witch.

A shout escaped as he flew through the air, spinning like the auger. It was impossible to block or recover, and he plunged head-first into the pit.

Then they both froze.

A pair of sturdy legs jutted out, casting about for leverage above the grasses. A muffled cry for help wafted up from the bottom of the narrow, muddy trap.

I don't want this.

Already trembling from the surge of essence gushing from James, Andrei raced to the pit and grabbed his ankles, managing to hoist him a few inches.

I'll get you out.

With legs straddling the hole, he girded himself to jack James up, slowly at first, but then with the agility and strength of a gymnast as he pivoted sideways, grabbed his torso, and planted James's buttocks in the hole, his head and thighs elevated by the mound of sodden earth encircling it.

He kneeled close and cleared mud from James's face and hair. Frightened hazel eyes stared back. His head lurched at an odd angle as his chest heaved.

I've failed. Why can't I do this? Andrei transferred to his father.

Radu's response was instantaneous.

You're still a whelp. It seems you aren't ready. Take simple essence and proceed with the plan. The captives are useful.

Andrei gently gripped James's chin. His words came soft and slow.

"We're in synch and I will temper any pain. I won't harm my twin. You have no secrets and that closeness feels different from everything else. My father didn't tell me."

The infusion forced Andrei into a ball beside the pit.

Rachel shouted into the lush, boggy, billowing void.

"James? Are you there? What's happening? Andrei? James? Don't leave me."

The patter of another round of drizzle was the only sound for what seemed a small eternity until the sputtering motor of the tree digger roared to life somewhere behind her and then faded as it drove away and died.

"Help me! James? Andrei?"

Rachel shivered in the ground and sobbed long enough that the weather shifted, and then the mist dispersed completely.

FORTY-FIVE

GERI WATCHED THE GIRL IN THE HOLE as her head pivoted above the mud, hidden in the tangle of field grass. Lulia squirmed in her mother's arms, quiet cries muffled by a pacifier.

Geri quietly circled in front so Rachel could see her. She offered a concerned smile.

"Thank God! Please help me, something made my boyfriend do this. Now he's gone." Rachel craned her neck, eyes wild with desperation. "Have you found him? His name is James. Call the police, we need help. Please get me out!"

"I'm afraid he went crazy. He attacked my son."

Geri spoke softly as she cuddled Lulia.

"His rage was frightening. He's obsessed with nonsense and tore into the woods. I've never witnessed a true psychotic break. I hope he gets the help he needs. We're all so worried."

"What are you talking about? Please get me out. I've got to find him." Her teeth chattered and tears left trails down her cheeks through speckles of mud.

Geri surveyed her burrow. "You're needed exactly where you are. I recognize it isn't pleasant, but you may be injured. You need to share your truth with the police. They need to see what he's done; they'd never believe it otherwise. Can I get you some water?"

Rachel looked up in shock and then screamed as loud as she could. When the echo fell silent, all that lingered was the rustle of the meadow. "Help, police!" came out as a whimper.

Geri waited for a hush to take hold and then spoke quietly.

"No one can hear you; no one can see you. You're alone in the middle of nowhere with field grass swaying above your head. Screams don't carry far."

Rachel's face froze in horror, and her eyes darted wildly as a snarl arose from somewhere behind her head. Snorts and rapid breaths came to her, step by step, and then an animal sniffed her hair. She felt her whole body shiver in the cool, clammy earth.

"Get it away from me, please, whatever it is," she whispered. "I beg you."

"Of course."

Geri stomped toward the beast, shrieked, and chased after it, all the while clutching her bundle tight. The woman crashed through the reeds and disappeared from Rachel's line of sight.

"Are you crazy? Where are you going? You can't just leave me!" Rachel cried out as she found herself alone again, sobbing beneath the windswept stalks that still sprayed droplets.

Dozens of feet away and out of earshot, Geri caught up to the creature hidden in the grass. She got closer, and it circled near her feet.

"Radu told me you'd learned. I've been most curious." Geri stooped down with Lulia held tight. "An excellent demonstration, but I want to see you properly before we go on."

The badger understood and wended his way through the tangle. A few moments later, Andrei's smooth, athletic form rose above the meadow. He held up a hand in greeting and beckoned her over.

When she reached him, Geri tilted the bundle and wiped a dewy sheen from the infant's face. "Let me introduce your sister, Lulia." She was sleeping, and Geri gently withdrew the pacifier. "Soon we'll be a family again."

Andrei smiled and stroked her cheek. "Nice to meet you, Lulia."

"You'll take her inside," Geri said, standing to face him. "First, tell me what happened."

Andrei surveyed the meadow. "The mortals are planted."

"You've done well. But something went wrong. Show me."

Andrei nodded and then silently strode toward his captive in the grass, with Geri and Lulia close behind. They made it to the second pit where James stared out from his muddy perch. His eyes followed Andrei and he brightened as the witch came close to stoop beside him.

"We're connected and he's not in pain."

Geri studied James's athletic body splayed across the hole. "He was yours. Why didn't you kill him? What were you thinking? I want to understand what went wrong."

Andrei gently pressed James's crooked neck to check his pulse. "I agree it seems I should have. My father dispatched his father to avenge a past humiliation. His mortal son, in turn, sought revenge. But in the end I couldn't do it."

Geri focused on her son's face. "Why?"

Andrei's eyes turned dark, and he shuddered as he stood from James's side. His features hardened in the gray light of shifting clouds as the storm cleared away.

"Our connection is strong, even now. There's empathy. You don't ever feel that?"

Geri's lips were tight, and she nodded slowly. "Of course, but out of necessity it's something you grow out of."

"With him I can't. He's my first, my Siamese twin. That's what I feel. How could I kill him? His emotions infuse me and he likes when I'm there."

Geri watched him warily. "Don't be naive, Andrei. The spell does it. He doesn't really care about you."

"There's a bond I didn't expect that he can't fake. And it spins fuel; there's desire."

"That's how it goes at first. You're new to this and confused."

"I don't want anything more. A kill would be gluttonous."

"Cravings swell over time. You'll learn when this burns out next week. Meanwhile, fuel from a kill replenishes for months. Are you getting enough?"

"I'm pumped and tingling with what already came through. I can hardly think straight."

Geri touched his shoulder.

"As time wears on more essence is required; a kill for the same effect. Such is the plight of our coven, the poisoned gift of black magic."

Andrei bent to touch James's cheek and their eyes locked. "It is a poisoned gift."

"It's our longevity balm against hell." Geri studied him as he stood. "Whatever you ignited certainly seems to have charged you for what's ahead. Your trial is not a failure."

James swiveled toward his mother.

"There's one thing more. The demon disappears when I go inside him. I feel the pressure release and calm. Maybe that's what I like so much."

"And that's what we must focus on. Travis and the danger he's put you in."

They faced off silently as the wind shifted, and Rachel's sobs wafted toward them.

"James, is that you?" she called out. "Anyone? You can't just leave me. Who's there?"

Andrei looked in Rachel's direction and then back at Geri.

"She's ready for you. The cords are strong." Andrei extended his palm toward Rachel. "Now she's yours." He eyed James. "His mother is now my father's."

"You've learned the foundations well."

She beckoned Andrei close to take the bundle. "Bring your sister inside; spend some time. Prepare yourself mentally for the trouble ahead."

Andrei held Lulia close. He studied her face for a moment and then turned to Geri.

"What's to become of Travis? He doesn't know about me."

Her emerald eyes narrowed. "You have the advantage of surprise. He'll be arriving soon."

She paused to survey the Malloy house, and the acreage behind it. "If he surrenders and joins us, he'll gain access to Lulia. But he will need to prove his fealty. And his ability to cure you."

Andrei looked up. "And if he doesn't?"

"You'll need to drill another hole."

Geri watched as Andrei nodded and started across the meadow with Lulia in his arms.

Beyond the meadow, wind rustling branches heavy with wet leaves picked up and overtook Rachel's sobs somewhere in the grass.

FORTY-SIX

PAULA STARED AT HERSELF in the mirror. With a fingertip, she traced the thin lines at the corners of her eyes. *I look like a crazy woman. Why are my eyes so red? I ache and creak and feel jet-lagged. I need to start everything over. How do I go back?* She tilted her head and put a drop of Lumify in each eye. She clenched them for a moment and relished the coolness.

Why am I standing here? She appraised her makeup attempt in the warm light of the bathroom mirror. *Oh right, I have to look my best; it's the last thing they'll remember.* She applied a touch more matte mauve to her lips and smacked them together.

A flash of panic didn't like the fuss.

This isn't right; it's Saturday afternoon.

But the anxiety flare-up ebbed, and she drifted back into the safety of her bedroom.

Paula explored the closet and honed in on a target remarkably fast. She plucked out the black slip dress that fell just below her knees. *I always feel good in this, elegant and modern and just enough.* The hanger dropped, and when she bent to grab it, the panic flashed again.

Something bad is happening.

She pulled the dress over her bra and panties and did a quick spin in the mirror. She felt detached but distinctly driven toward a prize that tempted from behind a red velvet curtain. What it was didn't even matter. The thrill of discovery was everything.

I'm finally living in the moment.

Another flash of panic.

There's a man downstairs. He shouldn't be here.

But again her unease abated, the flicker of awareness extinguished like a flame. She lifted her hair and let it spill over the spaghetti straps. *At least I feel a shred of happiness.* She dug out a bottle of Chanel No. 5 and spritzed her décolletage. *Wait, do I? Am I going somewhere?* She stubbed her toe on the leg of the bureau. *Shoes! I can't go around barefoot.* She ambled to the rack in the closet and after a longer deliberation than before selected black leather pumps.

From the edge of the bed, Paula shimmied into the shoes. She stood and surveyed the head-to-toe look, and a fresh pulse of panic flared when she realized she had no idea what came next.

Why am I dressed for dinner or a funeral?

All at once, fragments from her dream in the closet flooded in and she collapsed on the mattress. She remembered there were witches about and realized her heart was racing.

Katherine was right about the wraith in the woods, and Travis sent her. Aaron's drowning was no accident; a witch got him. And that's on me because I linked us to Travis in the first place. The stranger downstairs wants to help me. That's why he's here.

Now she knew what to do.

She approached the stairs and tiptoed down, straining to listen for the man's whereabouts. She peeked into the kitchen. The skillet she'd used to prepare eggs and Canadian bacon dripped in the strainer along with the mugs. The notepad and pen were centered on the empty table.

"Paula?" A voice from the living room called out.

She wandered toward the sound and found Radu spread-eagled on the hardwood floor in front of the couch.

"Is everything OK?" Paula asked as she click-clacked in, fresh, nicely scented, and fancy.

He shimmied himself up on his elbows as she entered and smiled. "You look nice."

He watched her for a moment and then lay back down. "My back's bad, and I beg your help. There isn't time to heal on my own. I need to handle Travis *today.*"

Paula's lips pursed as she studied him. "I saw what he did to Katherine."

Radu motioned to her to come closer. "It's time to learn all about him. You'll understand the urgency. Your contribution to his surrender will far outweigh the cost."

Paula perched on the seat cushion and leaned over to take him in. She felt a twinge of excitement when their eyes met. This stranger in her house was not just sexy and mysterious, but also at her mercy. What wasn't to like? Anxiety poked and prodded and sounded an alarm, but she shooed it away. Buzzkill. A soothing voice entered in its wake.

Fear holds us back.

She was living her best life like they want you to do in magazines.

"You look great; I'll say it again." Radu smiled and held her gaze. "Elegant and prepared for the journey ahead."

She enjoyed watching his thick lips pucker and shift as he spoke.

"Where are we going?"

"Just downstairs, but far enough to escape the misery wrought by Travis."

"Why do you hate him so?" Her eyes narrowed, and she was transfixed by his.

"He humiliated me and has placed my son in mortal danger."

Paula paused to consider the dream. "Katherine was tortured in the woods."

Radu nodded, and his jaw tightened. "Now you know about him."

Paula took a deep breath and exhaled slowly. "What makes you any different?"

"I've come to clean up his mess." His thin, black eyebrows arched. "Travis came here, to Sussex, to advance his family magic, and leased the Malloy house for its isolation."

She watched with fascination as he paused, the hard angles of his face sharp yet smooth.

"You were pulled into his orbit by the bad fortune of proximity. He seduced you as a diversion, a personal experiment, and in doing so, he pulled in your whole family."

Paula took in the shadow play on his face, fascinated that his eyes seemed to darken.

"Last night you witnessed Katherine's ordeal, what drove her to hide in the closet. I needed you to see for yourself, otherwise you'd never believe it."

Paula closed her eyes and came to a conclusion. "He subjected her to that torment."

Radu nodded and a tight smiled formed dimples. "Travis also entangled James and Rachel and their two friends. His experiments are reckless. We all need to stop him." He winced as he forced himself to sit, and a deep breath shuddered as he slowly pulled it in. "And I need your help before we all wind up dead."

Paula flinched and stiffened on the sofa edge for a moment before leaning in close again.

"How can I save us?"

His gaze was trained on her. "We need to amplify your essence, to maximize potency. It's how we replenish power. Then I can restore myself and be strong enough to finish this."

"Essence?"

"DNA in small doses, the life force itself in large ones." His eyebrows raised with the hint of a smile. "My son will die otherwise. It's the only way to save him."

Paula gasped and covered her mouth.

"James and Rachel are in up to their necks."

Paula's eyes filled with tears. She blinked long and hard and then rejoined his gaze. "Don't let him get my children."

"I need the strength to kill if Travis fails to fix this mess."

"What do I do?"

Radu strained forward, eyes black and cheeks hollow. "Will you help me up?"

Paula nodded but hesitated before rising from the couch.

What is this madness? Can I help a witch?

A stabbing pain singed behind her right eye, and she yelped.

"You needn't worry. I will make it all so easy for you, pleasurable even."

She waited for the sting to subside, and somehow recognized that resistance would bring pain. She got up and shuffled behind him. A glimmer of reason coaxed her to obey. It was little more than an inkling, but she went with it, this shred of herself. She stooped down and wriggled under his arms.

"Tell me what's next."

Radu guided her hands in front and their fingers locked. She lifted from behind with her arms wrapped around his chest until they were both standing in front of the picture window.

Paula almost pulled away, but it felt nice to have her arms around him. He smelled of pine and peppermint, smoky yet cool. Euphoria rushed in from somewhere, everywhere.

"You feel nice." She heard her words slip out with the earnestness of a drunken lover.

What followed cooled and soothed like ice crystals bobbing in deep, brisk river rapids.

I honestly want you to enjoy this.

Radu clasped her hands, and they took slow steps past the coffee table. Paula held tight, legs pressed behind his in lockstep across the room. In the hallway, she swiveled to one side and opened the door to the stairs.

They took them one by one, Radu managing with both hands on the banister.

Already your essence flows.

In the basement, Paula guided Radu to an oversize chocolate-brown leather couch. He lay back with an impish smile. Why did he look so appealing? Such a charming witch.

And now it begins.

Paula recognized temptation lay on the couch but had to let it simmer a bit. Something on the punch list couldn't wait. Without a word, she turned toward the stairs and marched up. She made it to the back door of the kitchen and froze for a moment in front of the screen.

A breeze wafted in, and raindrops pattered on the driveway, flowing in rivulets down the blacktop. She waited and stared and wondered what came next.

That's when the glimmer flashed again.

I need to run from the witch.

A stab behind her eye squelched the notion, and an instant later the rebellion evaporated into an epiphany. She knew exactly what to do.

Where does Aaron stash the rope?

Paula pushed herself out the door and into the drizzle toward the storage shed.

FORTY-SEVEN

THE ORB WAS RESET WITH essence and purpose. Travis needed to expel the demon. It would be his last chance to save Andrei and to salvage the promise of his parents' magic. He hated not knowing if the boy were friend or foe, especially after months of caring for him. Betrayal scalded everywhere. Even his magic burned. He had no idea if it would work at all.

He'd slept in spurts, though mostly dreamless, nothing supernatural. Maybe that meant Radu was still staggered? That would be a good thing.

A dreary morning hadn't inspired early action. It was mid-afternoon before he and Sorinah headed for the other side of town. Water pooled on the windshield when they turned the wipers off and parked in front of the Malloy house. Travis's backpack held the globe and a butcher's knife, padded with a few hand towels.

"I've come to renounce my ancestral magic because I've been misguided," Travis robotically recited as they climbed out of the car. He shot Sorinah a look. "That's our plan."

"And then what?" Sorinah scowled and slammed the door.

"They know I want Lulia, and Geri isn't opposed, or she wouldn't be here. I've already defeated Radu, but he still wants my acquiescence. Perhaps he's right about my family magic. My best defense is to free Andrei."

"What if he's a threat?" Sorinah glanced over the hood of the car.

Travis's face tightened as their eyes met. "He's the wild card. I'm sure he's here. We'll see how deeply he factors in. I'd like to believe Radu is the rot and still flattened in the grass."

They sloshed through puddles as they crunched the gravel drive and curved around the house to the back. Travis's nostrils flared as he steeled himself for an attack, senses peeled for any flash of movement or scent of a witch. They crept forward, and as they rounded the corner, Travis froze and grabbed Sorinah's arm, motioning toward the shed.

"It's the tree planter from the cemetery four years ago." His eyes raked over the tractor and the drill poised above it. "It shouldn't be here. And there's no sign of Radu."

Sorinah scanned the grounds and then silently pointed at a patch of black peeping through the shifting grasses in the meadow.

Travis licked his lips and nodded. "Let's go."

He took her arm, and they started across the soggy lawn before plunging into the waist-high thickets. They crunched through the overgrowth until they reached their target: an oasis of trampled grass matted with a ring of mud. And in the center James was splayed out over a circular pit, black nylon gym shorts wedged into the hole, knees bent over a mound of dirt, head cocked sideways with eyes wide and mouth agape. Mud speckled his light brown hair.

"James!" Travis got close and touched his forehead. "Can you hear me?"

His expression was blank and he blinked his eyes as they seemed to follow. Travis checked his pulse and breathing. Then he planted his knees in the mud and briskly rubbed the exposed skin of James's arms and thighs. "Can you feel anything? Can you see me?"

A contented stare was the answer, with another blink.

"He's entranced and I don't like his neck," Sorinah said as she stood behind Travis and surveyed the scene.

"I'm afraid to move him. What should we do?" His words trailed into a whisper, almost to himself.

"We wait until the spell breaks. Then we'll know more."

Travis gripped James's jaw and swiveled his head gently side to side to test for resistance or a flinch, but he flopped like a rag doll.

"I put him at risk, along with his family. It wasn't supposed to be this way. It's not what my parents intended. I can't control anything anymore."

Sorinah exhaled slowly and squeezed his shoulder. "Another witch is to blame for this."

His sharp features turned hard, dark, and sullen. "My experiments marked them. Why did I grant Radu mercy? This is his doing; I should have killed him."

He reached up and took her hand. For a moment they were still, eyes glued to James.

Sorinah could see his sadness, so she nervously cleared her throat, then whispered.

"We are not all bad, just as pure goodness scarcely exists. Like storms, we amplify the value of contentment because it never lasts. Pleasure and peace are fleeting for all creatures; it is a law of nature. We are part of that plan, and our path will clarify when we complete the cycle we've started, right here, on this ground. Steel yourself, there's important work to do."

The breeze shifted and the drizzle had slowed to a silent spray. But then the somber stillness was broken by faint and intermittent sobs. They froze and held their breath, eyes darting.

A hoarse voice wafted from somewhere in the grass. "Is someone there?"

Travis locked eyes with Sorinah, and they both jumped to attention.

"Rachel?" Travis called out.

The answer came quick. "Yes, I can hear you! I'm buried in muck. Please, help me!"

"We're coming!" Travis called out, and they pushed through the tangle toward her voice.

They honed in on her panting and scanned for another notch in the meadow. When they got close, they spied her head bobbing side to side on a neck craned skyward.

Travis raced in front and kneeled down while Sorinah stood guard behind them, scanning the grounds.

"You're safe now. I'll get you out." Travis gently traced her cheek. "Are you hurt? Is anything broken?"

"Thank God, no. I don't think so. Have you seen James? He's missing."

Travis glanced back at Sorinah, and then turned to Rachel and shook his head. He wasn't equipped to offer information, not yet.

"Who did this to you?"

"James did. He went crazy!"

Rachel's face flushed, and she broke down, struggling to catch her breath between words. "He pushed me in and filled dirt all around. I can't get out! It was like he was possessed. I couldn't stop him."

"Did he say anything?" Travis started to pull soil away from below her chin.

"He said it was just to hold me." Rachel's eyes were wild. "He was talking nonsense and spouted more about the hawk. And then he disappeared, and I heard him yell. It sounded like a fight."

Travis's eyes grew dark and narrowed. "With whom?"

"A guy named Andrei lives here with his father. He was drilling a hole when we arrived, then James took over. He got obsessed with graves and Sophia and then threw me in." Rachel sucked down a deep breath. "Then it got weirdly quiet until the tractor drove away. I think James ran off to hunt the hawk, maybe to get his gun from home. I tell you he was possessed."

Rachel's head rocked spasmodically, and it seemed she would hyperventilate, but then she whispered, "I can't believe he did this. It wasn't really him. It's this place."

Travis dug into his backpack and grabbed a hand towel. He gently wiped Rachel's face.

"A while later a woman came by holding a baby, but strange."

"Strange how?"

"She was pretty and nicely dressed, but not for a farm in a field in the rain."

Travis did what he could with the towel and packed it away to start digging.

"She said James attacked Andrei and then ran off to hunt the hawk. She wouldn't help me, as if being buried like this is nothing. Everything's off, like a cult, or it's haunted; it's true. She said I am evidence for the police. She said they're on the way to catch James."

"Shh, shh," Travis said and pulled handfuls of dirt away from her neck. "What happened next? Take your time."

Rachel composed herself. "A slathering animal came out from the grass and sniffed me. Thank God she chased it away. Then I heard voices, so others are around, but the police never came." She screamed the last part. "Please help me!"

Travis wriggled his palms between Rachel's shoulders and the wet earth, and attempted to reassure her with a few firm pulses. "First I'll free your arms." He turned to Sorinah to enlist her help and recoiled.

"*La naiba!*" He spat the curse out between clenched teeth.

"What?" Rachel's face froze.

"Damn, damn, damn."

Travis's heart raced as he watched Sorinah drift toward the Malloy house, halfway across the meadow, tips of her shoes grazing the top of the grasses. He jumped up and back from the hole, eyes dark and narrow.

"I've got to step away. You won't be abandoned—I promise— stay strong." Travis spoke without turning to Rachel and plunged after Sorinah.

"No!" Rachel shrieked. Then came a whisper. "Please don't leave me. I can't take it anymore."

"You have to hold on," Travis called out already halfway across.

Travis raced as Sorinah hovered above the lawn behind the Malloy house. Her arms were stiff with fists clenched by her sides, legs dangling uselessly.

The backdoor from the kitchen opened, and Travis watched as Geri sauntered down the stairs, arms spread wide as if to receive Sorinah in a sloppy, sisterly hug.

"Don't touch her!" Travis shouted as he strode onto the lawn.

Geri lowered her arms and extended her palms.

"Calm yourself, Travis." She smiled and came within reach of Sorinah as she floated.

"I had to bring you closer. I didn't want to startle you in the grass, and trudging through it is so unpleasant, especially after the rain."

Travis seethed as he caught up and stood next to Sorinah.

"Release her." His eyes channeled his fury, red-streaked chunks of obsidian. He squeezed Sorinah's hand, and she blinked furiously to acknowledge his touch.

"All in good time," Geri cooed. "I need to take a temperature reading. Hot? Cold? Indifferent?" Her brow furrowed as she took them in.

"James is paralyzed, and Rachel's buried up to her neck. Anything you might offer to mitigate my rage had better come quickly." Travis felt a bolt coiled to spring but forced himself to truss it. He folded his arms and gripped himself, muscles taut.

"We all need restraint." Geri exhaled deeply and shifted her eyes to Sorinah. "I will make you more comfortable. Please excuse the precaution." Geri lowered her to the grass, and Sorinah stumbled as she regained her footing. "I wanted to greet you when you arrived, but before I knew it, you were chest-deep in the meadow." She swiveled toward Travis. "You instigated this by disabling Radu. It all comes back to you."

Travis shook his head as he scoffed, "I didn't instigate a thing. He lured me here, and tried to kill me. I defended myself, and broke him. I should have gone further."

Geri's face was as pristine as porcelain. "He admits he got cocky showing off the hawk; the recklessness was foolish. He didn't try to kill you. You have to save his son." Her shift dress billowed in the breeze.

Travis's arms were tensed and straight down his sides as he took a step toward her. "I spared Radu, so he went after the neighbors. He had no right to touch them. They are mine."

"Yours?" Geri's eyes opened wide.

He was livid but the words came steadily. "My mortals, my responsibility, and my business because my magic brought them into this. No harm was ever intended."

Geri locked his gaze. "And Rachel? You were fine four years ago with a tainted ring on her finger and fine with inflicting her friends."

Travis shook his head and scowled. "She was meant to escape unharmed. You know it. Radu intervened and purposely messed things up."

"It turns out your pawns don't escape unharmed." Geri motioned to the meadow.

Travis glared at her. "I spoke to Rachel. It's clear James was under a witch's control. She said Andrei was drilling holes when they arrived."

Geri's straight-edge bangs hung low, but her eyes still were trained on him. "The boy needs to aid his father, whom you nearly killed."

"Radu lied to my face. He told me Andrei was a mortal, adopted as cover." He felt his rage building and forced it back. The heel of his Stan Smith ripped up wet grass.

Geri twisted a bit as she surveyed the grounds. "You weren't able to sniff him out while you held him captive? He was your patient for long enough."

The breeze picked up as grey clouds ceded to streaks of mottled blue.

Travis traded glances with Sorinah.

"Not yet, but I outed Radu." Travis turned and marched to the tree planter, stopped just beside it, and stared at Geri.

"Whose idea was this?"

Geri feigned surprise as if she'd only just noticed it.

"Radu said it was yours from last time, a donation to the town."

Travis glared back. "Andrei's in deep. I'd hoped it wasn't so."

If Geri were lying, her calm didn't betray a thing. She was an expert.

"Andrei merely obeys his father as good sons should."

"He's my patient. I know he's subservient." He knocked caked mud from the drill bit.

"James attacked Andrei who was forced to defend himself."

"And hit him with supernatural force." His words sounded like a threat.

"Andrei beat James in a fair fight." Geri's tone was nonchalant.

"He's in a zombie state."

Geri seemed positively shocked. "A trance or a broken neck?"

Travis's eyes radiated hate but he refused to answer.

She took the silence as an invitation to chime in with more. "James is the wild card here. He attacked Andrei and planted Rachel."

Travis took steps away from the tractor, toward the meadow. "I'm going to free them."

Geri moved toward him. "Not so fast, Rachel is spoken for."

Travis stopped and turned. "What?" The disgust on his face wasn't hidden.

"Her essence is needed."

Geri tossed her hair and smiled.

"You incapacitated Radu, after all. In coven terms, it's quite reasonable. And James is to blame; he buried her. Grief made him snap. And later they'll find him dead, killed by the hawk that got his father. A spooky, small town tragedy. Sadder still, Rachel expired before she could be saved."

Travis held his breath, fully aware he was seething. He strode back to face Geri with his nails digging into his palms, focused on the distraction to restrain himself. Sorinah recognized he was ready to blow and rushed over to squeeze his shoulder.

"They are off limits. What exactly do you want before I free them?" he said.

A soft smile crossed Geri's face.

"It's all so simple. Stop your ancestral magic, for the good of the coven. You are not innocent here. The demon you roused stalks Andrei." She hardened and held his gaze. "You must help him and renounce your family magic. Only then will you gain access to Lulia, and the mortals will be spared."

Travis leaned toward Geri and forced a placid expression as if facing a judge to assert his innocence. "I've already stopped. I never wanted to harm Andrei. I can't explain the intrusion. *I renounce the magic.*"

Geri raised her eyebrows in apparent approval and waited for him to continue.

"The neighbors go free. And the rest stops now."

"Andrei's not so simple," Geri scoffed, "the doctor's patient."

Travis bristled. "I care for him, the feelings are genuine and I believe they are mutual."

Geri shot Travis a look of scorn. "Care for? You used him as fodder to practice your magic, and now he's tainted."

Sorinah stepped forward to intervene. "We accept our part of the blame. The orb experiments will stop. We are in agreement."

Travis couldn't soften his baleful expression as he studied Geri. "I must have access to Lulia, and the neighbors go free now."

Geri no longer looked docile. "What about Andrei and your curse?"

Travis held firm. "I will fix it and reverse it if you'll leave me to it."

Geri shook her head and took a moment to find words. "This doesn't work that way."

No one spoke for a moment, and the stiff wind whistled as it ushered in larger breaks of blue. Geri's tone turned icy along with it.

"You fix him or you die. Can you?"

The turmoil in his eyes matched hers.

"I will give it my all."

"If you fail you die. And that might free him."

"You can't be certain of it." He took a hostile step toward her, fury sharpening his already chiseled features. "And why deprive Lulia of a father in the face of a better option?"

Geri furrowed her brow and glared. "What option?"

"My vow of abstention that already wears thin." Travis didn't flinch.

Geri shot her gaze to the sky and didn't look amused. "I'm not sure that's still on the table. You can barely mask your hostility. I don't believe you can bend."

Travis's chest heaved, and he clenched his fists. He knew he was trembling, and veins on his arms bulged as a bolt smoldered at the launch point.

He forced words forward. "What more do you want? Tell me now before I incapacitate you, free Rachel, and bring James home."

Geri scowled and locked eyes with him. "You need to prove your fealty."

Travis spat on the grass. "How, exactly? I always keep my word, unlike any of you."

Sorinah gasped and gripped Travis's shoulder as she pointed across the driveway.

His eyes trailed the end of her finger and stopped on the Malloy house.

"*La naiba,*" he barked and fought to contain the bolt.

A badger climbing the steeply pitched roof between the dormer windows of the attic pulled a white bundle with its teeth as it backed toward the peak.

Lulia's cries broke the silence as she was dragged along the shingles.

FORTY-EIGHT

PAULA LEFT THE ROPE IN a coil on the kitchen counter, then dried her hands with a towel as she stood in front of the sink. Focus and serenity had finally found her. And now the stranger's face was in the window, a reflection shimmering on glass. There was something magical happening.

I could stare all day.

With his soft smile and a wink, she knew everything was OK. She took the rope and started the slipknot. There was nothing to it.

Aaron taught me when we hung a pumpkin-headed scarecrow for Halloween.

She tested it, and the silky rope pulled through nicely, so she shifted her gaze back to the window. The reflection dissipated as if it had never been, and she knew it was time.

She checked herself in a small mirror on the counter above the junk drawer and gasped.

Is that me? I almost forgot my own face.

She decided she wasn't half bad and it didn't matter anyway so she went to the table with the rope and grabbed a chair with both hands. At the top of the stairs, she hoisted it up and carefully descended to the basement, steady in heels, black dress shifting.

Muted light spilled into the room from rain-flecked windows staggered just below the ceiling. Radu lay where she left him, but his feet were bare, and he'd propped himself up against a pillow sloping from the padded arm of the leather couch.

He smiled and waited for her to bring the chair close to his head so they could talk.

"Let's get the rope in place," was the first thing he said. Creases in his cheeks curved into dimples as he smiled. "The beam is just overhead. And then we can relax."

Relaxing was what she wanted, so Paula mounted the chair and looped the rope over the beam a couple of times. She pulled out the slack and tied it to leave the noose dangling a foot below the beam, and climbed back down, coiling the extra rope on the chair.

"It's dreary outside, but the patter sounds nice." Radu swiveled to his side and nudged back to make room on the cushion in front of him. "We can chat, I'd like to share...."

Paula held her breath and took a seat on the edge.

"...so we can feel closer."

His voice was calm, cool, and soothing, his scent pine and peppermint. The natural, muted light and rain made things cozy. But even so, Paula perched stiffly in front of him, careful not to lean back, careful not to touch, because that might be creepy.

Until a flashback hit her.

"You remind me of Travis," she managed, "the tingling, the attraction."

He shimmied higher on the pillow and waited. "Tell me more."

Paula relaxed, just a bit, just enough to graze his leg. "It's curious he's everywhere again. He was gone for the longest time, as if we'd never met."

His thigh pressed against her back. "All for his convenience."

Paula felt the warm firmness through the sheer fabric of her dress and leaned against it. This sharing was quite interesting. "He was always nice to me. It's odd you hate him."

"Travis believes he's something he's not: a man of virtue." Radu increased the pressure, just a bit. "But he fools himself and others. I'll show you how he does it. Can you picture him?"

Paula closed her eyes, and heard a whisper deep and low, in Romanian. Then came a prickling of excitement with a sprinkling of euphoria. She felt amazing.

"Yes, I saw him yesterday."

"Think back to the first time he seduced you."

She could picture it perfectly, and their positioning mirrored her vision. She was aware of an arm on her shoulder, and then it crossed over, so she slid backward. Good looks and muscle always helped. And then thighs spooned her from behind so she folded into them.

Paula's pulse rate surged along with her arousal.

Relax and recall his touch.

Paula welcomed the vision and didn't wonder where the voice came from. The melding of forgotten memories, sensations, and emotions with this new spin was fascinating.

Think of his body, his smell, his touch.

Paula shifted higher, to nuzzle against his chest, and his arms pulled tight.

Do you think you might want more?

She swiveled to take in his piercing gaze.

It would add another layer, another small victory.

"Why can I hear you?"

A flash of anxiety intruded and when she asked the question pain flared behind her eye.

"Shh, shh," he warned. "We have a connection." His voice cooled the stabs as if they never happened.

When she dared to open her eyelids, the wall with windows across from the couch warped and wavered like a funhouse mirror. She waited, frozen, unsure of what came next.

And then things steadied and she knew. She traced a finger over his lips.

He kissed it.

"I need you to choose," Radu whispered, his eyes locked on her. "Can you still see him? Please, I need to know. This part can't be faked."

Paula closed her eyes and strained to recall Travis's face, his build, the way he touched her, but nothing came.

She opened them, and Radu's enormous, black diamond eyes sparkled.

"He was here a minute ago. Now I can't even picture him; he's gone."

Why?

"You've taken over."

That's how he does it. I told you I'd show you.

"It's quite effective."

She caressed the stubble on his jaw. He flinched as she climbed on top, but already the pain was receding, flush with essence. She probed his chest and began to unbutton his shirt.

We both feel it. The desire is real and catalyzes everything. This part is nice.

Radu pulled her close, pressing his core against her silky dress with slow, rhythmic thrusts. His jeans felt smooth and firm like body armor. One of her hands toyed with the zipper.

Paula leaned in and kissed him, pine and peppermint enveloping her as his thick lips tightened and then expanded to invite a dive as deep as she wanted to go.

FORTY-NINE

TRAVIS WATCHED SORINAH SOAR over him and then hover near the attic dormer windows of the Malloy house, immobilized but able to scream, her caramel hair rippling in the wind.

He struggled to restrain a tempest that roiled inside, primed to launch a bolt to Geri's spine. His gaze darted between his mentor and the animal on the rooftop.

"I wouldn't be rash," Geri said with eyes trained on his grimace, "or Sorinah will drop like a stone and break. I can slam her down hard, as you did to Radu. I'm happy to adopt your simple yet effective technique."

Travis forced himself back, lips curled and teeth bared. "What are your terms?"

A smile tickled her lips. "I want you to choose: Sorinah or Lulia. It's a test of fealty."

"You're mad," he spat. "You're endangering your own daughter."

"Not as long as the beast grips tight and the fabric holds. The choice is yours."

Gravel crunched under his strides toward the house. His words oozed contempt. "You don't deserve to be a mother, and I will ensure you never take Lulia again."

That's when the tree planter parked next to the shed roared to life.

The auger shuddered and began to twist from its perch above the tractor, protruding like a spear and spraying clumps of mud.

Sorinah cried out as her trajectory abruptly reversed and then savagely halted just out of reach of the tip of the whirling drill. Her whole body rocked with the jolt and her neck snapped back as if rear-ended.

"Your daughter and a future with the coven…or Sorinah." Geri shouted with her gaze trained skyward. "Choose. You don't have long to decide."

Travis watched as the badger dragged his daughter toward the gabled roof peak with backward steps and jaws clamped on the edge of the white blanket. Her wails fought against the rumble of the engine.

Travis raced to the tractor and grabbed the controls. He knew the console well enough from his previous journey and tried to thrust the drill into the ground, but the lever and kill switch froze. He jumped down and locked his gaze on Sorinah, who looked stricken as her levitating body tottered toward the auger.

With all his strength he probed for Geri's invisible tentacles, fixated on them, and tried to repel them. Her intrusion blocked his normal pathway to connect with Sorinah, but he pressed against the barrier. He'd soaked in Sorinah's aura for decades; they were like family.

Grab my thread. He poked sharply until he felt his thrust pierce like an arrow through a seam between logs in a drawbridge. His strike penetrated just enough to ignite a reflexive response, and something deep inside Sorinah latched on. Geri cursed as Sorinah lurched in midair. Travis dug in deeper and repeated over and over: *Grab my thread.*

He felt a charge when Sorinah's energy locked on his.

Their union attacked Geri's invasion like antibodies on a virus. As they repelled Geri's tendrils, Sorinah wobbled near the drill point, but then plunged and shuddered to a halt just above the gravel. When Geri's hold broke, Sorinah swiveled to stand unassisted in front of the tree planter.

Geri seethed and curled her hands into claws at her sides.

"And so you have chosen."

Travis and Sorinah watched as she turned her attention to the Malloy house. Lulia shrieked as the creature dragging her disappeared over the roof ridge, and she tumbled over the peak and out of sight.

"You're mad," Travis said, "but I'm calling your bluff."

Geri turned and sneered at Travis. "You just sacrificed all rights to your daughter."

Travis's eyes were wild, and without a sound, he shot to the other side of the house. From the front lawn, he scanned the roof. There was nothing, so he raced to the bushes below the eaves and probed the grounds. There wasn't a trace of his daughter, not even a broken branch.

He circled back around, his senses strained for clues. Geri and Sorinah were exactly where he'd left them. He realized he was seething and needed a clearer head.

Geri raised her eyebrows and smirked as he approached. "So what's become of Lulia?"

"I'm betting you know exactly where she is," Travis scoffed. "The danger was faked, you can't fault my choice. It was a false test."

"One that you failed." Geri's expression went cold, and her eyes narrowed.

"Did I?" Travis folded his arms as he stepped closer. His chest heaved, and he dug his fingers into his biceps to help contain his rage.

"You've failed to honor your ancestors and used family magic to endanger your sole heir. The witches' pact is broken and you failed as a mother. You've betrayed your own blood, the one who would inherit and advance what the ancestors entrusted to you. A supreme duty has been squandered and it carries supreme shame."

"Save your moralizing," Geri spat; her face was flushed with anger. "You know nothing of which you speak. I've made sacrifices only a mother can make."

"You faked a miscarriage." Travis sucked in a deep breath and held it before continuing. "You deprived me of my daughter. Lulia does not know my face, my touch, or my protection. You betrayed us both, and nothing you can say will rectify it."

"Your hubris requires a correction I'd hoped to avoid, but your eyes must open." She trained her gaze on Travis and faced him squarely. "Radu is my husband, and we've been married all along. I was never killed in a crosswalk; that much is obvious."

Travis stiffened and shook his head. "You were married even during our contract and your pregnancy?"

"Yes," Geri said, "even while you conjured wraiths here in Sussex. When you returned to the coven in Bucharest, my death was faked, and the plan was put in motion."

"Why?" Travis fought to focus and to steady a rush of wooziness.

"Because of the humiliation and pain you caused him. Because of the danger you pose to all of our futures. He opened my eyes to it after his visits from the demon while in seclusion. I later witnessed his mastery of a brand new power: the hawk, the disguises."

Geri turned and pointed toward the forest beyond the meadow.

"Radu was instructed to return here to complete the cycle. We knew you wouldn't renounce your family magic without a fight, because your survival depends on it. Getting you back here required the deceptions."

Travis stoically studied her face. "It doesn't excuse your reckless mothering."

"It doesn't?" Geri snorted and shook her head. "You know nothing of the sacrifice it takes to withdraw from a family, to pretend to disappear, even temporarily."

"You abandoned Lulia?" Travis's eyes were wild.

"Not Lulia," Geri said and seemed to gauge his capacity to hear more. "Andrei is our son. I had to abandon him and Radu completely for the duration of our contract. I had to stomach you as our son's therapist even as you prepared to use your magic on him."

Travis couldn't find words and for a moment focused on the shifting clouds. Geri and Sorinah watched him and waited.

"He told me he was an orphan, a gypsy. I was trying to help him after losing two mothers."

"He's very convincing and quite gifted. He's already mastered Radu's new tools: disguising and shifting right along with his father." Geri pointed to the roof of the Malloy house. "Lulia was never in danger because she was in her step brother's care."

He forced himself to control the rage that would be lethal, exhaling slowly and scanning the grounds for any sign of the half-siblings that had disappeared over the roof.

"Where is Andrei now? And where is Radu? I deserve to see them face-to-face. I came here to foreswear my ancestral magic and to focus on saving Andrei. I am Lulia's father and have contractual rights. This betrayal goes beyond my ability to parse. I want them to face me. Where's my daughter?"

His face was dark and cold and hard and fixed on her.

And then she faded away to nothing.

A ring of fire sprang to life, spanning the width of the gravel drive and encircling Travis and Sorinah with a searing heat that radiated from the dancing orange flames.

Travis cursed and strained to look beyond the trap.

A few moments later, Geri emerged from the shed with a bucket in one hand, and Lulia in the other as if attending to errands.

She approached and stood on the grass, a safe distance from the flames.

"The ring will hold you until we are prepared to manage you. Andrei is watching and waiting and strengthening his resolve. Now that you know, he wants to see you, which galls me considering what you did to him, but he's more sensitive than I might like, a whelp. Radu will soon be fully replenished. He will join us shortly to accept your surrender. And to force you to save his son, or die."

She turned and started toward the meadow.

"Rachel?" Travis shouted. "Rachel!"

He waited a moment, but the only sound was the breeze in the trees, and the crackle of smoldering gravel. A mist rose from the flames.

He watched Geri's march to the meadow through gaps in the blaze and called after her.

"Rachel is under my protection; she's not his."

Geri stopped and turned, her voice echoing across the meadow grass.

"The girl's despair has ripened to potency. It is not against you, rather it is because of you that she was marked."

And then Geri went to Rachel.

FIFTY

RACHEL IMAGINED SHE HEARD someone call her name somewhere in the distance, but by now she couldn't separate reality from illusion. She was hungry and cold, and no one was coming. She realized that now; she would die here. Somehow the acceptance helped. Her teeth chattered, and when spasms of panic shook her, she wasn't sure words even came out.

"James?"

She held her breath and listened. It seemed the skies were clearing on a shifting wind, but now the breeze carried the soft cry of a baby.

Is that even real?

She'd steeled herself against madness by drifting into a daydream where none of this was happening. It was the only way to calm the shivers.

James didn't do this to me. He hasn't gone crazy because it wasn't really him.

She imagined she was floating in a mud bath on the banks of the Dead Sea. She'd never been there, but she could dream.

I'm completely still and meditating, and the mud warms my skin. The sun's breaking through, and I open my eyes to find James lying beside me, tanned and smiling. I doze off and when I awake, he's gently digging me out. Then we float together in turquoise, salty waters. He kisses me and holds me close and promises never to vanish again. Please, James, please.

A crunch in the meadow snatched Rachel from her reverie, and her eyes popped open. She scanned the grasses and gasped as the woman with the baby reappeared.

"Thank God you came back. Why would you leave me? Where are the police?"

Geri stepped into the clearing around Rachel's head and knelt on the matted grass in front of her, holding Lulia close. She rested the bucket beside them.

"I'm sorry, thing's got messy after James went crazy. The police are still looking."

Rachel's eyes were wild. "What's happened? Is he OK?"

Geri exhaled slowly and shook her head. "It's anyone's guess; all we can do is hope."

"Then, please help me. If you dig out my arms, I can do the rest." Rachel's eyes pleaded with the woman, who seemed perplexed. "Use the bucket."

Geri lifted the infant and whispered in her ear. She paused and then lay the bundle gently on the matted grass. Her eyes were trained on Rachel's as she chanted in a foreign tongue.

"What's happening? You're all insane." Rachel sobbed and squeezed her eyes closed. She scrambled for the Dead Sea and almost got there but her lids popped open when the woman answered.

"The potent milk of your essence shall nourish us both."

The witch stood and with both hands carefully placed the bucket over Rachel's head, and pressed it down.

"Essence primed is essence divine, flush with fear."

Rachel's screams were muffled under the plastic.

FIFTY-ONE

AS THEY PRESSED TOGETHER, swollen with rapture, Paula felt Radu's coolness stream down her throat and into her lungs as she inhaled deeply. She couldn't pull away and didn't want to. She held his breath inside for as long as she could, savoring the indulgence.

The vapors ease your departure from a mortal shell, and desire sweetens the journey. Let them infuse and transport you. Surrender to the pleasure. Melt into the inevitable.

Radu's lips were chunky and luscious and oscillated with just enough pressure to keep Paula hooked and nursing greedily as if the fount could dry at any moment. She was aware her fingers massaged him, but her focus remained fixed on his mouth and the intoxicating tingle of pine and peppermint.

He leaned forward and swiveled to sit while holding the suction. Paula moved in unison with his advance as he held her, and she took another deep drink.

We are both ready.

Paula felt herself nod while fastened tight, gulping him down.

Pleasure is fleeting. Our journey must continue.

Paula was sure it should. "I don't want this to end."

That's why it's so intense and precious. It cannot last.

"Maybe this time it will."

Would you like it to?

She certainly did and pressed closer.

"Why would it stop?" She pulled back and looked into his eyes. "What can we do?"

You can join me on the inside, forever.

Radu smiled, opened his arms, and lay back. Paula climbed on top of him and through her silky dress felt his arousal thrust against her belly.

Kiss me one last time.

Paula propped herself up, held his gaze, and then leaned in. The rush made her woozy as they rejoined. She wanted it all to last, this feeling, the excitement, his attention, and that taste.

Essence primed is essence divine, flush with desire.

She felt his firm grip on her hips.

This won't be fleeting.

Radu pulled back and locked his eyes on hers. His arms and chest glistened, moist and smooth, and packed his open shirt. He caressed her chin.

I will always carry a part of you. Will you join me?

Paula nodded. She would join anything he wanted.

Get into position quickly; it is time.

Paula knew what to do. She swiveled her legs to stand, and grabbed the back of the chair to jump up. At some point she'd lost her shoes, and the soles of her bare feet felt the length of rope coiled on the seat.

Radu swiveled sideways to watch as Paula positioned the slip-knot over her neck.

Your essence, Paula, changes everything.

Paula reached up and felt for slack in the rope. She glanced down at Radu, who lay on his side with eyes trained on her, deep-set, black, and bottomless.

Aaron's essence was spent against Travis.

Anxiety prodded Paula and took her by surprise. Aaron?

The chair wobbled under Paula's feet, and she clung to the beam.

James's essence fuels my son.

She froze to concentrate on his words. James?

And his fusion with yours will be unstoppable when I finish what's been started. Now, Paula!

A guttural moan marked his climax and a break in his restraints. Her anxiety shoved her through the crack she detected all at once.

Instead of kicking out the chair, Paula threw off the noose and leaped to the couch. A fire flared behind her eye as she grabbed the coil of rope and wrapped it twice around Radu's neck, forcing him to his stomach, and jumping on his back. She yanked it up with both hands, leveraging force with her feet dug into the base of his spine. She trembled as he rocked to buck her off, his arms uselessly trapped under his torso. He slammed her into the wall behind the couch, but she steadied herself against it, pressing down on his back, pulling as hard as she could as he gasped for air.

Reason surged in from wherever it had been barricaded, and Paula stomped on his ribs with one heel, keeping her other foot planted on his tailbone as he heaved and retched on the cushions. She felt his resistance weaken and wrapped more rope around her hands to take up the slack. His legs kicked frantically, and she stooped low for balance.

She yanked again with complete abandon and something snapped. Radu went limp and collapsed on the couch, toes wilting to the carpet, face in the leather cushion.

Paula wrapped more coils around his neck and hoisted him up, cranking side to side until his head bobbed like a flaccid windsock. She let it drop.

It took a while before she could move, but the glimmer told her to breathe.

She recognized it as a kernel of reason, hers alone, the instinct that saved her.

Paula jumped off the dead witch on her couch and folded into a ball on the floor.

FIFTY-TWO

TRAVIS TACKLED THE BARRIER OF FLAME, but it swatted him back, and he bounced to the gravel with the hair singed from his forearm.

Sorinah rushed over and helped him up. "Save your energy."

"I'm OK. Can you see anything?" Travis rubbed his shoulder and checked his backpack for breakage. The globe was intact.

"She ducked into the grass near Rachel," Sorinah answered and pointed.

The sun dropped lower in the sky, purple and orange streaking the clouds.

"Any sign of Andrei?" Travis craned his neck through breaks in the flames.

"Nothing, and I've been combing the house. He's still hidden."

"We are going to lose Rachel if we don't act fast."

Travis paced the perimeter of their fiery pen, senses straining to detect Andrei. The patient he considered intimate had managed to elude and deceive him and was now at large and dangerous. It burned as much as the flames.

"I don't know what I'm supposed to feel," Travis said as he looked toward Sorinah. "I cared for Andrei, but he played me all along."

"It's called hurt and betrayal," Sorinah whispered, and her lips tightened.

"There's also rage and frustration and regret."

"You're unaccustomed to grief; it's complicated and hard to shake."

There was a pause, and Sorinah watched as he bobbed and weaved to survey the meadow. She came close and took his hand.

"There's too much to process. For now, just compartmentalize the pain and tuck it away. Grief will dull you."

Travis squeezed her hand, steadied himself, and exhaled slowly.

She was right; he needed to focus. He shuffled to the center of the drive where the air was cooler. The flames themselves scorched only when breached, like a deadly electric fence. He took a deep breath, looked up, and noticed the dwindling sunlight. They had to break free. He closed his eyes to attune his senses.

But a shriek from across the meadow popped them open.

He froze and strained to listen, and then, all at once, the flames vanished, leaving only a ring of steam on the gravel. Something, someone, had granted them an opening.

"Rachel!" Travis shouted, and without a second's hesitation they bolted from the driveway onto the lawn. They'd fixated on Rachel's whereabouts and descended on the notch in the meadow concealing her pit. He crept up behind Geri with Sorinah at his side.

Lulia lay on the grass, wrapped in a blanket while Geri bore down on the bucket over Rachel's head. Travis rushed in and grabbed Geri, whisking her up and away from Rachel. Sorinah scooped up the baby and jumped back.

Geri screamed in frustration while fighting the paralysis of his binding spell. Her curses and squirming diminished as he immobilized her in the grass.

Travis dove for the inverted bucket and in a fluid motion pulled it from the mud and heaved it aside. Rachel gulped in deep breaths, eyes wild, and her face dripping sweat.

Travis kneeled in front of her. "We've got you. We'll get you out."

Sorinah sidled next to him with Lulia cradled in one arm.

"That woman..." Rachel trailed off.

Sorinah reached out and gently wiped her face. "It's over now."

Travis leaped up and strode toward Geri.

She struggled against his restraints and found her voice. "Radu has disappeared."

"To where? You had us trapped." Travis towered over her as she writhed in the grass.

Geri's eyes blazed hate. "He needs me; our connection was severed. Let me go!"

Travis leaned closer. "I thought he was here with you."

Geri managed to spit on his leg.

Travis ignored it and scanned the grass. "We're taking Rachel."

Geri's eyes fixed on his and narrowed. "She isn't yours." The hint of a smile curved the edges of her tight lips as a menacing growl stirred in the grass. Travis swiveled and shimmied sideways.

"Watch her!" Travis shouted in Geri's direction. Sorinah jumped up with Lulia and crouched low, coiled like a spring.

Travis trained his ears on the growl as it shifted directions. He veered away from the pit, trying to distance himself from the rest. He took a dozen strides through the tangle.

And then Andrei jumped him.

Pain tracked down Travis's back from claws and teeth like razors. He groped at the beast and thrashed as its jaws sank into his neck. He managed to grab a handful of bristly fur, yanked it with all his strength, and threw the creature across the grass. The badger rolled and recovered in an instant, crouching low with teeth bared and black, beady eyes locked on his target.

Travis marched forward and it pounced again, leaping with superb grace and slashing at Travis's chest before rebounding and plunging into the thicket.

"I'm going after him," Travis shouted as he tore bleeding into the meadow after the trail of crunches and rustles leading toward the Malloy house.

A scream from Rachel echoed across the meadow as Geri leapt and rolled in front of her with a wicked smile.

Sorinah stomped at her head, but Geri swiveled away, jumped

up, and then towered over the trio as Sorinah knelt with one hand behind Rachel's neck, one arm wrapped around Lulia.

Geri's words came measured and calm. "Travis couldn't hold me while under attack, and neither can you while shielding them. Be sensible, and hand over my child."

Sorinah hesitated, but then extended the bundle.

"I have no beef with you, Sorinah. I'd advise you to disappear, and quickly. We will overpower Travis. It won't take long, and there isn't time to dig the girl out."

Sorinah glared and a shadow crossed her face. She scooched in front of Rachel when her whimpers turned spasmodic, and Geri marched away with Lulia.

Travis made it to the lawn behind the house and scanned the grounds and sky. The sun was low and painted a purple and orange backdrop behind wisping, gray clouds that reflected dying light. He pressed the fabric of his shirt into the scratches and bites to absorb the blood and help them clot. Geri caught his eye as she glided across the meadow with his daughter, and he cursed, but it was Andrei he wanted.

A moment later the screen door off the kitchen clicked shut, and Andrei strode down the back steps wearing khaki shorts and a black tank top. As his patient approached, Travis tried to manage his fury and this time smelled the witch. They locked eyes as Andrei planted himself near.

"What's happened to the shy, skinny boy from my office?" Travis clenched his fists and felt the rumblings of a bolt churn in his core. He forced it back. "Your overnight transformation is quite remarkable, not to mention the creature."

"I revealed what you wanted to see." Andrei's piercing gaze raked over his therapist. "We're witches, Dr. Coman. It's allowed."

"How did you do it?" Travis needed to know something that burned. "How did you manage to hide from me?"

"Isn't it obvious?" Andrei folded his arms across a mounded chest. "The power streams from a higher plane than yours. You were never the one in charge. I had to play along."

Travis felt a surge of the emotion Sorinah had warned him about. "Why?"

"You humiliated my father. Isn't that reason enough?" Andrei raised his eyebrows and stared without blinking. "Sons obey their parents. A doctor should know that."

Travis pulled in a deep breath and blew it out slowly.

"We bonded in my office. *That* I know." He shook his head, and turmoil roiled his face. "I am sure you felt it too. Some things cannot be faked."

"I did feel it and was willing to forgive and maybe even tell you everything, but that was before you infected me with the globe." Andrei's voice cracked and his nostrils flared. "And now my father is missing. My connection with him died. I blame you because you broke him."

"He would have healed on his own."

Travis reflexively prodded the sphere in his backpack. He exhaled slowly and fought to keep his tone level.

"And the orb wasn't supposed to harm you. The intent was to uncover your torment so we could work on it. You fed me nonsense about a gypsy mother."

A disappointed look crossed Andrei's sharp features. "I wanted your sympathy. I admit I liked the attention, and I needed the story to hook you. I had to hide my parents."

Travis shook his head almost imperceptibly and didn't say a word.

Andrei watched him and pressed on. "Your magic doesn't care what I said. It grabbed me anyway. There's a demon in the orb, you suspected, but went with it nonetheless."

"I tried to neuter it completely. I am sorry I failed and will do my damnedest to fix you."

"It's too late for apologies." Andrei trained his eyes on Travis. "My father told me about Marku. He died a few weeks after your visit."

Travis stiffened and scowled. "I won't let that happen to you."

"What if you can't stop it?" Andrei's breaths were short and rapid, and his hands flexed by his sides. "Something channels to the Devil."

"I will find a way to undo it." Travis desperately wanted to believe it.

Andrei scoffed. "Meanwhile the demon watches, and I haven't much time."

Travis's heart raced, and he felt detente slipping away. "Let's work together, combine our strengths. We can fix it."

"I'd like to believe you." Andrei steeled himself and planted his legs. "But another look in that globe would make things worse. He's waiting inside." His eyes almost pooled tears. "I need to take matters into my own hands. When you die, your spell dies with you. There's that chance."

"It doesn't always happen." Travis wanted to be more useful alive than dead. "Let's work together, you and your parents."

Andrei's tone went dark. "My father's fallen silent, he's in trouble or dead already." Radu's son inched closer, livid and trembling. "You are keeping me from him. I need to put you down."

"This isn't the answer." Travis clenched his jaw and raised his palms.

"And neither is inaction." Andrei pulled in a deep breath, then stepped back.

"Then let's fix you first."

Travis lowered his arms as their eyes locked.

"Do it for your father. We might not get another chance. I swore I would. I've retooled the orb."

The young witch's brow furrowed, and confusion swept his face. "And if it doesn't work?"

"We try again until it does. I'll share the incantation. We'll all study it."

"No, then we kill you," Geri said as approached from the shadows along the side of the shed. She clutched Lulia to her chest.

Travis grasped the globe through the zippered pouch, and tossed his backpack. He shouted toward Geri. "You told me to free him, and this is the chance."

He checked his temper and looked Andrei squarely in the eyes. "Things are happening fast now. Where's Radu? What happened to James?"

Andrei's tone was calm and quiet. "James is mine, but he's more than just fuel. I like the connection. He's hurt but I keep the pain away."

"Release him." Travis's face was tight and cold.

"I can't."

"Why is that?" The globe started vibrating, and Travis used both hands to steady it.

"When I'm with him the demon quiets." Andrei's gaze was fixed on the orb. "I'm safe inside him, the dread subsides. Even now I'm somehow hidden."

Travis's eyes locked on Andrei. "Then let's do this while you're free."

He stepped toward his patient with the orb at his side.

"It will kill me." Andrei grimaced as he caught sight of color blooming inside the glass.

Travis planted his legs in front of him.

Coils of black light sprang to life within the sphere as he held it with both hands and lifted it higher. The globe shimmered and vibrated as he held it aloft.

"I will draw the demon out," Travis shouted over the crackle. "Work with me to expel it."

Andrei's eyes were fixed on the ultraviolet light, as Geri hurried near with Lulia.

"Get away from him!" she shouted, eyes trained on her son as she froze.

Already Andrei was transfixed and sluggish. He knelt, reached out, and locked his fingers around the crystal ball as he had in the office. His arms trembled as a muted violet glow washed over his face against the amber light of the gloaming.

The young witch's eyes were wide and words came quiet, slow, and forced.

"Get him out of me."

Andrei tilted his head to gaze inside, trembling, locked in.

"He's coming again. I feel it."

Tendons in his neck swelled as he strained to look away but couldn't.

"What kind of a doctor does this?" Geri froze and her lips trembled as she whispered, "What kind of witch?"

Then her son's eyes grew wide, and he stiffened, a look of horror on his face.

"My father is dead."

Andrei wheezed in a breath and blinked slowly.

"He's waiting for me in a cavern."

Geri cried out, but Andrei didn't seem to hear as beads of sweat dripped down his face. His eyes narrowed as he fixated on something deep within the sphere.

"He's calling out, trying to warn me. He's in misery. There are openings between the rocks, holes like windows. He's trapped. He's moaning. He knows I'm looking and doesn't want me to find him."

"Stop this. I beg you!" Geri shouted as she stood close, transfixed.

If Travis heard he didn't respond, he hung on each of Andrei's words.

His patient started again in whispers and breaks.

"I've never heard him cry. I hate it. I need to get to him no matter what. He is staring at the door—"

Andrei gasped and stopped talking for a moment.

"The demon waits behind it. The one from my dream with the face of the Devil. He stands with my dad, but it's me he wants. My dad was not expected. The Devil calls me in that deep voice of echoes. He knows my name. He knows exactly where I am."

Andrei choked and struggled to swallow.

"He sees me, right here, right now. He sees us all. He knows you are here. We have to get away!"

The young witch gagged.

Travis tried to speak, but couldn't form words. If he could cast the demon out, he would, but there was no opening. He had to wait for it; for now he was immobilized. Meanwhile, a potent stream of essence flowed from Andrei and replenished everything.

"It's going all wrong. The Devil just stares, like in the dream. My dad begs him to stop, but now it's time. We all know it."

Andrei groaned, and his lips trembled. And then the boy's eyes rolled up into his head.

The voice that followed was deep with an otherworldly resonance.

"You invited my notice."

Andrei stiffened on his knees, arms locked with the orb in front of his face. His eyes steadied and stared, wide and dark.

Geri screamed and rushed into the black light cast by the sphere. She clutched Lulia with one arm and embraced her son with the other.

Andrei gazed at the globe as if she weren't there, still as a stone sculpture.

That's when Lulia launched up and away from Geri's grasp.

Geri shrieked even as she frantically clawed for the outer blanket that unwrapped and dribbled to the grass.

Travis held his breath as he watched his daughter hover above the shimmering orb.

And then Lulia spoke in the same deep, reverberating voice that escaped from Andrei:

"And now the balance shifts."

FIFTY-THREE

ANDREI KNELT, CHISELED, SMOOTH, and glistening like polished marble, as he held the orb aloft, while Lulia levitated above it. Travis crept as close as he could and pressed against the back of his enraptured patient whose gaze never wavered from the spasmodic flashes inside.

Geri whimpered when the demonic voice again forced through her infant's lips.

"Cycles are slow and winding; evolution spans centuries. I cannot directly intervene, yet slowly gain traction. Only now, in this moment, has the magic advanced enough to recast edicts declared more than two millennia ago. The progress must not be squandered."

When the voice paused, a hush fell over the meadow but for a gusty breeze that shifted gray-tinged clouds in the filtered moonlight.

"For witches born of my disciples, ancestral magic is what ensures survival beyond a mortal lifespan. Replenishing and strengthening power is central to our existence. The impulse to master it is strong because of the allure of earthly delights. As it stands, we have no promise of an afterlife awash with pleasure. There is only tedium and, for some, misery."

Travis watched as Geri crept forward, eyes trained on Lulia. "Please, release her."

For a moment the only response was a crackle of thin lightning bolts bouncing within the orb. Then the voice resumed from the infant's lips. *"Your illumination is required."*

Geri nodded and waited, neck craned upward. She was trembling.

"Magic evolves in increments over generations, and by design, it spawns mutations. The variants break barriers and ensure our survival over oceans of time, strengthening magical threads that bind the coven's core. Stagnation begets extinction."

There was silence, and Lulia's eyes went crimson and blazed toward Geri.

"Why my son? Where is his father?" Geri's eyes were wide, her face stricken.

"The disciple has failed and his son has ripened."

Geri gasped and took a step closer. She grabbed Andrei's arm, but it didn't budge from the orb. "Not my son! What can we do? It is not his time. We have always been loyal."

It seemed a short eternity before the voice again passed through Lulia's lips:

"When the new order begins, they will be free again in a reversal of our misery."

"Yes, tell me what to do!" A flash of hope lit Geri's features.

"Already the magical variant has set our liberation in motion."

Lulia's gaze shifted to Travis.

He dared not to speak and signaled to Geri to remain silent. Secrets from the orb were finally revealing themselves. There might be a chance to bargain.

Lulia levitated calmly, cherubic, seemingly diverted as she hovered in front of him.

"The variant magic modifies the edict I have been bound to for two millennia. It grants me a process to elevate my lower stature under God."

Travis shuddered with a jolt of adrenaline.

"And for the duration, I've been forced into subservience with only ancient tools at my disposal: superstition, cunning, magic, war, hatred, predators, and disease."

Travis pressed his knees into Andrei's back so he might not feel abandoned.

Lulia's fingers brushed the globe.

Travis flinched but was transfixed by her burning eyes.

"The sphere is a portal to my awareness. Your parents uncovered the magical root, and you advanced it."

Travis froze.

"Tarnished souls have always been mine to claim, but they are often shielded."

Travis found his voice. "This was never the intention. The gateway to your awareness is accidental. Nothing in the incantation summons it." His heart raced, and he realized he could scarcely breathe.

Lulia swiveled in midair and glared.

"You don't actually control the threads behind any of it. That is my provenance."

There was a pause broken by the crackle of spasmodic bolts of light within the orb.

"I don't understand your intrusion," Travis managed. "Leave the boy to us."

"Your magic is a key mutation after centuries of evolution. Its root brings my awareness to bear before the mitigating fog that cloaks a mortal's death."

"It hijacks what was mine," Travis whispered almost to himself.

"Your sorcery is crude and complex but grants a veiled path to a new order, leveling unfair advantages."

The ends of Lulia's ivory blanket trailed and rippled on the wind.

"Every soul plucked from heaven dilutes the bias against me. Any soul with traces of evil will enter my sights without the tedious trial that always favors heaven."

Travis clamped his eyes shut.

"With the door to my attention open, there are no pardons or redemption or divine intercession; no fount of forgiveness that turns the other cheek. Heaven thieves souls at my expense. Now a correction begins."

Travis forced himself to interrupt. "My parents, my ancestors, envisioned a more benign means of empowerment, a more peaceful future."

"*It was never benign; that was their illusion.*" The Devil's voice was deeply resonant and firm, but not hostile.

"They were burned alive for their experiments." Travis kept his voice level.

"*And their sacrifice is rewarded.*"

"How?"

"*They were killed for advancing the magic I desired. They have a place near me; they are not in the depths. Fittingly, you have avenged them.*"

Geri cried out. "There must be some mistake! Their magic weakens the coven."

"*Alas, the mistake is yours, coven tradition is myopic.*" Lulia's crimson eyes locked on Geri. "*Their son, Travis, has marked Andrei, the son of Radu, their former oppressor. The sacrifice completes the cycle and enables me to bind the root to the coven's core threads. All replenishments, kills, and controls will invite my notice and my claim to tainted souls. The balance will shift.*"

Andrei groaned and rose to his feet, arms trembling with the sphere as an appendage. Sweat soaked the tank top mesh and dripped off his elbows.

All at once his focus broke from the globe, his eyes wide and focused on Geri.

"And now I join my father," Andrei whispered.

Geri screamed and grabbed his arms, trying to shake the globe free. Her son scarcely moved, grimacing, with legs planted in the grass. Then he hoisted the orb out of reach.

Andrei's neck extended and twisted toward Travis, veins and tendons engorged as he strained against an invisible force. His lips formed words, but nothing came. He sucked down shallow, rapid breaths as his tongue protruded like a purplish, exploring eel.

"Take me instead!" Geri leapt up and swatted at the ball of toxic light. "I offer myself."

Lulia drifted in front of her, the ivory blanket still trailing and ghostly.

"*The sacrifice of a mother,*" the deep voice responded as the infant stared. "*Why would I contemplate such a swap?*"

Geri froze with her eyes locked on her daughter. "He's young and vital and already more powerful than I, a warrior better utilized on earth."

Andrei began to choke and wheeze as his probing tongue snaked and curled. His head tilted grotesquely sideways.

"Please, I beg you!" Geri dropped to her knees and wrapped around Andrei's legs.

Travis watched as the glow in the sphere flickered and sputtered out. The orb flew from Andrei's hands and rolled in the grass as the boy doubled over and gasped for air.

"*A mother's fate foretold.*"

Geri seized up and shrieked. Her expression jolted from elation to misery and froze in the second before her neck snapped sideways with one violent thrust, and she collapsed in a smoldering, decaying heap. Singed fragments from her dress flaked off and sparked in the wind.

Travis lunged above Andrei as Lulia began to totter and then plummeted. He caught her and tumbled to the lawn beside the festering remains of Geri.

Andrei folded to the grass, panting, eyes locked on his mother.

He tried to stand and lurched toward her. "Thank you—"

Cries overtook him as he collapsed and rolled toward her writhing, rotting corpse.

Travis clutched Lulia close as her wails started. At the same time, he scrabbled next to Andrei and placed one hand on his shoulder. Andrei flinched, then melted into it. Travis embraced him with Lulia nestled in between, both step siblings gulping for air.

"She freed you."

"Look what he did to her," Andrei whispered as he pulled away to stare at his mother's remains, her stricken face frozen in terror with teeth clamped down on a blackened tongue. "I can't use his magic; I won't."

"We will find a way to honor her sacrifice."

Travis squeezed his shoulder.

"Try to absorb what's happened. Please, take your sister."

Travis held her out, and Andrei braced against her cries.

"Stay here and stay strong. I will be back soon."

He forced his legs to move and watched as Andrei settled next to Geri, clenched Lulia awkwardly, and broke down, his sobs joining his sister's.

"What will we do?" Andrei managed.

A shadow crossed Travis's face as he paused. He didn't know the answer.

"I need to salvage what's left."

Andrei looked up. "I'm sorry, I had to obey. Now everything is different. Save them, I'll be here."

Travis flinched against rotten vapors trailing from Geri's putrefying corpse.

"I'm sorry, truly, for all of this."

Andrei looked up with pain etched on his face, and then watched Lulia squirm.

"We're orphans now."

"So was I. You won't be alone, I promise. I will care for you both. We will find a way forward."

Travis scooped the globe from the lawn and stuffed it into his backpack.

"We were deceived. Your father recognized the danger of my family magic, but none of us knew what we were up against. I will find him."

"He's at the other house," Andrei whispered. "With James's mother. I helped him. I had to."

Travis hid a flash of panic behind a blank expression and turned toward the meadow.

FIFTY-FOUR

TRAVIS WAS WAIST-HIGH IN THE GRASS when he realized he was trembling. The spectacle of Lulia's possession shook him to his core. Witches were not immune to horror. And it was starting to sink in: he'd aided and abetted the Devil. His parents and their parents never had an inkling the magic they'd honed to pass to him was tainted. And his work to advance it sped it along. Was there a way out? Death would bring no reward, not with what was waiting, that much was clear.

He was simmering in a stew of fear, hurt, and betrayal. Radu and Geri and Aaron were the latest to feed the beast he'd unleashed. He and his parents were pawns in a larger struggle, as were all the witches in service to ancestors and the coven, but blind to the founder's motive.

And he still hadn't united with his daughter. It burned as much as the other fires, like what had become of Paula? His heart raced, and he picked up the pace.

He plowed in moon-lit darkness through the meadow grass until he heard voices. Rachel sat in the grass near the pit with Sorinah crouched beside her, rubbing her arms to warm them.

Travis stepped into the clearing and stooped down to touch Rachel's cheek. "You're free now. I'm sorry you've had to endure this."

Rachel smiled weakly, "I've got to find James."

"First take care of yourself."

Travis shifted to face Sorinah. "There's a new reality."

She nodded and could see the turmoil in his eyes. "That voice resonated across the meadow." Sorinah held his gaze until Rachel's shivers begged another rub down.

"It channeled through Lulia." Travis's face was sullen and severe. "My daughter defiled."

Rachel shuddered against the warmth of Sorinah's touch. "Strange voices, screams, torture; it's clear this place is haunted."

Travis took a deep breath and stood. "We'll get you out of here."

"I heard Geri shriek." Sorinah looked up at him. "What about Andrei?"

"He's in shock and trying to calm Lulia." Travis looked toward the house. "His mother took his place. Geri died like Marku."

"I'll tend to Andrei once I get Rachel to safety," Sorinah said. "You've got to help James and his mother."

"I'll find him and get him home."

Travis hoped it was true and couldn't offer more.

He scowled as he scanned the meadow in the moonlight then locked eyes with Sorinah.

He sucked down a deep breath and shifted his gaze to Rachel.

"You need food and a warm bath." He pulled two towels from his backpack, and left them on the grass next to Sorinah.

Rachel's face drained of color. "Please—" Tears came and she fought to hold them back. Then she whispered.

"This is all too much. It never stops. Where do I go? I can't face my parents. I'm not even sure what I'd tell them, or the cops. That James buried me and the old farmhouse grounds are haunted?"

"Shh, shh, this part is over now," Travis said and took her hand. "Get ready for the next. You still need strength. Sorinah will take you to Paula's house. I'm rushing there ahead. Move slowly, I'll wait as long as it takes."

Sorinah touched her cheek. "Let's get you up and away from here. Step by step."

She crooned gently in Romanian, a lullaby maybe, seemingly to herself.

"I'm sure James is at his mother's," Rachel whispered as she tried to stand, but her knee buckled, and she collapsed with a grimace. "Right?"

Sorinah massaged the leg that had turned to jelly. "Not so fast."

"He has to be." Her neck craned, and the girl's eyes darted above the grass.

Travis waited for her breathing to slow before answering. "We don't know what we'll find there."

Rachel's expression turned to mashed clay, and she covered her eyes.

"I've infected him; he was with me," she whispered. "I'm the black widow."

"Shush," Sorinah countered. "It isn't you." She squeezed closer and held her tight as tears came in a rush. She tucked the mortal's head into a nook on her shoulder.

Rachel's lips trembled against her neck.

"Get to know me, and you're dead."

FIFTY-FIVE

TRAVIS SPIRITED AWAY SILENTLY in the moonlight and found James planted in the pit, his head twisted sideways and nested in the mound of dirt.

"Can you hear me?" Travis whispered as he jumped down beside him, leaning in close to check his vitals.

James's eyes fluttered open. His lips were parted, but no words came, only a groan.

"Don't try to talk," Travis said. He had limited time and few options and his adrenaline surged. "Can you move?"

James's knees bumped together and his fingers clawed at the dirt.

"That's great. Brace yourself, I'm taking you piggyback."

Travis fixed his gaze on James as he rose from the pit, his body stiff as it hovered above the grasses. Travis swiveled and girded for James's weight as his legs clamped around and his arms draped over the witch's shoulders. Travis jiggered James's position and held tight as he started through the meadow toward the stagecoach road.

"That's it, I've got you. Try to relax," Travis said. He felt James's breath against his neck become a rhythmic volley of low groans between strides.

His mind raced as they trekked through the woods toward Paula. He didn't know if she were alive or dead. And bringing her injured son into whatever waited wasn't an option.

As he neared her property and the forest began to thin, Travis lingered near the tallest pine at the edge of the woods. He crouched low and James was lucid enough to tense his legs for landing as Travis swiveled and laid him carefully on the bed of needles in the clearing behind it.

"You'll rest here until the paramedics come. I'm getting your mother."

If James heard, it wasn't clear. He seemed to focus, but then his lids closed again.

Travis gently stroked his cheek and felt for steady breaths, but had to press on. What if Paula were even worse? Now that he was near whatever Radu had in store for her, his heart thundered in his core.

He jumped up and surveyed the grounds behind her house as he approached with eyes wide and ears tuned. He sniffed for Radu and listened for anything beyond determined crickets and the persistent rustle of leaves.

Lights were on in the kitchen as he climbed the back steps and peered through the screen. He tested the lock, and then kept the door from crashing behind him. He stopped, listened, and surveyed the room.

A notebook on the kitchen table caught his attention, and he went to it.

Katherine,
I was wrong to doubt you. Everything you said is true.
The wraith in the woods is as real as the fire that burns
her soul. Travis conjured her. This I learned in the closet,
and it's entirely my fault. I brought him into our lives. I
was vulnerable then and fell for his powers of seduction.
God save me from the witches all around us. They've
embedded themselves nearby, lurking in plain sight. But
my death will set us free, a mother's greatest gift, the one
thing that will deliver my children from evil. For none of
this would have happened if it weren't for my weakness

*and my mistakes. I feel so guilty because he tried to kill
you and four years later hunted down Aaron.
My heart aches and there is only one escape.
Your mother*

His pulse raced, and Travis shot to the hallway. The door to the basement was open, and light pooled from somewhere beyond the bottom step. He crept down, pausing when his keen ears picked up breathing. He took the rest of the stairs in pairs and swiveled at the bottom.

Paula lay frozen on the floor with arms wrapped tight around her legs, knees pressed to her chest and shivering in a black satin dress.

"Paula?" Travis whispered as he reached down to touch her shoulder.

Her eyes opened slowly, but she didn't answer, and she didn't seem to see him with her gaze trained on the couch. The carcass of an enormous black hawk lay on the leather cushion. A noose dangled from a ceiling beam, and the end of the rope trailed under the raptor in a tangle. A kitchen chair was overturned in front of the couch.

She unclasped her hands and shifted to sit. She looked at him and shook her head.

"Am I dreaming?" She ran a hand over her face and then through her hair. "I'm so confused. I know you're wrapped up in this, so please, you have to help make sense of it."

Travis moved in closer and stooped low. "Take your time; tell me everything."

Paula pulled in a deep, unsteady breath. "Radu was here, and he talked about you. I remember snippets, but nothing's clear except I was going to kill myself. And it wasn't scary, it was a duty."

He responded quietly, "I read the note on the kitchen table."

Paula rubbed her eyes. "What note?"

"It doesn't matter now." Travis sat next to her, and gently put his arm around her. She didn't pull away. "Tell me more."

"It started last night in the kitchen. I remember waking up in the closet, and Radu was there when I crawled out. There were visions of Katherine; she was chased through the woods by a ghoulish woman, now I know and Radu blames you." Paula paused to study his face. "Why did you do that to my daughter?"

Travis shook his head. "Her fear was temporary, and wiped away. I needed the fuel to fight Radu."

She pointed to the dead hawk splayed on the couch. "He was there, I swear it. I killed him, and then I was on the floor. But when I woke he was gone, even his boots, and that thing got in." She stopped and covered her eyes. "It was a nightmare, or I am insane, or both."

"Keep calm, and take some deep breaths," Travis said as he stood.

He collected a pair of black pumps from the floor, and Paula clutched them while she adjusted the straps of her dress. "Look at my outfit. There was a whole plan."

He guided her to a wooden bench across the room from the couch, and they both sat.

She closed her eyes. "Let me try to grasp this." She blew out a breath and raked a hand through her hair. "I wanted to be nicely dressed for my own funeral. I was going to hang myself there, from the beam." She pointed and her arm trembled.

"What did he do to you?"

"I liked him and he seduced me and it turned sexual. I can't tell you exactly how that happened." She leaned back and stared at the ceiling. "He mentioned Aaron and James and I snapped out of it, just for an instant, just long enough to jump on his spine and strangle him with the rope. I think that's how it went, and I'm lucky, or there I'd be."

Paula held back tears; her eyes fixed on the dangling rope.

"His back was hurt and I used it against him. For that critical instant I could act, his hold on me broke, and I strangled him as hard as I could so he couldn't get up."

She turned toward Travis. "I've never killed anyone. When he stopped struggling and went limp, I collapsed."

Travis steadied her trembling hands. "You're very strong; you stopped him."

"Why do you know him?"

"He's an enemy, and he lured me back here to get revenge."

Paula shook her head to clear it, and exhaled sharply. "He blamed you for everything. It's strange how that comes through, the sense of competition with you. But he was evil and you are against him so I want to trust you; I've got nothing else right now."

Travis squeezed her hand. "He was setting you up to look crazy, and me as the villain."

Paula shuddered. "If the bird weren't here, I'd think it was all a dream."

"The memories will fade, and don't try to make sense of them." Travis pulled her close, then took both her hands. "You need to be strong because there is more to bear."

Travis paused to gather his thoughts. There was only one way he could manage.

"James is injured, his neck might be broken. Rachel said he tore after the hawk on the stagecoach road and he's lying beneath a tree at the edge of the forest."

"Oh, God, no," she whispered and shook her head. She took deep breaths and motioned toward the couch. "This hawk, the one that killed Aaron?"

Then she covered her eyes. "What's it doing here?"

Travis waited for Paula to peek out.

"Is he OK? Take me to him," Paula whispered.

Travis nodded and held her hands gently.

"We'll call an ambulance."

Paula stared at him for a moment and then at the hawk. She sucked in a breath through trembling lips, her face ruddy and stricken.

She jumped when knocks at the door in the kitchen broke the silence and carried down the stairs.

Travis turned toward the raps. "Rachel was heading here to find James."

"Let's go," Paula said as she wiped away tears.

Travis watched as Paula stood and held herself, eyes darting around the basement. He guided her up toward the kitchen, and then hung back as Paula went to the door.

Rachel stood outside the screen. Streaks of mud mottled her face and bare limbs where it had been hastily wiped away. Sludge had saturated her cotton shorts and polo. She forced a smile as she stood, shivering.

Paula opened the door. "What happened to you?"

Rachel took steps into the kitchen. "James? Is James here?"

Paula turned, and they both stared at Travis as he sidled near the table.

He bowed his head. "He's groggy behind a tree on the stagecoach road."

"Oh, God, I felt it." Rachel looked dazed and expressionless. "I know this feeling."

"Take us to him," Paula whispered, eyes locked on Travis. She rushed to a cabinet to pull out flashlights. Rachel followed as they filed down the steps and toward the backyard.

The clouds had mostly cleared, and moonlight flooded the lawn as they marched toward the forest. Travis led the way, his flashlight beam carving a path through the darkness.

"Why did you leave him?" Paula asked.

"He's hard to carry. And I had to check on you."

Travis forged ahead until his beam wobbled up the trunk of a towering pine. Paula and Rachel caught up and watched as he circled around and froze.

All eyes locked on James, who lay beneath it in a pool of light.

Paula screamed, so Travis switched it off. They waited in the dark until she shined one herself. He was still as a corpse, and the beam quivered as she trained it on his face that bent to one side, almost touching the ground.

Paula rushed to her son and knelt down. She stroked his face and shuddered through sobs.

"My poor baby," she repeated, over and over again.

His eyes fluttered, and opened, and his lips formed the faintest smile.

"I have a twin," he whispered.

"What?" Paula asked, bending close. "Say again?"

Rachel dashed forward and took his hand. Travis spotlit them from behind, and at the edge of his circle of light lay a great, black, dead hawk.

Then Paula noticed it.

"My God, it's the one from the couch."

FIFTY-SIX

PARAMEDICS SUSPECTED A BROKEN neck and shock as they prepped James for transport to the ICU. He could move but didn't speak again. They encouraged Paula and Rachel to defer a visit to the hospital until morning. Tests would start immediately, and there was no point in arriving before a doctor could review the initial results. For the night it was best for all to rest.

A fat saffron moon hugged the treetops as police lingered near and asked questions.

Rachel was still streaked with mud, inconsolable, and unhelpful. She spoke in fragments and vague snippets about "a haunted meadow" and "a mud pit" and then "getting ditched" when James "bolted to hunt the hawk that killed his father."

"He was possessed by evil," she added. "It wasn't him. He took off and left me. Something wicked got inside him."

They took notes and nodded solemnly and moved onto Paula.

"Things keep happening to my son," Paula told the two officers.

"Wasn't he reported missing by you Friday morning?" one of them asked.

"Yes, but they turned up later. There had been a party; they spent the night." Paula appeared flustered and strained for details. She looked toward Rachel for support but got a blank stare. "Travis just found him an hour ago. James had been hunting the hawk."

"This Travis?" The cop eyed him.

Travis nodded and tightened his lips.

Paula interjected, "He's a friend and neighbor."

The other officer flicked his flashlight beam toward the knoll behind the tree.

"Strange the hawk flew off when we got here." He folded his arms and shook his head. "It seems it wasn't as dead as you thought."

Paula sputtered and appeared perplexed. A vision flashed, a feeling of déjà vu that she'd seen the same hawk earlier, dead on her couch. She'd been certain, she'd studied its markings, orange beak, and poked its bristly feathers, but of course, it was impossible.

"At least everyone saw it. I'm not crazy," she managed.

The cop eyed her. "Why would it be crazy?"

"I honestly thought it was dead." Paula exhaled slowly and held her lips tight. "I'm feeling confused. As you might expect, I'm overwhelmed."

He shifted back to Rachel. "You say something was wrong with him. Can you elaborate?"

Rachel paused to consider. "When he ran off he was crazed."

"Crazed?"

"He left me in the mud and took off and I heard a shout." Her eyes darted to each of their faces.

"So he was distraught?" The officer's face was flat.

Her eyes pooled, and all she could manage was a nod.

He pressed on. "I ask because he fell head first, which suggests a dive, a deliberate act."

Paula held herself tight and tried to steady the sway. "His father died a week ago. We've all been distraught. But are you suggesting an intentional jump, like suicide?"

His brow furrowed as he paused. "That or a just a bad accident; forensics will help."

The paramedics were already wheeling James on a gurney on the stagecoach road toward the house. Paula watched for a moment and then clamped her eyes shut.

"I'm very sorry; we can follow them out. For now, we've got what we need." He shot a look at Travis and Rachel and then back to Paula. "He's responsive and there's every reason to be hopeful. You'll know a lot more in the morning. He's in good hands."

The cops led them along the path and out of the woods. The trio followed them silently onto Paula's property. A few steps more, and one paused with his eyes on the treetops.

"Maybe the hawk startled him. He could have been near its nest. They don't attack otherwise." He turned and continued the march to the driveway. "You found it near his body, so it seems they went down together before it recovered and flew off."

"A hawk attacked my husband on the lake, and then he drowned," Paula countered.

"That's very strange, indeed," he shot her a sympathetic glance.

They walked the rest of the way without speaking, and the trio waited by the kitchen steps until the ambulance pulled out of the driveway with lights flashing, followed by the cops.

"Let's get inside," Paula said as she led them into the house. "I've got to check the basement." She was breathing fast. "Why is it stuck in my head there's a hawk on the couch?"

They followed her into the hallway and filed down the stairs. Paula rounded the corner and raced across the room. The end of the rope lay strewn across an empty couch.

Paula sucked in a long, slow breath that shuddered the whole way down.

"Of course, there isn't a hawk," she said and shook her head. "What's scary is that I thought there would be."

Travis came up behind her. "You're exhausted and need to rest." The witch waited for Rachel to join them. "The mind plays tricks when it's overloaded. And you both need to eat. I'm sure Rachel would love a bath."

He reached up and unwrapped the noose from the beam and it fell to the carpet.

"Let's put that away." He grabbed the loop, undid the knot, and coiled the rope.

Paula watched and pondered. "We used it for Halloween. There was a pumpkin-headed scarecrow we hung from the oak out front."

Travis righted the chair from the floor. "I'll bring these upstairs."

After a long moment, Paula shifted toward Rachel. "Let me draw you a bath."

Rachel surveyed her streaky arms. "I would love that. And I don't want to be alone."

"Of course, neither do I." Paula took steps toward the stairs and then froze. "Did we just find James in the woods? Is my precious son going to be OK? It's impossible to tell what's real and what's a dream."

Rachel choked and sucked down a breath. Paula and Travis locked their eyes on her.

"It's all a dream; that's what I keep telling myself. A nice lady brought me here; she was like an angel; she wiped me down. She knew I was looking for James and cleaned my phone. I don't even know who she was or how she found me." She made it to Paula at the base of the steps. "Maybe I'm dead, and she was an angel."

"Eat, rest, and don't ruminate on what can't be controlled. Be good to yourselves." Travis clutched the chair and the rope as he followed them up. "James needs you in the morning."

Paula led Rachel into the hallway toward the bathroom while Travis headed to the kitchen and put the chair in its spot under the table.

Rachel followed Paula, and they stopped halfway in the dark, leaning against the wall. Travis listened from the stillness of the kitchen.

"When I think it's just a dream," Rachel said, "I pinch myself and bite my lip, but I'm really here." There was a pause. "I don't deserve to be. My friends are gone. The ones I loved most. I shut down after Mia and Sophia, and so did James, and that bonded us until being with me almost killed him, too. I am the poison."

Travis heard a volley of gasps, and then sobs started.

"Shush, no, you're not," Paula managed.

A moment passed, followed by a loud thump against the wall.

"I'll never be happy again," Rachel whispered, "not like before."

"That's gone for me, too." Paula's voice cracked and she hesitated. "I don't even believe in it anymore. I did before, but it was only temporary. I see that now. Happiness always erodes. So if it tries to return, I'll know it's false and fleeting, nothing more than an illusion."

The hallway went quiet except for uneven breaths.

"Aaron drowned in the lake. We found my son broken in the woods. How could he have fallen? Did he do it to himself? I'm foggy and numb and if James is disabled—"

There was a spasm on the floorboards.

"My God, Katherine! I need to call her." Paula's voice trailed off.

"Shh, one step at a time," Rachel said. "We'll make a list, together."

"A punch list, details to remember. Wait—"

After a few beats, Rachel dared to whisper. "Yes?"

"I felt a glimmer. But like so much else, it's gone." Paula quieted, and then there was shuffling, and Travis heard a door click shut.

For a while, the only sound was the hum of the refrigerator until voices resumed from inside the bathroom.

"We'll do this step by step. Leave everything on the floor, and I'll wash it."

The pipes clanked as hot water began to flow from the basement to the tub.

"I'll bring you a robe and get dinner going. Soak as long as you want and call out if you need anything."

Water gushed from the spigot with the soothing rush of a waterfall.

Travis studied the notepad on the table. What purpose could it possibly serve? He tore out the page plus the indented one under it and stuffed them in his pocket.

His mind raced, and all at once the otherworldly voice that bellowed from Lulia's lips echoed in his head and made him cringe. Hell was unleashed and waiting for him and he was to blame.

It's my magic that's poison, not you, Rachel.

He listened to the burble of hot water and the creak of floorboards overhead as Paula padded to her bedroom upstairs to change out of her favorite dress.

Travis wanted to linger long enough to say goodnight, but what would it matter?

By the time Paula and Rachel made it to the kitchen, they'd forgotten he was there.

Apparently he'd slipped away with the paramedics.

And wondering about James took over. So much else was gone.

FIFTY-SEVEN

TRAVIS SAW LIGHTS ON, so he crept up the back stairs, and peered through the window. Sorinah was feeding Lulia with a bottle at the kitchen table while Andrei sat across from them.

The dead hawk lay on the top wooden step, exactly where he'd transported it. He bent to gently probe Radu's remains: nothing but a carcass of bristly feathers on a thick wing.

Travis knocked and quietly opened the door, jaw clenched as he approached the table.

"Did you bring him?" Andrei asked. The chair creaked under him as he pushed back, his eyes wide and his face sullen.

"He's just outside," Travis said.

Andrei stared out the window. "I know he's dead. I saw him in the globe."

Travis nodded grimly. "Come with me."

Sorinah looked up and locked his eyes before he reversed course and waited for Andrei to join him on the back steps.

Travis watched as the young witch kneeled beside what was left of his father.

"That's it?" His voice broke. "That's how it ends?"

He caressed the feathers, and his face flushed, eyes pooling. His bottom lip trembled as he cradled the broken animal and then lifted his gaze to Travis.

"So what now? Do you kill me, too?" He flinched and then shrugged. "You can do what you want. I don't even care."

Travis reached out and squeezed his shoulder. "I do care."

The young witch was shaking, so Travis placed his hand below the carcass to help him guide it back to the wooden step.

Travis's tone was flat and steady. "We can bury him first thing in the morning, your mother, too, in the meadow pits."

He watched Andrei stare at the hawk.

Travis waited a moment, and then whispered, "I'm so sorry. I didn't want any of this, especially for you. Take as long as you need."

Andrei's eyes narrowed and shifted slowly to Travis's troubled face, where they froze for a while and everything got quiet.

"I'm going inside you," the young witch stated. "You did it to me, and now it's my turn. I bit you on purpose."

Travis held his piercing gaze. "Go as deep as you like. I want you to trust me."

Andrei closed his eyes and Travis felt the stirrings of connection, the charge of revealing himself without uttering a word. He wanted to share everything after months of sessions. Swings from love to guilt to fear to anger and back. There was nothing to hide and this intrusion was welcome, raw, and emotional.

It wasn't clear how long Andrei lingered, but his face flushed and then he whispered, "That helps a lot. It's complicated for me, too. You can check if you want."

When he'd composed himself, Andrei took a deep breath and wiped his face as he followed Travis back into the kitchen. They sat across from each other at the table while a bond thickened.

Sorinah was the first to break the mood, addressing Travis. "We had a long talk. Andrei was aware of the possession of Lulia while he was trapped in the globe."

Andrei studied their faces and then found a quiet voice.

"My parents didn't know about any of it, I swear."

Travis reached over the table and took his hand. Andrei's eyes blazed panic, and for an instant, Travis thought he might lash out, but the grip held and then strengthened.

His patient continued. "They worried about the coven. They thought you were dangerous."

Travis exhaled slowly and furrowed his brow. "It turns out they were right."

Andrei's tears broke through his defenses, and he pulled away to hide his face. Only the buzz of the old refrigerator masked his sobs.

"So what happens now?" he whispered when he was ready.

Travis studied Sorinah for a moment, and then pivoted to Andrei.

"We will form a family: you, Lulia, Sorinah, and I."

Sorinah's lips tightened as she rocked Lulia. "Through shared pain and blood, it is destined. This clash is older and larger than us, and together we are bound."

Andrei pushed his hand to the middle of the table. "I want to stay with you."

His new guardians took it.

Andrei's face flushed, and his lips formed the slightest, stiff smile. "Do we go back to Bucharest?"

Travis swiveled toward Sorinah and paused. "We will make a plan together after we collect ourselves. We will tend to your parents. I will do what I can to assist the neighbors."

Travis's eyes shifted dark and slow between their faces.

"I have no will to continue. I presumed my magic was elevated, not a ladder for the Devil's ascendancy."

Sorinah scanned his face. "What does that mean for this new family?"

Travis froze, and the silence lingered until Sorinah broke it.

"Here, take your daughter," she said as she stood and held out the bundle.

Travis smiled and lifted Lulia, pressing her nose to his face. He pulled her close and for the first time smelled her, kissed her, and touched her cheek. He whispered between pauses. "I am your father, Travis. You've already met Sorinah and Andrei. We are your family."

He pulled back her beanie and caressed the fine patches of raven hair. Then he settled back and cradled her on his shoulder.

"What will we do? The magic my parents left me is not what you need."

Sorinah reached over and touched his arm while Lulia seemed content to sleep. Andrei locked his eyes on the trio as Travis continued in a whisper.

"The time has passed that I need such vigor. I was driven to avenge my parents and then advance their work." He took in their anxious faces. "I won't use the tainted magic."

"And what of the Devil's plan?" Sorinah asked.

"I will shield her from all of this. She's never fueled, and she never will."

"So she won't be a witch?" Andrei asked from across the table.

"No," Travis said and shifted his gaze between them with his lips locked tight.

"The root of your magic has already been woven into coven threads," Sorinah said.

"And so it will advance without my assistance."

Sorinah raised her eyebrows. "Go on."

Travis studied them, his face like stone.

"The threads will soon infiltrate all coven magic, and mortals stricken by witches will also face the Devil's eye and his claim to tainted souls. There is no stopping what's been unleashed." He held a deep breath. "The implications are clear. They are insurmountable, and I must change course or have no honor."

"You can't hide from the demon," Andrei whispered. "I know how he watches."

"I'm not needed now. His plan is in motion, and I will be forgotten."

Sorinah's eyes were wide. "You can't give up entirely."

Travis didn't speak.

Sorinah waited a moment before attempting another tack.

"You need to survive for Andrei, for Lulia, and for me."

Travis rose from his seat, careful not to jostle Lulia, who was asleep and nestled at his neck. He maneuvered behind Sorinah, and Andrei sidled close to wrap an arm around them.

For how long they lingered, he wasn't sure. And then he answered.

"I will subsist, my time tethered to Lulia's mortal lifespan."

"That sounds a bit drastic," Sorinah whispered.

"We'll find another way," Andrei said.

Travis forced a tight smile and squeezed them back.

"I've done enough damage already."

"You can't blame only yourself," Sorinah said.

"I'd like to believe in redemption," Travis said. "If not, I deserve what awaits me."

He closed his eyes to ponder, to prolong the moment and savor it.

It had always been so, the specter of hell, but the ordeal made it all real. He was born a witch and had needed his parents' magic to survive, but it advanced an evil no one could have foreseen. No innocents were supposed to die, not Mia, not Sophia, not Marku, and not Aaron. He never wanted that, but it happened anyway. And the pain of those forced to muddle through would never heal. He knew that about Paula, James, and Rachel.

In that incongruity lay a sliver of hope, a possible exit.

It was the magic, not him.

A few hours earlier, he'd hated Andrei for attacking James, but found a way beyond it not to forgiveness but understanding and acceptance. His former patient was not *only* evil; none of them was. They were taught from childhood how to survive as witches.

Redemption was the key, exactly what the Devil's eye would bypass, a mitigating force the demon seized upon to quash. Maybe none of the witches had to accept the fate they assumed was destined by birth. Redemption might lie in a trajectory that didn't require immortality as an antidote to hell.

Travis found his voice.

"For mortals, the value of life comes from its brevity. Our magic prolongs it but aligns us with evil. There is no other choice; our survival dictates it; black magic empowers it."

"A poisoned gift," Andrei said. "My mother told me. I felt that with James; I wanted to save him."

"A witch to overcome it would define goodness," Travis stated.

Sorinah kept silent as Andrei pondered his words.

"Maybe that is the way out." Travis's lips tightened to the hint of a smile. "Redemption as an off-ramp to an otherwise bleak eternity."

Andrei clamped his eyes shut for an instant and then locked them on Travis.

"I saw my father's misery. He begged me not to follow."

A stillness hung in the room until Sorinah broke it.

"It would require the courage to die, to abstain from magic and wither as a mortal, with no guarantee."

Travis's eyes widened to piercing, obsidian orbs as he considered.

"Perhaps that's more than we had from the beginning."

He pulled them close, and it felt like enough.

FIFTY-EIGHT

Six weeks later

TRAVIS PULLED INTO PAULA'S driveway just before noon on a sultry day obviously favored by horse flies. Even if it were cooler, he'd vowed to never walk the stagecoach road again. Too many bad memories haunted it and him.

He parked behind a packed moving truck and watched as two men loaded a bureau into the back amid neatly stacked boxes and padded furniture.

Paula surveyed it from the kitchen steps and walked to greet him where he stood in front of the laurel, out of the way of the movers.

"Looks like it's going well," Travis said and extended his right hand.

She smiled and took it, and he covered hers with his left.

"Yes, we started early," she said. "Before the heat gets worse."

"Headed to Burlington, you said?"

Paula nodded curtly.

"A smaller place with two guest bedrooms, one for Katherine whenever she comes back east, and one for James." She shifted to survey the progress in the truck. "I'll be going back to work, and the commute will be shorter too. I need to get away from here."

Travis took a step back and folded his arms. "I understand. I wish you well."

Paula did a slow circle, neck craned to the airless, cobalt blue sky.

"It's dark even now, midday."

Travis watched, but there was nothing to say.

"It will never get lighter, so the best option is to leave, same for James and Rachel."

Travis pulled his lips tight. "Where are they?"

She breathed slowly and deeply and held his gaze.

"James is back at school. Rachel quit Old Gold and moved in with him. I'm sure she'll find something." Paula shuffled nervously in the driveway. "They plan to move to Boston when he graduates in May. They're already looking."

"How's his neck?"

"As breaks go it was lucky, so I'm cautiously grateful. He's out of the brace with no lingering physical issues to speak of." She paused. "But there's something...."

Travis stiffened as he waited for her to continue.

"He thinks he has a twin, Siamese even. Then he looks in the mirror and knows it's impossible. He makes Rachel check him for scars from the separation operation."

He struggled to find words. "Conjoined twins? Sounds a bit off. I hope it passes."

Paula nodded slowly with her jaw locked tight. "His doctor says it will. Something to blame on his blow to the head. I hope so, too, because he thinks someone's inside him."

Travis flinched and tried to hide it.

"Brain and spinal injuries are so tricky. Give it time."

His eyes shifted toward squeaks on the brick sidewalk as the movers wheeled two boxes from the front door and lined them on the back of the truck. *AARON* was written in black Sharpie.

Paula stared as they secured them with the rest.

"I saved his things for last. I'll leave them taped shut somewhere, probably forever."

She covered her eyes and rubbed her temples, then a dispirited look took hold.

"I sometimes get flashes of dread, and then nothing, it's the damnedest thing." Tears pooled and intensified her doleful expression. "Like veiled memory snippets from a childhood far away. But horrific and vivid enough to rattle me."

As she trailed off the workers approached cautiously. They told her they were almost finished if she wanted to check around and then headed inside for a bathroom break.

"I have to be going now," Paula whispered, dazed and flustered. "I need a moment, alone, one last time in the house." Her face constricted as she turned to the kitchen steps.

Travis watched her disappear behind the screen door.

That's when the craving hit in broad daylight.

He inched toward the boxes at the back of the truck. It would be so easy, an instinct assured him, to open one and start again, with just one t-shirt. Conjuring Aaron that evening with Paula gone would be harmless enough. The fear of a complete stranger would replenish him and then evaporate with Aaron's ghost. The plan had always been solid. Already he was weakening, and abstinence was only just beginning.

He fingered the tape along the seam of the box. A flash of what he'd felt while the globe spun riches out of Andrei struck all at once, potent and exhilarating.

Travis gushed like a steam pipe through gritted teeth and pushed himself away.

He doubled over to suck in deep breaths, and on the blacktop faced a new reality. Redemption would never come easy.

Travis regained his composure and made it to his car without looking back.

When he arrived at the Malloy house, he found Sorinah in the kitchen at the table in front of his laptop. Andrei stacked suitcases in the living room, while Lulia squirmed on the couch.

He immediately approached Andrei. "Are you still connected to James?"

"No." The young witch looked annoyed. "I thought we agreed to abstain. Why?"

"He thinks he has a Siamese twin. Someone who's inside him."

Andrei's brow furrowed in confusion. "It was like that for me, too. But I'm out."

Travis locked eyes with his unofficial son. "Promise me."

"I swear. Any spell would interfere and attract the attention of doctors."

Travis nodded with a tight smile and headed to the kitchen. They both knew he could probe if he wanted to. He came up behind Sorinah, and she shifted so he could read the screen.

"It's good we return tomorrow," she said. "Already it's begun."

There was a report out of Bucharest. A series of murders spooked local authorities because of their grisly similarities: twisted necks and tongues oddly stretched and blackened. Police speculated a serial killer or cult, Orthodox priests something more sinister: the beginning of end times, the work of the Devil, the apocalypse foretold.

Their eyes met, and it took Travis a moment to find words. His mind shot to the box at the back of the truck. Taming temptation might work for him. But not for witches with no other options. He owed them more after all he'd learned. Mortals were in this, too.

"Overreach will betray the coven. Intemperance was always a danger. The Devil's gambit is flawed; now we will be exposed and hunted. I can't hide from the war that's started."

He was resolute as he squeezed her shoulder.

"I need to retake my magic."

Sorinah turned to face him. "And so a new cycle begins. We will help you."

His eyes grew dark and flecked with crimson as he nodded.

"There's more to redemption than fighting temptation."

He got on his knees to face her.

"Traces of Aaron were boxed at Paula's, and I was lured by the access. The cravings will never stop; it's how we survive. But abstention isn't enough. For redemption, the intruder must be blocked, and the magic recast. We are changing sides."

He lifted himself and slowly steered Sorinah away from the

bleakness on the computer screen and toward Andrei and Lulia in the next room.

"None of us asked for the hell that awaits. I will reclaim what the Devil hijacked. The coven will take a stand."

The step siblings watched silently as their parents approached the couch.

Travis needed to believe he could fix his magic for their sake.

For now, hope would have to do because withering away without a fight was wrong.

That, at least, he knew.

The dependents were something he'd never had.

They loved him and it changed everything.

No way he was leaving them to the Devil.

ACKNOWLEDGMENTS

I STARTED WRITING *The Pawns* just before the pandemic hit. I am incredibly grateful for the unwavering support and encouragement of my spouse, Mauricio, through illness and dark days.

This book is dedicated to my mother, with much love. I remember her reading *Centennial* by James A. Michener when I was little. I thought it was the thickest book I'd ever seen; I think it still is. She nurtured a love of reading along with a robust library habit. I checked out every *Hardy Boys* mystery from the Essex Free Library before I got old enough for Agatha Christie, and then Stephen King came along with *Carrie* and *'Salem's Lot*. I was hooked.

https://www.essexvt.org/153/Essex-Free-Library

I would like to thank the Jericho Writers Club in Oxford, UK for tons of spot-on advice. The emails from Harry Bingham, who heads the group, are often a lifeline.

https://jerichowriters.com/

I owe a huge debt of gratitude to Julia Houston, a writer and editor in New Orleans. Her careful work on my manuscript was indispensable, and she helps me grow as a writer.

https://www.juliahouston.com/

ABOUT THE AUTHOR

RON GABRIEL IS A magazine industry veteran who worked for *Seventeen*, *The New York Times Upfront*, *Cosmopolitan*, *US Weekly*, and *Rolling Stone*. He grew up in northern New England where he loved exploring old graveyards and places rumored to be haunted. Late nights he devoured horror fiction from Stephen King, Anne Rice, and Peter Straub. He has a B.A. in Journalism from the University of Maine, and an M.F.A. from the School of Visual Arts. He is an active member of the Horror Writers Association.

The Pawns is his second novel.

To learn more about Travis's parents, and how Rachel, James, Mia, and Sophia got pulled into Travis's orbit, check out *The Banished: Book One of The Bucharest Witches*.

Please visit www.rongabriel.nyc to keep in touch. I love hearing from readers.